THIN ICE

PINE COVE BOOK SIX

HJ WELCH

Memory Lane
Pine Cove Book Six

PROLOGUE – TWO MONTHS AGO

KAMRAN

TROUBLE JUST WALKED IN THE DOOR, AND NOT THE FUN KIND.

Fuck.

Kamran Amir tried to ignore the feeling like a bucket of ice water had just been tipped over his head as he watched the unfortunately familiar figure of Chaz Bolt stalk through Pine Cove's only gay bar.

How the hell did he find me? Kamran thought desperately. He glanced at his friends, wondering if he could hide under the table without them asking too many questions.

No. He needed to nip this in the bud. Whatever Chaz wanted, Kamran wasn't going to give it to him. Not ever again. This was his home now, and he wasn't going to be chased out of it like he had been Seattle. He could do this. He could tell his ex-boyfriend that he'd wasted his time coming here. Chaz could just forget all about Kamran and Pine Cove right now.

"You all right, buddy?" Kamran's friend, Angel, asked over the pulsing music. They were squeezed into one of Aquarium's booths with some of their other friends, but a quick glance around the table told Kamran that no one else had noticed him freaking out.

"Uh, yeah," Kamran told him, shaking himself and trying to muster a convincing smile. "I'll, uh, be back in a second, okay? Watch my stuff?" He jutted his chin to where he'd put his wallet, phone, and keys on the table.

"Sure," Angel said with a frown. He clearly had questions, but luckily, he didn't pry. Kamran hoped he never would.

He liked to keep his past firmly away from his present. It was nobody's business the shit he'd stupidly gotten up to before, and he wasn't going to let Chaz ruin the good thing he had going on in his new home.

Apologizing to his friends, he clambered out of the booth and made his way through the crowd to the other end of the bar where Chaz had propped himself up, looking around like he was thoroughly amused. Kamran took a moment to observe his ex from the other end of the bar, pretending he was waiting to be served.

He gritted his teeth. Objectively speaking, Chaz was still hot as hell. The white shirt he wore clung to his muscular form and showed the dark ink he had all over his chest and arms. A wisp of hair was just visible where the top buttons of his shirt were undone, and he bit a toothpick between his teeth like the goddamn bad boy cliché he was.

It was three years, give or take, since Kamran had last seen him. Since he'd foolishly agreed to do his then-boyfriend just 'one tiny favor, baby.' Kamran grimaced as he recalled that moment. This was why he didn't date. Of all the people to have made an exception for, Kamran's idiot heart had decided Chaz Bolt was the one to risk it on.

He'd shaved his head since Kamran had left Seattle, and thankfully Kamran could say he preferred him with hair. The last thing he needed was for his dick to get confused if Chaz was here for a booty call. Kamran would sleep with just about anyone, but Chaz was one hundred percent off-limits.

It wasn't like Kamran had been hiding from him. He didn't shout about where he lived, However, it probably would have been pretty easy for Chaz to work it out. But Kamran had thought they'd had an agreement. After everything that had gone down, Kamran had made it pretty clear that he'd leave Chaz alone if Chaz did the same.

So why the hell had he walked into Aquarium on a Sunday night in January like it was no big deal? Kamran refused to think for one second it was a coincidence.

"What can I get you, hon?" Oliver, the cute bartender, asked Kamran, pulling him from his anxious thoughts.

Kamran blinked at him. He was a cute twink with purple-and-teal hair. They'd had a couple of fun nights together, and Kamran liked him because he wasn't clingy or weird after. "Oh, sorry, man," he said, shaking his head. "I'm okay for a drink. I was just going to go talk to my, uh, friend over there."

Oliver winked at him. "Sure thing, gorgeous. Catch you later."

As he moved to serve another customer, Kamran decided to stop fucking around and just go and face Chaz. What was the worst that could happen?

Well, he knew the answer to that. In fact, there were a couple of less than desirable outcomes, but there was no getting around it. It was time to go face the music.

Smoothing down his T-shirt, Kamran made a beeline for Chaz. "What are you doing here?" he demanded without preamble as soon as he got close enough.

Lazily, Chaz turned his smoldering eyes on Kamran, who tried very hard to convince his cock not to jump to attention under that hot gaze.

"Baby," Chaz rasped, grinning around his toothpick. He

3

then took it out and rolled it between his fingers. "Damn, you look good. It's been a while. I've missed you."

"Well, I haven't missed you," Kamran said with conviction. Just because his pants were getting a little tight didn't mean he'd completely lost his mind. Yeah, sex with Chaz had been mind blowing, but everything else – like, his personality, morals, and lifestyle choices – were a dumpster fire. "Why are you here?"

Chaz twisted so he was leaning against the bar with one hip. "I told you. I missed you. I thought we could catch up."

"My number hasn't changed," said Kamran pointedly. The hairs on the back of his neck were standing up. He didn't trust Chaz as far as he could spit. "But it doesn't matter, because there's nothing to catch up on. I told you we're through. I leave you alone, and you leave me alone. We had a deal."

Chaz licked his lips. "Deal's changed, baby." He reached out to touch Kamran's hip, but Kamran batted him away, staring mulishly at his ex. "Whoa, chill out," he said with a laugh that grated on Kamran's last nerve.

"You need to leave," Kamran bit out. "Whatever you want, the answer's 'no.'"

Chaz considered him a moment. "You really think you can say 'no' to me?" he asked. There was a dangerous tone to his words that sent a shiver down Kamran's spine, the bad kind.

But Kamran wasn't going to be intimidated. "Yes," he hissed. Then he blinked. "I mean…no…I'm saying *no*," he said firmly.

Okay, maybe he was a bit intimidated. He'd be a fool if he wasn't. Chaz was bad news, and the company he kept was even worse. Kamran was disgusted at himself for ever thinking Chaz's bullshit was sexy.

"Come on," Chaz purred, looking Kamran up and down

like he was a boa constrictor and Kamran was a mouse. "You're the best driver I know. No one can handle a car like you. It's just one tiny favor, baby."

Boom. There it was.

"That's exactly what you said last time," Kamran spat, jabbing a finger in Chaz's face. "But you didn't tell me the whole truth. I didn't know what I was getting into. Now I know better, and I'm not getting involved, you hear me? Find someone else."

Chaz sighed and rolled his eyes. "You're being a pussy," he said, shaking his head. "It's just a little driving."

Kamran leaned in close, staring Chaz dead in the eyes. "It was just a little *bank robbery,* and that security guard got a little *shot,*" he growled.

Chaz rolled his eyes again. "The guy lived. What are you complaining about? Besides, we got away, thanks to you." He groaned and brushed his hand over his crotch. "Jesus, baby. Your driving always turned me the fuck on. You saved us that day."

Kamran swallowed and refused to cast his eyes down. He didn't care if Chaz was hard for him. He didn't care that Chaz was the only one who'd ever called him baby and told him he was good at anything. He didn't care that realizing Chaz had just been using him for his skills had broken his heart into a million pieces. He *did* care that Chaz had turned him into a criminal that day, and Kamran wasn't going to jail for anyone.

"Find someone else," he growled.

He went to turn away, but Chaz shot his hand out like a bullet, grabbing Kamran's arm and squeezing it like a vise. "I'd *hate* for the FBI to get your name somehow," he said, his words laced with fake concern. "Wouldn't that just be terrible?"

Kamran's heart felt like it jumped out of his chest, but he

gritted his teeth and tried not to let his panic show on his face. "If you turn me in, I'll give them your name in a heartbeat," he spat, shaking Chaz's hand off him.

But Chaz just laughed and shrugged. "You'd still go to jail. I've done time before, no big deal. But a pretty baby like you?" He whistled over the music. "They'd make mincemeat of that fine ass, which would be a tragedy, but I guess I'd be willing to make that sacrifice."

Kamran shook his head. "You're bluffing," he said. "I just drove the car and had no fucking clue what was going on. You were the one with the gun. And with your previous convictions, that would be three strikes. You'd go away for *life.*"

Chaz narrowed his eyes and curled his lip. "Then you'd better keep your fucking mouth shut, hadn't you, princess?"

"I will if you leave me alone and get another driver," Kamran snapped.

He didn't feel good about protecting Chaz and his crew, but Kamran had no one else to look out for him aside from himself. Protecting Chaz meant he kept himself safe – in theory – and Kamran consoled himself that the security guard had indeed recovered and the bank had been insured.

But damn, he felt like shit about it all.

Chaz seemed to be weighing his options as he glared at Kamran. "Fine," he said eventually. "If you're too chicken shit, then you miss out on the fifty grand it would have earned you." He laughed coldly. "I seem to remember you didn't complain about the payday last time. Did you ever get that Mustang you were always jerking off over?"

Kamran did his best to keep his cool. His most prized possession was parked right outside. That must have been how Chaz had known to look for him in here.

And yeah, taking his share of the stolen money hadn't been his proudest moment, but he'd been broke back then.

The cash had meant he could move to Pine Cove, where he could drive *legally* for film and TV, as well as Uber in the downtimes. He'd crafted a whole new life for himself here, and he wasn't going to let Chaz sully it.

"Keep your money. I don't need it," he said, only lying a *little*.

Sure, his apartment was the size of a shoebox and had a funky smell he could never quite get rid of, but it was all his, and he usually made rent each month. Usually. But no matter how tempting a surprise bonus was, getting tangled up with Chaz again would never be worth it.

"Forget you ever came here," he told Chaz.

Chaz shook his head. "You're making a mistake. You never were the smartest one, though. You'd have been screwed without me doing everything for you. Baby, I'm sorry. You don't have to do the job. But can't we just have one more night? I miss you *so* much."

Kamran bit the inside of his cheek and said nothing. As much as he'd been lured in by Chaz's lavished praise, he could also cut Kamran down with a single sentence. He was a manipulative asshole. Kamran was ashamed at how pathetic he'd been to fall for his wiles. But when you'd been told that you were nothing your whole life, it was kind of understandable that a guy could fall for all those sweet nothings like they were honey.

Chaz was the only person that he'd ever made the mistake of getting close to, all because he thought that finally somebody loved him. He'd never made that mistake again. And he wasn't going to back down now.

"Fine," Chaz snapped, dropping his flirtatious act. "I'll find another piece of ass in this tacky dump." He sneered as he glanced around Aquarium before looking Kamran up and down. "I hate to break it to you, princess, but you were and still are easily replaceable."

"You'll leave, now," Kamran said, sounding far braver than he felt. Inside, he was a quivering wreck.

Chaz rolled his eyes one last time. "Whatever," he scoffed as he pushed himself away from the bar. "The job's not for a couple of months. Call me if you come to your senses and change your mind."

Kamran opened his mouth to assure him that would never happen, but Chaz had already melted into the crowd. Kamran hoped he would leave as promised and wouldn't key Kamran's car – his absolutely pride and joy – on the way out.

It took about thirty seconds for Kamran to finally exhale and sag against the bar for support. He raised a trembling hand and scraped it down his face. That had been the last thing he'd expected that evening, and it was going to take a while to get over the shock. Chaz had no place in his life now, and Kamran had to remind himself that was the way it was going to stay.

He was safe. He had friends and just enough money to keep himself going. He was all right.

But the bone-deep knowledge that he wasn't loved ran through his entire body. Sure, his friends liked him a lot, he was pretty certain. They at least tolerated him and laughed at his jokes, so that was good enough for Kamran.

But when he wanted to, Chaz had treated him like a prince, as if he was the most precious and important person on the planet. After being kicked out and disowned by his whole family at fifteen for being queer, Kamran had to admit that had felt so, *so* good.

But it had never been real, and he had to remember that.

As luck would have it, Oliver came his way again and caught his eye.

"Hey, man," said Kamran, his voice only catching a little. "Could I get a shot of that cinnamon stuff? The one that burns like a motherfucker."

Oliver raised his eyebrows. "Rough night?" he asked. There was kindness in his words.

Kamran nodded. "Nothing a little hellfire won't fix, though." And just like that, he plastered on his trademark cheeky grin and winked at the cute bartender. "Say, you don't have plans after work, do you?"

Oliver smirked. "Anyone ever tell you that you're a big ol' ho?"

Kamran licked his lips and quirked an eyebrow. "All the time, beautiful."

Oliver shook his head and laughed as he poured Kamran his drink. "Okay, you can have a pity fuck later, but *only* if you don't have too many of these." He pushed over the shot. "No one likes a messy drunk. I'll add it to your table's tab."

Kamran grinned and saluted him with the amber liquid. "You're the best."

Because if he masked it with alcohol and sex, Kamran might not feel the gaping hole in his heart. He might forget that he might know how to use his dick and drive like a demon, but that chasm inside him was the thing that made him unworthy of love.

Kamran Amir didn't get to be loved.

So he got drunk and laid instead until Chaz Bolt went back to being the bad memory he deserved to be.

LEE

"I'M ON VACATION, DUKE," LEE MARSHALL GROWLED OVER HIS Jeep's engine. He kept his eyes on the road as his boss sighed over the phone's loudspeaker.

"I thought you didn't even want to go on vacation," he said slyly. "You *never* take time off work."

Lee shifted his muscular bulk on the leather seat. Technically, Duke had a point there. "Well, I am now," he said firmly. "For a whole week, so call someone else."

"We think we've got a breakthrough in the Charles Bolt case," Duke said in a teasing tone, like he was dangling bacon in front of a salivating dog.

Damn him. Vacation or not, Lee absolutely wanted to know about any developments with that asshole. They'd been trying to get something, *anything* to link him to a string of armed robberies over the past few years in the Seattle area, but while they had a lot of circumstantial evidence, there was nothing concrete to really nail him.

Lee ground his teeth as he carefully indicated and switched to a slower lane on the freeway. "Okay, what?" he finally asked.

Duke chuckled. "So predictable," he said, the smile clear in his voice. "That's why you're my best guy, Marshall. You *are* the job. You can never switch off."

Lee bit the inside of his cheek and refused to let his words get to him. He knew that Duke meant it as a compliment, but other people...

Well. Other people had accused Lee of being a workaholic and left him for their personal trainer.

Lee shook his head. He wasn't thinking of Billy right now. He was thinking about Chaz Bolt and the hundreds of thousands of dollars he and his crew had stolen over the years. Not to mention the people they'd hurt and terrorized. He was scum, and he deserved to spend the rest of his life behind bars.

He grunted, indicating that Duke should continue.

"We've got a name. Someone who Chaz might have made contact with back in January. We think this guy might have been involved in the First National robbery three years ago."

"The driver?" Lee asked, his interest piquing. They'd never gotten any leads on the getaway driver on that particular case, and it didn't seem like they had worked with Bolt on any other jobs.

"Bingo," said Duke. "A guy named Kamran Amir. Thirty-three. American citizen. Got in a little trouble as a kid – looks like he was homeless for a couple of years in his late teens – but he seems pretty straitlaced on paper after that."

"So what makes you think he's our guy?" Lee asked.

"He and Bolt dated for several months," Duke explained. "Then it appears he left Bolt just after the First National job. Guess where he's living now."

Lee wasn't one for guessing. He preferred facts. But Duke liked to make his agents work through the problem. So Lee rolled his eyes where his boss couldn't see him.

"Seattle?" he suggested.

All the robberies they were almost certain were connected had taken place in several other neighboring towns and cities, but the first ones had been in Seattle. That was why Lee's branch of the FBI was handling the investigation.

"Nope," said Duke with a singsong tone. "Try a little closer to home."

Now it all made sense. This was why Duke was calling Lee and not one of the half-a-dozen agents on the job who weren't currently trying to start their vacation.

"Pine Cove?"

"Yahtzee!" Duke cried, making Lee wince. He could just picture him spinning around in glee on his office chair. It was after six on a Friday night, so most sensible people had left for the weekend. Like Lee had attempted to do. But Duke was just as much of a workaholic as Lee was, and he'd revel being all alone with his files and reports, spinning on his damn chair.

"Kamran Amir lives in Pine Cove now?" Lee asked incredulously. Technically, his parents' home was between Pine Cove and Penny Falls, but it was Pine Cove where Lee had gone to school and hung out at the weekends.

"Is it really that surprising?" Duke asked. "You moved from there to here. People go the other way, too."

Lee wanted to argue that there were *plenty* of small towns in the Pacific Northwest and Amir could have relocated to anyone of them. But he'd chosen Pine Cove because...

Oh *shit.*

"The driving," Lee said excitedly, his brain whirring.

"See, Marshall," said Duke smugly. "This is why you deserve this promotion. You're fucking smart. Yes, Amir is still driving, just for film and TV now. And Uber, apparently." His pause suggested he was reading through his file. "Okay, Bolt's credit card statements suggest he was in your little podunk town for just one night. He used it at somewhere called Aquarium and a motel."

"Aquarium is the biggest gay bar around the area," said Lee, shaking his head as he couldn't help but reminisce.

He'd been there several times when he'd come home during college. It was cute in a kitschy way. That was back when Lee had been horny *all* the time and hadn't minded hooking up with random strangers. Before he'd become dedicated to his career. It was an entire lifetime ago.

"Okay," said Duke, his tone back to business. "I know you're heading to your folks' place, but can you swing by this guy's address first? If he knows anything about Bolt – what he's planning now, what happened three years ago – I want to know it, too. We can offer him immunity for the part he played if he can get us a conviction."

Lee sighed.

It wasn't like he was desperate to get home. Sure, he loved his parents and siblings, but this was going to be a whole huge family affair. A week-long celebration for his mom and dad's fortieth wedding anniversary. Ten *looong* days of organized fun, and every cousin, aunt, and great-aunt asking why he didn't have a new boyfriend yet.

As much as he'd promised them and himself that he wasn't going to work, there was a part of him that itched for the comfort of his job over the endless stretch of interrogations he was going to face.

Surely, it wouldn't matter if he put that off for a few more hours.

"No problem," he said as he changed lanes again, making his way toward the exit. He was about twenty minutes away from home, but he could reroute now and head toward town easily. "Send through the address."

Duke snorted. "That's my guy," he said as Lee's phone pinged with a new email. He'd pull over once he got off the freeway and program in the address to get him to Amir's place. "You know," Duke continued, "if you play this right and we finally catch Bolt and his crew, you could really have a shot at that promotion."

Lee rolled his eyes again and tried not to get his hopes up. "You always say that," he grumbled.

"This time I mean it, Marshall," Duke said, and Lee had to admit his voice did sound sincere. "You've done excellent work on the Bolt case. We're so close to getting him for good. See if you can rattle something out of this Amir character, take your family vacation, then come back so we can kick ass and finally close this case. All right?"

Lee exhaled and shook his head, trying not to get his hopes up too much. But maybe if he finally got that promotion he'd been chasing, it would make all the long hours and lonely nights worth it.

"Sounds good, boss," he said, resisting the urge to smile like a buffoon, even though he was alone. "Oh, is there any local law enforcement I should liaise with?"

"Yes, good thinking," said Duke. Lee heard several clicks of a mouse and the ruffling of papers. "Ah, yes, here we go. A Detective Lucy Padilla. But hopefully, you won't need anything from the local PD if Amir cooperates."

Lee hummed and frowned as he pulled into a gas station so he could park and input the new address. "Any idea if Amir is *going* to cooperate?" It would be nice to know what he was walking into.

But Duke made a dismissive noise. "I mean, they broke up. And it looks like Amir didn't come back to Seattle with him in January. So maybe this guy hates Bolt's guts. But that doesn't mean he's not an asshole. If he's who we think he is, he was still an accomplice in an armed robbery that could have earned him some serious Gs. I'd proceed with caution."

"Always do, boss."

Lee said his goodbyes and busied himself updating his GPS. He didn't really need a map to get him home. However, he liked to know what the traffic was doing. But he didn't recognize Amir's address off the top of his head. He wrinkled his nose as it came up. If Amir had gotten any share of Bolt's money, he hadn't spent it on a fancy place. That was the only area of Pine Cove that could be considered rough. Lee reminded himself not to make judgments, though, and got going.

He blew his cheeks out as he got back on the road. After college, he hadn't been back into the heart of Pine Cove since. When Lee did find time to visit, he usually just went to his parents' house for a night. He hadn't felt much need to relive his younger days. He liked moving forward, always. But he knew his family had probably planned some activities in the town he'd grown up in for this week, so maybe this would be his chance to reacquaint himself with everything.

It was kind of strange driving through Pine Cove. Even at night, Lee could see enough to spark his nostalgia. In fact, he surprised himself by taking a short detour just so he could cruise down Main Street. His heart gave little pangs as he recognized the Rise and Shine bakery, the Sunny Side Up diner, and the quaint boardwalk with its arcade.

He remembered his buddies Swift Coal and Rhett Perkins. They'd all played football together and had spent hours at the arcade drinking iced slushes and smashing each other's knuckles playing air hockey. Lee wondered what they were doing now. Heck, would they maybe be in town?

Suddenly, the idea of reaching out and catching up with some old buddies appealed to Lee. He barely had time for Facebook usually, but if it meant he could escape his well-meaning but meddling family for a few hours, he realized he was quite on board with the idea of reconnecting in person.

As it happened, he passed Aquarium anyway on his way

through town. But he wanted to try Amir at home first. It would be much easier to have this conversation in private if Lee was going to get any information out of him. He chewed his lip and pondered what kind of scumbag he was going to have to deal with. Or maybe he'd just been a victim of circumstance.

Lee shook his head to himself. In his line of work, the kind of people who tended toward armed robbery were not cute fluffy bunnies. He was going to have to be prepared for this guy to fuck him around.

He reluctantly parked his Jeep at the base of Kamran's apartment block and got out. There were a few other vehicles parked around the base of the building, including a beautiful Mustang that caught Lee's eye. He questioned what such a gorgeous car was doing in this part of town. The owner was taking a risk leaving it out in the open like that.

He shook his head. It wasn't his concern. The car didn't look to have been vandalized at present, so Lee pushed it from his mind. He jogged up several flights of stairs as the elevator was busted. The halls smelled musty, and several of the lights were out, but it wasn't the worst place Lee had been, not by a long shot. Still, he was eager to get back to his car, considering he had his laptop and suitcase for the family retreat inside.

But he pounded several times on the door before he accepted that Amir was either not at home or was ignoring any callers. Lee chewed his lip and debated calling this Detective Padilla but decided he didn't want to get into a big thing tonight. Besides, Padilla probably wouldn't thank him for spoiling her Friday night.

Lee's parents would be hurt if he was late for dinner. He checked his watch and considered what to do. He still had a couple of hours until his mom had requested he be there, so he figured he could still swing by Aquarium and ask around.

He rubbed his chin as he made his way back down the stairs, feeling the prickles there from the growth after he'd shaved that morning. He had to look neat for work, but part of him was tempted to grow his beard out over the next ten days. He'd probably have a decent amount of stubble by the end of the week.

But no one to rub it against.

He growled at himself in disappointment as he began driving back to the gay bar. He was too busy with work to be worrying about a boyfriend. Maybe after he got this promotion…

Then what? Billy had been right, he thought bitterly as sad thoughts of his ex drifted through his mind. It was never enough for Lee. He was always chasing the next case, the next conviction, the next promotion. He'd neglected Billy and driven him away.

But Lee's heart ached because he knew what he wanted, what he craved. The thought of a sweet, stable guy waiting for him at home made him want to keen with longing. He craved a *home* and someone he loved to breathe life into the space between those four walls. Maybe some kids, a dog. Lee bit his lip and imagined what kind of guy might fit into his little fantasy. Someone monogamous like Lee, who liked long-term relationships. Maybe a younger guy who'd had his heart broken once or twice who Lee could wrap up and shower with love.

He was embarrassed to discover a lump in his throat. Lee coughed angrily. "Focus on the job," he told himself as he looked for a parking spot on Main Street. It was a Friday night, so it wasn't easy. "Bag Bolt, then the promotion. Then you can maybe think about starting to date again, you big fool."

The trouble was, it was as if being back home in his small town was giving him funny ideas. Surely, Pine Cove was the kind of place to meet a sweet guy who liked a simple life of puppies and baking, not the hustle and bustle of Seattle. Guys there just wanted to fuck and run, in Lee's experience.

"You are not here to look for a boyfriend," he reminded himself sternly as he finally found a parking spot a couple of blocks away from the bar. "You're here to try and get information on a suspect in a case. A case that could make you a special agent. Get a grip."

Angrily, he snatched his keys from the ignition and locked the Jeep. He breathed in the cool March air as he walked with purpose back to Main Street. There was a fat moon hanging in the sky behind fluffy clouds that drifted by in the night. The familiar scent of pine filled Lee's lungs, and he allowed it to settle him.

He was here to do his job, and if he knew anything, it was that he was *excellent* at his job. And once he'd accomplished that, he was going to go home to his folks and be a dutiful son. He'd smile and nod, even after the tenth time someone asked if he was going to settle down already, and god help him, he was going to relax. His mom had plenty of activities planned for their vast family to take part in, and Lee was pretty sure a few afternoons of walking, touch football, and fishing would do him the world of good.

This vacation was precisely what he needed to center himself. He loved his job, but he wasn't an idiot. Billy had been right. He needed a better work-life balance, just *slightly.* He could take a break from the office this week and recharge his batteries, coming back stronger than ever.

After he dealt with this Amir guy.

Aquarium's doors were open, so Lee could feel the bass throbbing from a whole block away. He remembered that the bar was pretty chilled during the week, but as it was Friday night, it was already heaving with a short line outside. Lee debated standing in line, but he really didn't want to keep his folks waiting any longer than he could help it. So he nodded at the bouncer as he approached and flashed his badge.

"Any trouble?" the guy asked, looking Lee up and down.

He shook his head. "Shouldn't be," he assured him as he entered with another nod. The guy narrowed his eyes but then let him pass without further comment.

Ah. Lee realized he had a problem.

The place was packed, as expected, but all Lee had was Amir's driving license photo, which never looked much like the person in real life. If he was here, it was going to be pretty difficult to see him. He sighed and decided to try his chances at the bar. Pine Cove wasn't all that big. If he was lucky, Amir might be a regular.

He made his way through the throng, looking over the sparkly blue walls and tanks of real, colorful fish. He chuckled, remembering that they even had aquatic life in the men's rooms. More than once, he'd had a drunken chat with a guppy while he'd washed his hands.

He didn't exactly push his way to the front of the crowd at the bar, but his size meant people kind of naturally parted for him anyway. He was soon pressed against the counter, catching the eye of a cute twink with teal-and-purple hair. Not really Lee's type, but he had a big bright smile that warmed Lee's heart regardless.

"What can I get you, handsome?"

Lee gave him a tight smile back. "Actually, I was looking for this guy," he said as he held up his phone with Amir's photo. "I heard he might be around."

The twink's eyes went wide. "Kamran?" he asked in concern. "He's not in any trouble, is he?"

Lee shook his head and flashed his badge discreetly. "No, nothing like that," he assured the bartender. "I just have a couple of questions for him, that's all."

"About what?" someone demanded from somewhere near Lee's elbow.

He turned around to see a stunningly beautiful Asian guy dressed in booty shorts, glitter, and not much else. A beefcake placed his hand on the peeved guy's shoulder.

"Is Kamran okay?" the muscle guy asked. Both men gave Lee intense stares.

Whoa. So much for worrying whether Kamran was a regular in here. What was this? Cheers? Did everyone know his suspect? Lee didn't think they'd seen his badge, though. Just heard his question. So he tried to play it cool.

"No, everything's fine," Lee said with a smile he knew probably didn't reach his eyes. "But if you could point him out to me, I'd appreciate it."

The glittery guy scowled. "You don't know what he looks like?"

But the beefcake chuckled over the loud music. "Maybe it was dark and this poor sap doesn't remember who rocked his world." He winked at Lee. "You looking for round two, buddy? You wouldn't be the first."

"Or the last," Glitter added with a sinful giggle. "We love him, but oh em *gee* what a ho."

Lee opened and closed his mouth. These people assumed he'd had *sex* with Amir. He sounded like a real player. Lee tried not to wrinkle his nose and make any more snap judgments about this guy. What did it matter to Lee if Amir slept around? Lee was here for work.

"Uh, yeah, sure," he said, playing along. "You couldn't help a guy out and point me in the right direction, could you?"

Glitter snorted. "Sure, but you better be quick unless you want a *really* full bed tonight."

He and Beefcake laughed as they indicated where Lee should look, then cozied up together at the bar to order drinks for themselves.

Lee frowned, not sure what they meant, but as he cast his eyes to the corner where they'd pointed, he understood.

The most *stunning* guy was between two more hunks who were running their hands over his chest and back. They grinned down at him as he flashed cheeky grins between them, biting his lip and fluttering his eyelashes.

His skin was tan, and his thick hair dark. He had a perfectly sculpted small beard that ran the length of his square jaw, and his damp T-shirt clung to a lithe torso as he shimmied between the much bigger guys. He wasn't short exactly, but the other men were built more like Lee was. They definitely didn't skip leg day.

But it was Amir's eyes that made Lee's heart skip a beat and his cock swell in his pants. Those dark eyes just *sparkled* with mischief and mirth as he flirted with the bigger dudes. But there was something honest in them, something warm.

Lee mentally slapped himself and bit his tongue. He was here on an official investigation, not cruising for a good time. Who cared that Amir took his breath away? He was an accomplice to bank robbery and probably rotten through and through. And even *if* Lee were there for pleasure instead of business, Amir was the polar opposite of the kind of guy Lee would be looking for.

So Lee rubbed his hands on his thighs, willing his cock to calm down, and prepared to interrupt the threesome that was apparently about to happen.

And he absolutely definitely didn't feel jealous of anyone who was going to spend the night in the same bed as this gorgeous man later. Because Lee didn't do hookups. Lee didn't lust after criminals. And he certainly wasn't interested in the *suspect* he was approaching.

His cock might not have gotten any of those memos, but at least his brain was listening.

Sort of.

2

KAMRAN

"ALL THIS FUSS OVER LITTLE OLD ME," KAMRAN SAID, fluttering his eyelashes as he traced his fingertips down the rippled chests of the husbands he very much hoped to be sandwiched between before the night was through. These guys were fresh meat and apparently very keen to find a new friend to play with. Kamran licked his lips, unable to imagine anything better.

"Excuse me, gentlemen," a low voice rumbled over the pulsing bassline. "Kamran Amir?"

Kamran caressed the side of one of the husbands' jaws, lazily turning his attention to the guy who had said his name.

He wasn't sure what he'd been expecting, but this guy almost made his future bedfellows look scrawny. He was a mountain of a man, clean-shaven with piercing blue eyes and light brown hair. He met Kaman's gaze with a blazing intensity.

"Who's asking, handsome?"

The guy bristled. He was all buttoned up in a fancy suit that Kamran immediately wanted to spend hours peeling off him. He wondered if his new friends would be down for a fourth.

Kamran smirked. Nah, something about Mr. Suit screamed an allergy to group sex. In fact, he looked distinctly uncomfortable as he narrowed his eyes at Kamran. Maybe he wasn't even queer and had stumbled in here by accident.

No, the way his eyes helplessly flitted to look at the hands running down Kamran's chest informed him that this guy was definitely into dudes in some capacity. The question was, in what way? And how fast could Kamran figure out what that was?

"You jealous of our prize, friend?" one of the husbands asked in a teasing voice. "Because you might have to come back tomorrow. My man and I are only in town for one night, and we have some *serious* plans for this pretty boy here."

Kamran shivered, his balls tingling and his dick throbbing. He was so in the mood tonight to be bossed around. Being vers was the fucking best. But being fought over by three mountain men might be even better.

"Now, now," he said, pinching the chin of the husband who'd gone all deliciously caveman over him. "There's plenty of me to go around, I promise."

Mr. Suit cleared his throat, a blush creeping onto his creamy skin. *Oh.* Kamran suddenly had several vivid fantasies about bossing *him* around. Or maybe he was one of those shy types that turned savage in the bedroom. He certainly had the build for it. Jesus, the guy was a hulk.

"Mr. Amir," Mr. Suit finally said. Apparently, it had taken him a while to find his voice. He swallowed, his sharp Adam's apple bobbing. Kamran wanted to bite and suck at his neck until Mr. Suit wasn't so composed or stuffy with Kamran's marks littering his pale skin. "My name is Agent Marshall. I have a few questions for you. About a Charles Bolt."

He flashed an FBI badge, and all the blood drained from Kamran's body. If he hadn't been squashed between two chests made of granite, he was pretty sure his knees would have gone out from under him.

The FBI wants to ask about Chaz? FUCK!

"I, uh, I'm not sure I can help you there, sir," he said evasively.

Shit. He should have asked how the guy knew his name. Kamran had been too busy thinking with his dick.

He tapped one of the husbands' bulging arms and smiled up at him. "I'm a little *busy* right now," he said, trying to signal to his hookup that they should ignore the federal agent.

But the husbands frowned at each other, then down at Kamran. "The FBI?" one of them repeated.

Kamran's heart sunk. As if they'd protect the little fuck boy they'd just picked up for one night only. Kamran's skin flurried with goose bumps as coldness washed through him. He felt sick, all those drinks he'd had already threatening to come right back up.

"I hate to interrupt your evening," Marshall said, his eyes flicking between the husbands. "But I must insist on a few minutes of your time, Mr. Amir."

Kamran opened his mouth to tell him to fuck off, but fear stopped him. He didn't know if Chaz had betrayed him after all or if Marshall even knew anything.

"Yeah, okay," he said in a small voice. "It's all right, teddy bears," he said to the husbands as they protested. "I'm sure I'll be back soon. Why don't you get us all some beers, and we can have a dance before you take me to your fancy hotel."

He managed a wink, but he felt like someone else was operating his body as he fumbled to pick up his leather jacket from where he'd left it on the back of a chair. He pushed through the crowd.

"Mr. Amir?" Marshall called after him.

"Outside," Kamran snapped over his shoulder, finding his fight at last. "You've got five minutes."

Suddenly Mr. Suit didn't look delicious anymore. He looked fucking threatening, and Kamran had to struggle to breathe properly as he forced his way through the throng to get out back.

Aquarium had a gorgeous patio area covered in fairy lights that was quieter than the main bar. The dozen picnic tables were packed with people, so Kamran didn't even try to sit down. He just shoved his arms through his jacket and stood under one of the heaters so he wouldn't shiver as he spoke to the FB-fucking-I.

"I need your help, Mr. Amir," said Marshall directly. Apparently, the cold night air had done him some good as he didn't look nearly as flustered as he had been before. "Can I confirm that you know Charles Bolt?"

"Chaz? Yeah," said Kamran with a hollow laugh. "Asshole. Unfortunately, I dated him for a while until I found out what a loser he was."

Marshall's eyes searched Kamran's face, and he tried not to fidget under the scrutiny. "Has he been in contact with you recently?"

Kamran licked his lips, weighing his options. "Yeah," he said with a shrug, averting his gaze as he looked over the crowd of people enjoying their Friday night – like Kamran had been until a few minutes ago. "He came here, actually. A couple of months ago. He begged me to get back together or even just hook up. I told him no way, and he fucked off again."

That was all true, at least. Kamran just left off the part where Chaz had asked him to commit a felony. *Again.*

Marshall narrowed his eyes and appeared to consider something. "Mr. Amir, I want to assure you that we are after

Bolt here, not you. Any involvement you have in his past transgressions would be overlooked if you could help convict him and any of his co-conspirators."

Kamran's heart skipped a beat. An immunity deal. Was that what this guy was offering? For a second, Kamran went to open his mouth and ask what exactly that meant. But then he stopped himself. If he did that, he would be admitting his own guilt. Maybe that was precisely what Marshall was trying to get him to do?

"What past transgressions? He skip out on some parking tickets or something?" Kamran asked with a smirk. "You interrupted my hot date for some library fines?"

Marshall scowled, clearly not amused. "We believe Mr. Bolt has orchestrated over a dozen armed robberies, and I have it on good authority you were involved in at least one of them. But like I said, if you help us out with what you know, we could offer you immunity."

A shiver passed through Kamran's entire body. *Fuckity fuck FUCK.* They had information on him...but not proof? How could he find out without tipping his hand?

He couldn't. Not without knowing for sure that these guys wouldn't turn around and throw his ass in jail too – or worse. Kamran didn't look all that brown, but his name sounded very un-American. He didn't trust a bunch of suits any more than he did Chaz. As usual, he was completely on his own.

"Look, man," he said, keeping on the defensive "I know Chaz was a piece of work, but I don't know any details. I don't want any trouble. I'm sorry I can't help you, really. But all I know is that the guy came crawling back to me for sex. That's it. He didn't give me any blueprints to any vaults or instructions on how to find his super-secret lair or whatever."

Marshall growled, and Kamran tried telling his cock that *wasn't* a sexy sound. This guy was the *enemy.*

"Let me be clear," Marshall said. His blue eyes felt like they were piercing through Kamran's soul. "If you don't help us, I can't protect you."

Kamran ground his teeth and took a step forward, getting up in Marshall's face. He ignored the spicy cologne that wafted off him, resisting the urge to inhale deeply.

"If you'd have left me alone, I wouldn't need protecting," he said, jabbing a finger at Marshall's face. "I left Chaz because he was into shady shit. What do you think he'll do to me if he finds out I've been talking to the FBI? It won't matter that I don't know anything and therefore told you nothing. He'll still be very, very angry."

Kamran did his best not to tremble. He'd largely kept away from Chaz's business operations, but he was pretty certain it was linked to organized crime, and Kamran had absolutely zero desire to find out what those guys did to snitches.

Marshall sighed, then scrubbed his hand over his jaw, almost smooth aside for a day or so's growth of prickles. "We have the chance to put a dangerous man away for life," he said. His voice was so low his words only just reached Kamran's ears over the thrum of dozens of conversations and the pulse of the bassline from inside the bar. "This is important."

"You have fun with that, then," Kamran said cheerily, slapping Marshall's shoulder. "Sorry, not my problem. Is that all?"

His heart was racing. A part of him really did want to spill his guts and tell the feds every rotten thing he knew about Chaz. But no one looked out for Kamran except Kamran. He wasn't going to jail because Chaz tricked him so many years ago. What judge in their right mind would believe that? 'I swear, your honor, I just drove the car!' No, that was aiding and abetting, and Kamran's life might not be perfect, but it was a whole lot better than prison.

"Wait," Marshall called as Kamran turned to go. For some reason (Kamran blamed his still *very* interested dick), he actually stopped and looked at the agent again. Marshall slipped his hand inside his jacket pocket and pulled out a business card. "If you remember anything…anything at *all…* call me. The offer of immunity still stands. I'm serious when I say I want Bolt. You're insignificant."

Ouch. Well, what else was new?

Kamran plucked the card from between his thick fingers and forced himself not to imagine what a strong grip Marshall must have. "Okay. I still don't have anything to tell you. But if you feel better leaving your number with me, big guy, that's cool. If I'm ever desperate for a booty call, maybe I'll look you up."

Marshall spluttered, and the pink blush bloomed up his neck again, but Kamran didn't stick around to enjoy the effect his words had had on the FBI agent. Instead, he spun on his heels and marched straight back into the bar, trying not to let his nausea get the better of him.

The husbands had obviously been waiting for him, as they were still in the exact same spot with an ice bucket of brews on the table in front of them. But the last thing Kamran wanted to do now was be bossed around. Be vulnerable. He caught the eye of one of them and held his hand up, shaking his head and not breaking his stride as he headed for the door. They looked disappointed, but he was sure they would get over it and find another guy willing to be their third.

Kamran had been used enough for one evening.

"Leaving already?" Jimmy, the bouncer, asked. He was always weirdly aggressive with Kamran, like he was trying to flirt, but it came out more like bullying. Kamran didn't want to get blacklisted from his favorite bar, so he put up with it. But tonight, he had no room left for bullshit.

"Yep. See you later, man," he said as he stormed out onto Main Street.

He wrapped his arms around himself and tried to swallow the lump in his throat. Had he just made a huge mistake? Marshall's card felt like it was burning a hole in his pocket.

Part of him wanted to talk to someone. That would mean fessing up about his shameful past, but right now, Kamran was really scared. Would Marshall change his mind and take him down with Chaz now that he'd refused to cooperate? Or would he just use Kamran to get information, then throw him to the wolves?

He got his phone out before he realized he didn't know who he could call. Scout and Emery were his best buds, but they were back in Aquarium having a date night. There were several other people inside their friendship group, including their newest addition, Angel. But he had his own shit going on, and besides, this wasn't the kind of thing that Kamran wanted to explain over the phone. He didn't want *anyone* to know what he'd done. Ever.

Usually, he'd hail an Uber to take him home after a night of drinking, but he had a hunch the walk would do him good. Ironically, he was feeling pretty sober again after that encounter and might have been okay to drive, but as it was, he didn't have a choice, as his car was at home. So he zipped up his jacket and began marching his ass in the direction of his apartment.

By the time he trudged up the stairs and unlocked his door, he was in a real funk. He'd promised himself a night of pizza, TV, jerking off, and sleep. But all he did was fall onto his sofa in the dark apartment, still fully clothed with his shoes on, face-planting into the cushions with a groan.

"Fuck you, Chaz Bolt," he said vehemently.

It had been bad enough when he'd broken Kamran's heart, but now he was tormenting him years after the fact. Worries warred inside his gut as Kamran tried to convince himself he'd done the right thing.

"You need a beer, cheesy carbs, and a horror movie," Kamran said to himself. "This will all feel better in the morning."

But he didn't move off the couch. Instead, his keys dropped from his fingers onto the floor, and he let his eyes drift closed. His frayed nerves gave way to rest, and Kamran let it consume him. He allowed the gloom to soothe him as he chased a sleep that would make his fears go away, just for a little while.

Indeed, for a short time, he dozed, feeling almost peaceful.

Until the hand over his mouth woke him up immediately.

He cried out as someone clamped their hand down harder and hauled him to his feet. Terror flashed through Kamran as his eyes swung wildly around the apartment. There was another person there, judging by the swinging flashlight beams.

"Take whatever you want," he cried out as the guy let his mouth go to shake him. "I don't have any cash, but there's a PlayStation, and, uh…"

Whoever was holding him yanked him closer, his cigarette breath making Kamran recoil in disgust. The other person swiped at everything on the kitchen counter, sending appliances and jars of coffee to the floor with a crash. Kamran would have hoped the neighbors had heard the clatter, but people were always fighting and breaking stuff around here.

No one was going to be calling the police.

"Like we'd rob this shithole," Cigarette Breath said with a malicious chuckle. "Nah, Kammy. We're here on behalf of Chaz. He'd like to know what you said to the nice FBI agent tonight."

Fuck – what? How could Chaz know about that?

"Who? What?" Kamran spluttered as the other asshole took something – maybe a baseball bat? – to Kamran's TV. "Oh, come on, guys! I don't know anything! I didn't say anything!" He struggled against the hands holding him, feeling sick from the lights swinging all over the place. There were sounds from the bedroom, and Kamran realized there must have been a third person. Were they going through his clothes? "What the hell are you looking for?" he squawked.

Cigarette Breath laughed again, the twisted fuck. "Nothing. The boys are just blowing off steam." He leaned closer, his smile a snarl mere millimeters from Kamran's nose. "Chaz told us to come fetch you like the good puppy you are. He wants a word."

Panic flooded Kamran in an instant. He didn't think. He just kicked viciously and swung his fist at the guy's head. He got lucky, slamming into both his shin and his head, and Kamran used the opportunity to break free.

He only had a couple of seconds' advantage, but that was all he needed. Kamran was the type of guy who'd planned emergency escape routes from his apartment in case of a home invasion one day. It seemed like the kind of shit that would happen to him, and here he was.

Cigarette Breath stumbled backward, caught off guard and pinwheeling his arms. He didn't cry out for a second, giving Kamran another slight advantage. Adrenaline thumping through him, Kamran snatched his keys from the carpet by the sofa and lunged for the window he never locked, thrusting it upward. The shouting was right behind him, but he didn't let fear hold him back or make him second-guess anything. He just grabbed the drainpipe and half slid, half fell the few stories to the ground.

"Fuck!" he cried as he rolled over the asphalt, jarring his shoulder and tasting blood in his mouth. He spat it out as he scrambled back to his feet, charging toward his car. Those assholes hadn't followed him out the window, just like he'd hoped. They were probably too big. But he'd bet his last dollar that they were running down the stairs after him.

He threw his ass in the driver's seat, his heart racing as he pulled away from his apartment block without turning the lights on. He was a skilled enough driver that he made it several blocks before he risked switching on the beams and slowing his speed just a little.

He hit the steering wheel and let out a primal roar. "Fuck, fuck, FUCK!" he hollered.

He choked back a sob and rubbed his hand over his face. He was so screwed – he didn't know what he was going to do, where he could turn. He couldn't risk going to any of his friends in case he put them in danger. If Chaz caught up to him and fucked him up, it would kind of be his own fault. But the likes of Emery and Scout were *good* people. They didn't deserve this shitstorm.

Eventually, he calmed down enough to pick somewhere to drive to. He steered his beloved Mustang through the winding road that cut through the pine forest the town was named after, bringing it to a halt at his favorite peaceful spot that looked over the lake from about a hundred feet up. Shaking, Kamran got out of the car and slammed the door before going to rest his ass against the hood, looking out over the moonlit waters.

He *loved* his stupid life here. It wasn't much, but it was his. He didn't want Chaz to run him out of town, but what choice did Kamran have? He wasn't going to let Chaz hurt him, and he *certainly* wasn't going to help with whatever job he was planning. Which left…

"Oh no," Kamran croaked. He unfolded his arms and reached into his pocket with a trembling hand. He had precisely *one* option left.

Even if Agent Marshall was the very last person he wanted to call right now, he was Kamran's only hope.

3

LEE

Well, that hadn't gone as planned.

Lee was used to dealing with less than favorable individuals, but Amir...he'd really rubbed Lee the wrong way. He wasn't the first to act like he didn't give a single damn about Lee's case – morally corrupt felons didn't tend to have a yearning desire to aid the greater good. But Amir was probably the first to turn Lee down *while also flirting*.

Lee had been left in the courtyard feeling distinctly ruffled after Amir had stormed off. He practically vibrated with frustration, and after standing in a daze for a minute or more, he'd finally shaken himself and marched straight to the bar. He'd been just about ready to order when he'd remembered he was driving, so with a sense of deflation, he'd ordered a Coke.

For a few minutes, he scanned the crowd, looking for Amir, but he'd seen nothing. Either Amir was still there and staying well away from Lee, or he'd already left.

Lee felt like he had an itch he couldn't scratch. He wanted to get one last word in with Amir, but that wasn't going to happen. He was a rat who'd fled a sinking ship, Lee was sure.

The thing was, he mused as he snagged a bar stool and nursed his soda, was that he had no idea why he *cared*. He'd butted heads with plenty of perps who didn't want to help him. Some he'd been able to encourage to do the right thing, others not so much. But ultimately, they all went on with their lives, and Lee didn't give them a second thought once the case was done.

But Kamran…

Uh – Amir, he scolded himself with a frown. The guy's name was *Amir.*

Anyway, perhaps it was the flash of fear that Lee was absolutely certain he'd seen in Amir's eyes, just for a second when Lee had said Bolt's name. It had to have been fear for his own self-preservation. Lee would bet his badge that Amir knew more than he was letting on. And if he didn't want to let Lee help him, that was his problem.

But Lee's gut had got him this far in his career, and he knew better than to ignore it. Something deep inside him was telling him there was more to Kamran Amir than all the flirtatious bravado on the surface would suggest.

Or perhaps that was just wishful thinking on Lee's part. Perhaps he was just the next in a long line of gullible men to get suckered in by those beautiful eyes and that wicked smile. Lee might not be into hookups, but he was still only human. A human who hadn't had sex with another man in far too long.

He swirled his paper straw around his drink, watching the ice cubes bob, and tried to convince himself that he wasn't going to jerk off later that night, replaying every delicious thing Kamran had said before he'd realized Lee was there to see him on official FBI business.

Amir. Fuck, he needed to get a grip on himself.

Or he needed a drink. A real one.

He sighed and decided to stop putting off the inevitable.

His folks would be expecting him soon, along with a whole host of other family members, and Lee needed to shake off this funk so he could smile and play the dutiful son role.

Preferably with a large glass of red wine in hand.

He made eye contact with the cute twink bartender and nodded to say thanks. The guy winked and waved. "Come back soon, cutie," he cooed over the music.

Lee smiled in return, but he didn't think he would come back. Right now, his gut was telling him he'd only spend any future time in Aquarium swiveling his head, looking for a certain someone. He grunted in annoyance at himself as he made his way out the door and started walking back to his Jeep. It had obviously been a long, *long* time since anyone had given him blue balls, and he was just mad about it.

Not that a *suspect* was someone he should be thinking about inappropriately. But Lee convinced himself that if he was never going to see the guy again, an inappropriate thought or two couldn't hurt.

"Jesus," he muttered to himself as he left the throbbing bassline from the bar behind. "Who are you, and what have you done with Agent Marshall?" Maybe he really was getting into vacation mode already.

He rubbed his head and wondered if he should call Duke back now. But he decided against it. Because apparently, he was an absolute fool who wanted to give Amir a day to change his mind and call him. Or at least a few more hours.

Lee rolled his eyes at himself. Would he really feel better about his stupid little crush if the guy was less of a jerk? It wasn't like Lee *knew* Amir in the slightest. This whole attraction was based on a few infuriating, flirty remarks and the rest was pure physicality. What did it matter if he was a petty crook or...?

Or...Lee was back to that fear. This niggling feeling that

there was more to Amir than met the eye was getting really annoying.

He blew out his cheeks as he approached his car. He rolled his shoulders and cracked his neck. "Family mode, family mode," he muttered to himself. "There's no point taking a vacation if you're going to be preoccupied with the Bolt case the entire time."

He unlocked the car and started trying to list his older sister's kids' names from oldest to youngest. But the trouble was she just kept popping them out, and he hadn't even *met* the youngest yet, so he'd sort of lost track. Was Mia, the eldest, eight or nine now?

He finished programming in his parents' address (the app said no traffic, at least), and he put his key in the ignition.

Just as his phone rang.

He sighed and fumbled to get it out of his pocket, expecting it to be Duke chasing him for an update. But the caller was unknown. For a split second, Lee's heart leaped – actually *leaped* – as he thought it could be Amir. But that was ridiculous. It had been less than an hour since he'd left Lee in the courtyard, and he was probably in naked ecstasy with that muscular couple by now. Something that Lee was *not* going to visualize unless he wanted to break something.

"Agent Marshall," he answered.

"Uh, yeah. Hi."

Lee sat up straight in his seat at the distinctly rattled-sounding voice. The guy was breathless, and his words were scratchy. *Shit.*

"Amir?"

"Yeah, look," he said tersely. "Something's happened. Can we talk?"

"Of course," said Lee, looking around out of habit to make sure no one was around. "How can I help?"

"Not over the phone," said Amir. "Can you meet me? I'm

out by the lake. I kind of...well, I don't want to go back into town right now."

Coldness washed through Lee, and he resisted the urge to ask what had happened again. Kamran had said he wanted to talk in person, so that was what they would do.

"Where are you?" Lee asked firmly. "I can meet you. What's the address?"

Amir exhaled. "Fuck. I don't know. It's Ridgepoint View. If you take the main road out of town and—"

"I know it," Lee interrupted. "I grew up here. I can be there in about fifteen minutes. Will you be all right until then?"

Amir scoffed. "I mean, I might freeze my ass off, but I'll be here," he grumbled.

Lee realized he was smiling at hearing Amir bitch. He couldn't be in that much trouble if he was complaining. But then Lee remembered he was working and wiped the smile off his face.

"Don't move," Lee said, then ended the call.

He didn't bother trying to input the location into the GPS, as it didn't really have an address. It was just a local place that everyone knew – even Lee, despite not living in the area for many years.

So he just started the car and set off, his heart thumping loudly in his chest. What had happened to spook Amir? He'd been pretty adamant in his refusal before. Why had he changed his mind?

Lee shook his head and put his brain back in charge rather than his heart or his cock. He dialed Duke as he drove. He didn't pick up, but Lee left him a voicemail to tell him what he was doing. That way, if this was a trap set by Amir and Bolt, at least Lee's superiors would know where to look for his body.

But as Lee approached the turnoff, he only saw one car in

the dirt parking lot. It was too late for sightseers and too early for teens making out, so for now, he and Amir were alone.

Lee killed his car engine and got out at the same time as Amir exited the stunning black Mustang that Lee had seen parked near Amir's apartment building. "Oh, wow," he said without thinking. Apparently, his heart had taken over from his brain again. "That's your car?"

Despite looking tired, Amir smiled and nodded, trailing his hand along the paintwork. "Yep. This is my baby," he said with warm pride. Then he pulled his hand away and fixed Lee with a stern glare. "So thanks for almost getting me killed, you asshole."

Lee stopped in his tracks and blinked at Amir. They were both standing between their cars, a few feet between them. Amir crossed his arms. Lee frowned at him.

"Uh…what?"

Amir scoffed and shook his head. "I *told* you Chaz wouldn't be happy if he heard I was talking to the FBI. I don't know if he's watching you or me, but his goons just showed up at my place, trashed it, and tried to take me to see the bastard with the promise of some really fun pain. If you'd just left me alone…" He broke off, muttering under his breath.

Lee's feet moved forward without any consultation from his brain. He reached out and touched Amir's shoulder. "Are you all right? How did you get away?"

Amir shrugged, but he didn't throw Lee's hand off. "Jumped out the window and shimmied down the drainpipe." He shook his head and looked up at the cloudy sky. "Fuck. I didn't want *any* of this. Look – is that deal still on the table? Because apparently none of you assholes will just let me get on with my life."

Lee swallowed and took his hand back. *Maintain distance,*

genius, he berated himself. "Immunity is absolutely still on the table," he assured him. "So is protection. We can get you somewhere safe, away from Bolt and his people."

Amir made a clicking noise at the back of his throat. "Yeah, whatever," he said. "If I have to choose the lesser of two evils, I guess you're not threatening to have me beaten right now." He licked his lips, then met Lee's gaze.

There was that fear again.

"I won't let anything happen to you," Lee assured him, startling himself with his own sincerity.

"Whatever," Amir repeated. "Look, he tricked me."

"I'm sorry?"

"He tricked me," Amir repeated. "He told me he was picking something up and he needed a lift home. He didn't tell me what he was picking up was *three hundred thousand dollars* with the assistance of a handgun. I didn't know, I swear. He yelled 'drive,' I drove, and by the time I worked out what had happened, it was done." He huffed, his breath coming out as smoke. "I broke up with his sorry ass that same day – not that you probably care about that. But...I really didn't know, I swear."

"I believe you," Lee said, surprised to find that he really did. "Okay...here's what we're going to do..."

"ARE YOU KIDDING ME?" Lee demanded through the phone several minutes later.

But Duke never joked, not about work.

"I don't know what to tell you," he said on the other end of the line. "It's a Friday night. You're in the middle of nowhere. Either you bring him back to Seattle where we can babysit him, or—"

"Or I babysit him here," Lee said.

He pinched the bridge of his nose as he paced along the railing by the lookout point. It really was a stunning vista with the forest rising up all around the lake, the moon and the clouds reflecting on the water, the town lights twinkling to the right, and the mountain looming to the left.

It was no big deal, really. He could make the three-hour drive to Seattle, deposit Amir, go back to his apartment, then return here in the morning. But it was the weekend, and Lee knew it would be a nightmare to get Amir set up somewhere safe if he really was afraid of Bolt's people finding him again. His trusty gut was telling Lee not to let the guy out of his sight, but…

"Sir, I'm supposed to be on the way to see my family right now. Tell me what to do here. Put him in a local hotel?" That would qualify as letting him out of his sight. Lee sighed. "I guess I could stay with him. My folks would understand…"

"Could you take him with you?" Duke suggested.

Lee stopped pacing.

"Have you spun around too many times on your chair?" he asked sincerely.

Duke laughed. "Look, it's just until we get things straightened out. Can't you just tell them the truth? That you need to bring a little work home with you?"

Lee thought of his mother's disappointment after he'd promised so faithfully that he'd take an honest-to-god vacation. He thought of his father's bitter resentment at being reminded that Lee had wanted to do something so uncouth as go into law enforcement instead of joining the family business.

"I can't bring a suspect home with me," he said, rubbing his forehead and covering his eyes. "I just can't. But my gut says he's in danger and I should take care of him. So I'll find us a hotel where we can hunker down – I can pay for it – and—"

"Don't tell them I'm a suspect."

Lee whirled around and saw Amir had crept up behind him and had that dangerous sparkle back in his eye.

"Uh, what?" Lee said, aware of just how dumb he sounded.

"Look," said Amir, raising his eyebrows. "I'm freaked the fuck out, and I want *you* watching out for me."

"Why me?" Lee asked, mindful that Duke was hanging on the other end of the line.

Amir laughed. "Because you are the size of that Jeep over there! Because *you* promised to keep me safe, and you're not passing the buck that easily. Nope. You want me to help you out? I'm sticking to you like glue. So bring me home to meet your folks and tell them I'm a friend from work or a boyfriend or something."

"A *boyfriend?*" Lee repeated. He definitely didn't squeak. Uh-uh.

"A boyfriend?" Duke piped up with interest. "Oh, Marshall, that's kind of genius. You could keep him protected *undercover.* If he's with you, pretending to be your guy, it won't look suspicious if you never leave his side."

"But—!" Lee spluttered. This couldn't be happening. "No, sir, that's insane! We just met an hour ago. I can't spring him on my folks – my entire family! No one will believe it for one thing."

"Look, I'll be straight with you, Marshall," Duke growled down the phone. "I want Bolt, and I want him bad. I don't see a problem with this solution. In fact, it's perfect. Unless…I don't know, is he really hideous? Cough twice for yes."

"N-no. It's not that," Lee managed to stammer. It was pretty much the *opposite* of that. "It's…"

It's that I thought I was never going to see him again, so I've already had inappropriate thoughts, and I don't think I can close that Pandora's box again.

43

"Good," Duke steamrolled ahead. "Sorry if this puts a kink in your vacation plans, but like you said before, you never take vacations anyway."

"No, *you* said that," Lee grumbled.

"It'll give you a good chance to find out everything he knows about Bolt," Duke continued. "And if you *really* can't stand him by the start of next week, I'll see what I can do about protective custody here. Unless you think he's a flight risk?"

Lee turned back to glance at Amir, who seemed like he'd been holding his breath. As their eyes met, Amir smiled and looked hopeful, like a puppy.

A really *sexy* puppy.

Fucking hell.

"I'll be good, I swear," Amir said, holding up his hands as if he was giving a peace offering. "I'll play along with your family. I'll testify against Chaz. Just…don't throw me to the wolves, okay? Chaz was mean as a snake when I knew him, and he can only have gotten worse. I'm at your mercy, Agent Marshall."

Lee swallowed as his damn heartstrings tugged. "Okay, fine," he groused to both Amir and Duke. He tried not to let his heart soar too much when Amir broke into a beautiful, grateful smile. "Let's see if we can make this work. But we are setting some ground rules," he said firmly to Amir. "And you owe me extra vacation days," he added to Duke.

But Duke had gotten his way, so he just laughed. "Like you don't have about a hundred stacked up over the years. That promotion is looking *real* sweet right now if you can pull this off. I know you're my guy, Marshall."

"I'm a gullible fool," he said with a sigh. "I mean it. Extra vacation and a serious shot at that promotion."

"You got it," Duke said.

Then he closed the call.

Lee exhaled and slipped the phone into his jacket pocket. Then he met Amir's gaze.

"Okay," his new charge said with raised eyebrows. "Now what?"

Now what indeed.

4

KAMRAN

ON A SCALE OF ONE TO TEN OF BAD IDEAS, THIS WAS PROBABLY an eleven.

What had Kamran been thinking? Well, he'd probably been thinking that he wanted to avoid a lot of pain, among other things. And the best solution for that was hiding behind the biggest, scariest guy he could find. Lucky for him, he had himself an Agent Lee Marshall.

"So your name is Lee," said Kamran from where he was leaning against his Mustang with his arms crossed. "You're an FBI agent from Seattle, and you've come home for a big family reunion."

"For my parents' fortieth wedding anniversary," Marshall grunted. He also had his arms crossed as he rested against the big black Jeep he'd arrived in. The thing was like a tank, which made sense because so was its owner.

Kamran narrowed his eyes at him and tried not to shiver too much as a cold breeze blew through the forest. His adrenaline was wearing off, and he could feel himself crashing. But they each had to drive their cars to Marshall's folks' house, and Kamran wasn't going anywhere until he knew what he was walking into.

Of all the cockamamy schemes he'd gotten himself into over the years, this had to be the most bizarre. But Marshall had said that his boss liked the idea, and Kamran really liked the idea of having a human brick wall between him and Chaz's goons for the foreseeable future. He'd meant what he said. Marshall had promised to protect him, and Kamran was going to hold him to that.

Even if that meant playing house.

Kamran could be a great boyfriend, he was sure. He'd watched all his friends doing it. He'd hung out with the Coal clan and Perkins posse enough to understand that some families really did *like* their kids, even the queer ones. Heck, they even *loved* them.

"So how many people are we talking here?" Kamran asked. "And it's, like, a whole weekend thing?"

He was already worrying what would happen to him when Marshall handed him over to someone else, but he'd cross that bridge when he came to it. So long as he didn't have to sleep in his car tonight, Kamran wasn't thinking that far ahead.

Marshall sighed and rubbed his eyes. When he looked back at Kamran, he could see how blue they were, even by moonlight.

"It's a full vacation," Marshall explained. "From now until next Sunday."

"But that's, like, ten days?" Kamran cried in surprise. "What the hell are you going to do for all that time?"

"We," Marshall corrected wearily. "This was your bright idea. *We* are going to spend time with my parents, siblings, their partners and kids, as well as my aunts, uncles, cousins, second cousins, and lord knows who else."

Kamran became aware that his mouth was hanging open.

His brow furrowed as he stared at Marshall in disbelief. *"All those people? Under one roof? Who are you – the Kardashians? Do you live in a castle?"*

Was it his imagination, or did Marshall look uncomfortable? "We have, um, guest quarters. It's, uh, good. With all those people, there'll be less focus on us. I hope. Less questions."

Kamran shook his head. "Oh, no. Are you about to tell me you're closeted? If they're assholes, I'll take my chances sleeping in my car."

He meant that.

Sort of.

Luckily, Marshall shook his head emphatically. "No, they're not homophobic. I've been out since my early twenties. Half my cousins are gay, for real. That's not it. Besides, it's family. They have to love you no matter what, right?"

Kamran narrowed his eyes. Normally, he didn't let remarks about family and unconditional love rattle him. But he was on his last nerve, and this guy had just turned his life upside down.

"I wouldn't know," he said peevishly, looking out over the lake. "I haven't spoken to a single member of my family in eighteen years. They don't know if I'm alive or dead, and I don't think they'd care either way."

He looked back at Marshall, and some of his anger melted away at the expression of pure horror he saw there.

"Fuck, I'm sorry," Marshall croaked. He sighed and rubbed the back of his neck. "Your file said you'd been on your own as a teen, but I didn't know the extent of it. I'm sorry."

Something strange fluttered through Kamran. He wasn't used to talking about his past, let alone receiving sympathy for the shitty way his family had treated him. Chaz certainly hadn't cared. But this stranger seemed really caught up about it.

"It's okay," he said with a shrug. "It was a long time ago, you know? I have a found family now."

He chewed his lip and wondered if that was really true. He really liked his friends, but they were all coupled up now. Sometimes it was hard not to feel lonely, even when he was surrounded by people. He put on his party face, of course. He'd never let them see he was unhappy. But not for the first time he thought about what it might be like to have someone – more than one person, even – love you unconditionally.

"That's good," said Marshall. "I'm glad you found your people. Family isn't just blood."

Kamran was done talking about this. He'd rather deal with the more pressing matters at hand.

"Okay, so your family aren't aggressively homophobic," said Kamran, only partly relieved. "Then what is it? I can tell you really don't like this plan." Kamran couldn't blame him. Kamran wasn't the 'take home to Mama' kind of guy. "Look, I meant what I said. I'll behave, scout's honor." He saluted by his head. "I really don't want Chaz anywhere near me. If that means making small talk with Aunt Mildred about cats, I'll do it. Just, um…"

Don't leave me! he wanted to scream. Just for once, Kamran wanted someone to give a damn about him, even if it was only because he had dirt on Chaz. But there was also a small, pathetic part of him that desperately wanted Marshall to see something worth protecting. He seemed like a decent guy. It would make a nice change to have someone like him give a crap about Kamran.

Marshall sighed again. "Okay, so the thing is, my family cares a *lot* about me," he said, sounded pained.

"Oh, no. How tragic," Kamran drawled deadpan.

Marshall rolled his eyes. "They're going to ask us a

million questions. If our story isn't airtight, they'll work it out. And I don't want to lie to them, all right? It's a shitty thing to do. If they find out I brought a sham boyfriend home, it'll break their hearts. They're still cut up over my last boyfriend not working out."

Kamran blinked, not quite sure he was understanding. "You're worried about hurting their feelings?"

Marshall shrugged.

Kamran laughed. "Because I'm a no-good criminal who's no way near good enough for Prince Lee Marshall. Right, sure, I get it."

Marshall frowned. "I didn't say that," he said defensively.

"You didn't have to," Kamran grumbled. "Whatever, it's fine. I told you I'd be on my best behavior, and I mean it."

But Marshall still looked put out. "No, Am—Kamran. I mean it. There's nothing wrong with you. And you said you just got tricked by Chaz that one time…unless there are other crimes I don't know about?"

"No!" said Kamran hotly, angrily crossing his arms again. "I did some shit when I was a minor, but mostly I'm a regular, normal guy."

Marshall appeared to relax. "Exactly. That's good," he said before shaking his head. "I mean, that's good for me. I mean —" He growled in frustration. "That's the kind of guy I like to date. But – okay, yeah – my family is rich. *Really* rich. And my dad has certain ideas about who I should date. It took me months to bring Billy to meet them – almost a year. When I show up with someone I haven't mentioned one syllable about, they're going to smell a rat and probably ask even more questions."

Kamran, yet again, wasn't following. "So you tell them they're too nosy and should mind their own business."

Marshall *definitely* looked noticeably uncomfortable at that concept, and Kamran tilted his head in fascination. He knew his friends cared what their families thought of them and their life partners. He also knew that the Coals and Perkinses desperately wanted all their kids to be happy. But this was something different.

"You want their approval," said Kamran heavily. "And I'm not going to get you that. Well…shit. I'm sorry I'm just a lowly Uber driver and not some billionaire."

"We're not billionaires," Marshal said quickly before wincing. "Well, I think my cousin Graham is, but we don't talk about that."

"Oh, yes," said Kamran, putting on a fancy British accent. "One *mustn't* talk about money. It's simply not cricket!"

He was making jokes to cover up the sting of yet again not being good enough for someone. It was what he always did, so it came naturally to him. But the fact that Marshall was so out of his league upset Kamran more than it should have.

Because if it was just for one night, if it was just for fucking, Kamran could have pretended he was good enough for Marshall. But if it included discussing ponies and knowing which was the correct dinner fork to use, Kamran was severely out of his depth.

Marshall dropped his arms and looked up at the moon. "I'm worried about hurting my mom's feelings. She wants me to be happy, and she'd never understand me tricking her like this. I'm worried that my dad is going to be cruel to you because he's a stuck-up jackass, and he's not the only one in my family. I'm worried whether or not I can keep you safe if Bolt's men have put a target on your back. And I'm worried that I've agreed to the dumbest idea in the history of the Bureau because I'm desperate to get a promotion, but now I'm going to fuck it up and get *fired* instead."

Kamran raised his eyebrows. "That's a lot of worries," he

said. "No wonder you're buttoned up so tight in that suit. Otherwise, they'd all come tumbling out."

Again with the jokes. But if he didn't make fun, he might have to acknowledge that Marshall had just admitted that he was worried about his dad being *mean* to Kamran. Kamran could understand him wanting to keep him safe – if he was going to be his witness, Marshall would want him alive to actually testify. But why the hell would he care if his dad said something unpleasant to Kamran? Kamran was a tough guy. He could deal with an asshole dad. Hell, he'd lived through growing up with his own one well enough. But why would Marshall care about that?

Marshall made a sort of grunting noise that could have been a laugh, then glanced at Kamran. "No flirting," he said. "I mean it. This is a business arrangement."

Kamran scoffed. "Oh, handsome, if I were flirting, you'd know about it."

Marshall quirked an eyebrow. "Oh?"

Kamran responded by fluttering his eyelashes and going all coy. "Why yes, Mr. Tough FBI Man. You'd probably notice by the way I was on my knees, begging to suck your cock. I bet you've got a *huge* one."

Much to his delight, Marshall's blush was visible in the moonlight. "None of *that,* I mean it. No...no dirty talk or anything. Absolutely *nothing* physical is going to happen between us. You're my responsibility."

Kamran huffed and rolled his eyes, dropping the act. "Okay, fine. But you say you want your family to believe we're really dating, and I can do that. But it'll have to involve just a little bit of PDA." He threw his hands up. "I'll keep it totally respectable. I promise."

Marshall rubbed his temples and groaned. "Okay, this is really happening. We should probably stop wasting time and get going. There's no sense in putting it off any longer."

Kamran laughed. "Whoa there. Aren't you supposed to be the hotshot FBI agent? How about we work on our story for two seconds. How did we meet? How long have we been dating?"

What made a guy like you settle for a guy like me?

Kamran pushed that unhelpful thought away.

At least Marshall had the decency to look sheepish. "Okay, good point," he mumbled. "Huh, we met..."

"On Grindr?"

Marshall scowled. "At the gym. In Seattle. If they think you're from out of town, they won't go nosing around Pine Cove for gossip. And we've been together since..."

"January," said Kamran, getting into this little roleplay. "We bonded when all the other casuals gave up on their New Year's resolutions and quit coming. Of course, I'm more of a cardio guy, and you're more into bench pressing...well, me."

He grinned wickedly, delighted when Marshall cleared his throat and looked away. Kamran might not be good enough for him and his snobby family, but he got a kick out of knowing that at least he was affecting him in the pants region.

"See, that wasn't so hard, was it?" he teased. "I bet you took me to a fancy restaurant and got all gentlemanly. We kissed on the first date, but you wouldn't sleep with me until the third."

"My family do *not* need to know details like that," Marshall spluttered.

Kamran chuckled. Despite the massive crappiness of his evening, he was honestly having a little fun.

"I'm a method actor," he said with a shrug, then licked his lips. "This may shock you, but I don't actually *date*. Especially not since Chaz. I'm more of a 'different person every night' kinda guy. So I need to know these things if we're going to be believable." He waggled his eyebrows. "Oh, and I personally don't like labels, but to be clear, I'll bang anyone willing with a pulse. Man, woman, people who are both or neither or in between. You can tell people I'm bi if that helps, though. I bet you're one of those serial monogamists. One long-term relationship after the other?"

Marshall grunted. Kamran took that as a yes.

"And you're gay?" he prompted. He just had a feeling.

Sure enough, Marshall nodded. Just like Kamran had thought, they were totally opposite.

"So…you really don't date?" Marshall asked.

Kamran shrugged. "Nope. Too much hassle." *And heartbreak.* "But I guess you're *extra* special, and I gave up my playboy ways and promised not to dick down anyone else." He crossed his heart. "Any tattoos I should know about?"

"No," Marshall snapped. "Okay, you. You, um, drive Uber?"

"Is that not good enough?" Kamran asked. "I remind you I *could* tell them I work in the movie business, but you don't want them knowing I live here in town."

Marshall blew out his cheeks. "*I* don't care what you do. *I'm* not a snob. But things might go smoother if we embellish a little." His face suddenly lit up with a grin that could almost be described as mischievous, and excitement bubbled up through Kamran like Champagne. "You want to play make-believe? Why don't we tell them you're an up-and-coming NASCAR driver?"

Kamran spluttered out a laugh. As much as the idea thrilled him, it was preposterous.

"Because I'm not?" he suggested. "And a three-second internet search could prove it? Also, I'm broke. What few things I have are back at my place, and I'll be lucky if they haven't ripped, smashed, or burned everything in there by now." He rubbed his chest, suddenly sobering up. "Fuck. I don't even have a *phone* charger. I have what I'm wearing and my car…that's it."

He didn't even register that Marshall moved until he'd placed his hands on Kamran's shoulders. He'd done that before, but now was different. Now, Kamran wanted to lean into that touch. He wanted Marshall to wrap his enormous arms around him and make the whole big bad world go away.

But he couldn't make it go away, and Kamran shouldn't want to let him do that anyway. Still, he didn't shrug off the touch. He'd had a really crappy day, and he needed a little comfort, even just for a moment.

"I can get one of the tech guys to work a little magic and have your fake profile online before we even get to my parents' driveway," Marshall said, his voice a low, soothing rumble. "And I'm so sorry about your stuff. We can see what's left soon. I can send someone over, or we can go ourselves when we know it's safe."

Kamran scoffed and rolled his eyes. "I doubt there will be much worth saving. Besides, none of it is, y'know, nice. I can't pretend to be something I'm not."

He became aware that Marshall was rubbing his thumbs in strong circles against Kamran's collarbones, and he had to work really hard not to let his eyes flutter closed or groan.

"We'll go shopping tomorrow," Marshal said. "I'll get you new stuff."

"What?" Kamran spluttered. "No, you can't—"

"If this is going to work," Marshall interrupted firmly, "then you have to look the part. Besides, you can't spend the next several days in the same clothes. Think of it as an apology for me leading Bolt's men to you. You're right. They wouldn't have trashed your place or tried to take you back to Seattle if I hadn't barged into Aquarium, flashing my badge, and generally behaving like a bull in a china shop."

Kamran felt his lips twitch, but he refused to smile. "Well…I guess you *do* owe me for that," he grumbled. "I could *let* you take me shopping. If I'm going to be your bae, I suppose I should look the part."

For a second, Marshall seemed to bask in his triumph. Then he dropped his hands and stepped away.

Kamran resisted the urge to pout.

"Okay. Right," he said awkwardly. "So that's a yes to NASCAR?"

Kamran considered him a second, feeling odd that Marshall – as an FBI agent – wasn't just telling him what to do. He was asking Kamran if this was okay.

"Yeah," he said, nodding as a smile crept onto his face. "That could be really fun, and I'd know what I'm talking about."

"Excellent," Marshall said.

He rubbed his hands together, then blew on them. Kamran had a fleeting thought about wanting to keep them warm himself, then shoved it away. Marshall had said an emphatic 'no,' and Kamran would respect that.

Mostly.

"Okay, well," Marshal continued, "that's probably enough to get going. We'll have time to, uh, get to know each other over the next few days."

"Totally," said Kamran, feeling his anxiety flicker. "Because you're not going to leave my side, right? You're going to be my twenty-four-seven muscle."

Marshall laughed half-heartedly. "It certainly looks that way. Okay. Do you want to follow me to my folks?"

For all his bravado, nerves fluttered in Kamran's belly. Convincing some fancy family that he was really dating their son seemed almost as scary as dealing with Chaz.

Almost, but not quite.

"Ready when you are, Agent Marshall."

Marshall fixed him with a stern look. "You better get used to calling me Lee – *Kamran*. Trust me, the fewer reminders we give my family that I'm in the FBI, the better."

"Why—"

"It's getting late," said Marshall – *Lee* – checking his watch. Which – now Kamran was paying attention to – he could see was a damned fancy one. "Follow me, and we'll get to them in about twenty minutes."

It was ridiculous because driving was Kamran's favorite thing in the whole world. But in that moment, he kind of wished he could get in Marshall's car and just be a passenger for once. To just be carried along and not have to think...

But there was no way in hell he was leaving his baby abandoned by the side of the road. So he nodded at Marshall, then moved to the other side of the car, getting inside and starting the engine.

"Time to pretend I'm somebody," he muttered to himself as he began following Marshall back down the road.

5

LEE

LEE SPENT THE WHOLE DRIVE MULTITASKING BETWEEN TALKING with the tech guy who (luckily for Lee) didn't have a social life so was happy to whip up an online profile for Kamran's shiny new NASCAR career on a Friday night, and watching Kamran's headlights obsessively in his rearview mirror.

He tried telling himself that Kamran wasn't in any danger, and he certainly knew how to do something so simple as follow Lee down some quiet country roads. But Lee was rattled, and nothing seemed logical to him right now.

Kamran was really not what he'd been expecting. He was smart and tough and…yeah, okay, he was hot as sin. But Lee honestly was trying to close the lid on that Pandora's box as best he could. This was a *business* arrangement. They'd put people in protective custody and witness protection before. This wasn't entirely unusual.

Except *nothing* about Kamran was usual. Lee had known there was more to him than met the eye before, and he'd been right. Of course, there was a chance that he was playing Lee for a total sucker, but Lee's gut was having very strong opinions about the hurt and pain he kept seeing flashes of.

Between talking on the phone, watching the road and Kamran behind him, and debating what the hell he was going to say to his family, he almost managed not to think about what Kamran had said about being on his knees for Lee.

Almost.

He snarled and adjusted himself in his seat. He only had a few minutes until they reached the estate, and the last thing he needed was an inappropriate boner.

"Think of your promotion," he said to himself between taking deep, cleansing breaths. "This is a job, nothing more. You can do undercover work. You've been trained for this."

But despite what he told himself, he hadn't had any kind of training that would prepare him for Kamran Amir casually mentioning how he'd beg to suck his cock. They didn't cover that in the Bureau handbook, funnily enough.

As they turned left and started making their way down the driveway, Lee felt his nerves rising, and he glanced in the mirror at Kamran's car as much as he paid attention as to where he was going. He knew this private road like the back of his hand, though. He'd learned to drive up and down here when he'd been fifteen, after all. He was much more preoccupied by what Kamran might be thinking. He wished he could see his face and try and guess what was going on in his head.

Lee had never been particularly comfortable with his family's wealth, not when he'd gotten older and realized people treated him differently because of it. And expected Lee to treat *them* differently because he had never wanted for anything.

Well, that wasn't exactly true. But he'd always been able to afford whatever he wanted.

He chewed his lip as the house came into view, *really*

wishing he could gauge Kamran's reaction. He'd made it pretty clear that money was a button issue for him, and Lee kicked himself for putting his foot in his mouth earlier and making it seem like Kamran wouldn't be good enough for Lee because he wasn't affluent. Lee didn't give a shit about that. He had more than enough money for the both of them. He only cared that the men he dated were happy.

But yes, there were several members of his family who would judge him, and that was precisely why Lee thought very carefully before he ever brought a guy home. They'd liked Billy with his job in IT and parents who spent vacations skiing in Aspen with them. But Billy hadn't liked Lee in the end, so the point was moot.

"Urgh, it's all moot! He's not your boyfriend!" he said in exasperation to himself as the two cars got closer to the four-story mansion. It had been a hotel back in the nineteen twenties and had been remodeled several times since, so it had hints of several different design styles. But Lee would be an idiot not to acknowledge that the towering columns, enormous windows, and marble fountain and statues were intimidating.

However, it didn't *matter* if Kamran was intimidated so long as he was *safe*. Because he wasn't here as Lee's boyfriend. He was here as his witness. *Urgh.* Apparently, Lee's brain and his heart weren't communicating effectively, because he was still a ball of nerves that not only his family would only discover his lie but also that they would treat Kamran like crap.

He pulled his Jeep around back into the parking lot that was filled with cars, indicating how many members of his family had already arrived. Officially, they were having a casual reception tonight because some people weren't getting here until tomorrow. But to Lee's eyes, the place looked pretty damn packed.

After he killed the engine and pulled the keys from the ignition, he closed his eyes and exhaled. "Look at it this way," he muttered. "At least no one's going to be hounding you, asking you why you're still single. They're going to be asking when I'm going to pop the question instead."

He grimaced, but he was wrenched from his thoughts with a lurch by the pounding on his window. Clutching his heart, he opened his eyes to see Kamran grinning like a maniac outside his door.

"This is your parents' place?" he cried, his voice muffled through the glass. "Holy smokes!"

Lee blinked at him, confused by the U-turn. Kamran had seemed intimidated by Lee's wealth before. Now he was excited. He sighed. Money changed people. Kamran probably had dollar signs in his eyes. This was another reason why he got to know a guy before dating them. Because he didn't want to lie awake at night wondering if the guy was with him just for his money.

He popped his neck and rolled his shoulders, then got out of the Jeep to greet the excitable Kamran. "You like it?" he asked.

Kamran blew a raspberry. "This is going to be so much easier than I imagined."

Lee paused on his way around to the trunk and frowned at Kamran. "Huh?"

Kamran jutted his chin toward the house. "You said some of your family might treat me like dirt? Well, anyone who comes from this kind of money is living in an alternate *world*. I don't care if some duke or viscount thinks I'm a loser. They'd probably turn their nose up at Prince James and Theo Glass, am I right?"

Lee felt his eyebrows rising, remembering the choice words some of his relatives had uttered when the English prince had married a commoner. "Uh, yeah," he said weakly. "Probably."

Kamran nodded. "So this'll be fun, right? You just point out which ones are naughty or nice, and I'll either schmooze 'em or lose 'em."

Lee popped the trunk and sighed. "Please don't aggravate anyone," he said, already feeling a headache coming on. This guy was a whirlwind. How was it possible that they'd only just met a couple of hours ago? He'd managed to push almost every button Lee had in that short time.

Where was that large glass of wine Lee had been craving?

"Fine," said Kamran with a pout. "I will be aggressively nice to the mean ones and pretend to agree with everything they say."

Lee slung his laptop bag over his shoulder, closed the trunk, then picked up his suitcase. He'd just tell anyone who asked that Kamran's stuff was in there as well, and they could sneak out tomorrow and go shopping for actual supplies.

He narrowed his eyes at Kamran, honestly not sure what to expect when they got inside. The guy was all over the place, ricocheting like a pinball. Lee was certain that the fear, the pain, he'd glimpsed had been real. But everything else? It was like Kamran had different masks to play different characters depending on his ever-shifting mood. Playful. Snarky. Sexy. He had a persona for everything.

Who was the real Kamran Amir?

Lee doubted he'd ever get the chance to find out, even if they were going to spend the next several days together.

"I would have thought you'd be intimidated," said Lee as they started walking around the house. "A lot of people are. I wouldn't blame you," he added hastily.

But Kamran shrugged. "Yours is the only opinion I care about, and that's because if you like me, you'll protect me better," he said, waggling his eyebrows at Lee. That really should have been annoying and not attractive. 'I said I can't pretend to be someone I'm not, but I realized on the drive over that's *exactly* what I can do here. It's like taking a vacation from my life!"

Lee felt his mouth twitch in half a smile, but his heart also panged. Was Kamran really that eager to get away from his life?

"Just...don't go OTT," he warned. "I had my guy set up your profile. You're now a driver in the regional weekly series at Evergreen Speedway, and you live in north Seattle. The key to subterfuge is to just give a few little details away but then keep it vague. No one's going to want an entire back story from you."

He really, *really* hoped that was true, but it sort of depended on how many gin and tonics his aunt Ginny had consumed.

"So what are your parents' names?" Kamran asked as he craned his neck and looked up at the house as they circled around to the enormous front door. Lee had thought it had been huge as a kid, but even as a very large adult, it still seemed big to him. A slight feeling of trepidation shivered down his spine, but he did his best to ignore it.

"Cheryl and Donald," Lee said, switching his suitcase to his other hand and wiping his right one against his pant leg. The last thing he wanted was a damp palm when he shook his dad's hand. "Let's just say this was a last-minute, spontaneous decision for you to come, okay?"

Kamran scoffed and continued half-skipping toward the door as his gaze traveled up and down the period columns. "Forgive me, *Lee*, but I don't think you have a spontaneous bone in your body. How about we say that I surprised you and that's why I've hardly got any stuff with me. Because I'm a little scamp who does things willy-nilly."

He flashed that gorgeous grin Lee's way, and Lee did his

very best not to shiver with lust. But when Kamran smiled at him like that, he wanted to do wicked things to him. He wanted to protect him with his last breath. He wanted to hold him and keep him safe...

Lee wasn't sure if that was his brain or his dick talking, but he shooed the thoughts away. That grin was just for show. It didn't mean anything.

"They are going to wonder how the hell we're a couple," Lee said, shaking his head as he crunched over the gravel driveway.

Kamran grinned again. "Don't you know anything about romcoms? Because opposites attract. Not to mention that I've got a really tight—"

Lee thanked whoever in the universe was on his side that when the front door opened and his mom and dad appeared, Kamran shut his mouth in an instant. Then he whirled around and yanked Lee to his side in a fierce hug, grinning like a crazy person.

"Leopold?" Lee's mom asked, blinking as she peered out into the darkness. Of course the driveway was tastefully lit, but behind her and Lee's dad, several chandeliers blazed in the entrance hall. In fact, all the windows glowed with warm, inviting light, and the sounds of laughter, chatter, and the tinkling of china, crystal, and silverware drifted out to greet them.

It took a second for Lee to realize that his mom had used his full name. Kamran, of course, picked it up right away.

"Oh, it's _Leopold_, is it, hon?"

Lee turned to him and widened his eyes, trying to remind Kamran that they'd agreed that he wouldn't be too over the top. But that sparkle was back in his eyes, and this time it looked borderline dangerous.

"What's going on, Leopold?" his dad asked.

He was a tall man. He'd been bigger in his prime, but he

still cut a pretty imposing figure in his silk shirt and immaculately tailored pants. His mom looked like the pocket-sized, perfect wife as usual in her cashmere sweater and pearl necklace. They'd never gone into politics, like certain family members, but they had the look for it.

Lee gritted his teeth but decided to have a conversation later, reminding them *yet again* that his name was Lee, not Leo or Leopold or anything else. Just Lee. But for now, he had bigger concerns.

"Mom, Dad," he said, hugging Kamran to his side and trying not to sweat despite the chilly night air. "I hope you don't mind, but I have a bit of a surprise for you. This is—"

"Kamran," Kamran said, vaulting forward with his hand outstretched, thrusting it at Lee's dad. "Lee's boyfriend. It's a pleasure to meet you. I've heard so much about you!"

Lee watched as his dad shook hands on autopilot while he cast his gaze over Kamran's shoulder to raise his eyebrows at Lee. "Boyfriend? Well, I wish I could say we'd heard anything about you at all."

Lee bit the inside of his cheek, feeling the disapproval radiating off his dad. Kamran was already blacklisted because Lee's dad would assume that because Lee had kept him secret, there must be something wrong with him. He didn't stand a chance.

So it's a good thing this is all fake, isn't it?

Lee ignored the voice in his head and instead watched in mild horror as Kamran spun and threw his arms around Lee's mom. "It's my fault. Blame me," he said cheerfully as he practically lifted her off her feet. "I wanted to keep my shnookums all to myself. But when I heard there was a big party happening, I figured it was about time I came and said hello!"

When he finally released Lee's mom, he wrapped his arm

around her and beamed back at Lee as if waiting for him to join in.

"Oh, Leo," his mom cried in delight, looking up at the man who had just accosted her. "You have a young man? Why, that's just *wonderful!*"

Lee managed a smile that he hoped wasn't too much of a grimace. That was one word for it.

Where was that wine?

6

KAMRAN

"Oh my god, this is so good," Kamran said around a mouthful of his third fishy pastry thing. Or was it his fourth?

Either way, he took a gulp of Champagne to wash it down and grinned at Lee's Aunt Ginny. She was a skinny woman in a lime-green cocktail dress with bright red hair, clinging to an ice-cold glass of gin and tonic, looking through thick, round glasses at Kamran like he was the most fascinating thing at this whole crazy party. Or the most disturbing. Kamran really wasn't sure of anything here, but he was kind of having fun regardless.

The redbrick exterior of the house combined with the white columns and wrap-around balconies had made Kamran think that this place was going to be all quaint and old. But the inside of Lee's family home was startlingly modern. Everything was chrome and gray leather with sleek cream finishes and fancy light fittings.

His parents had seemed stunned speechless at the door, which was probably how Lee had managed to hustle them over the threshold and into the party itself without any further discussion. Lee had dumped his cases by the foot of the stairs in a reception room of some sorts, then had steered Kamran straight to the drink table, which also happened to be by the buffet.

Kamran discovered that after all the adrenaline earlier, he was now absolutely starving, which was how he had ended up parking himself by the food with a plate and a glass of bubbly filled to the brim. He might have been worried about what Lee thought of him if Lee hadn't been doing exactly the same thing.

Maybe they had a teeny tiny bit in common after all.

Except Lee had red wine and was going straight for all the carbiest, meatiest things he could find. The man probably ate four thousand calories a day – not that Kamran was thinking about his physique. Okay, yes, he was. He'd had a long hard day, and now he felt like Eliza Doolittle in My Fair Lady, mixing with all the rich folk and their absolutely delicious food.

It was possible that the Champagne was giving him some false confidence, but whatever. Chaz thought he was *nothing*. A dog to be summoned what he saw fit. Now here Kamran was, with the best witness protection ever.

How had he gone from hurtling down his drainpipe to this in less than two hours?

He decided not to question it any further and filled up his glass once more.

"So…how long have you boys been dating?" Aunt Ginny asked. She tucked an aggressively red curl behind her ear and sipped from the straw poking out of what Kamran could only describe as a goldfish bowl of gin and tonic. "You seem…cozy."

Kamran tried not to preen as Lee's grip around his waist tightened. Through his pleasant alcohol buzz, it was becoming increasingly difficult to remind himself that this was all for show. It also seemed irrelevant. Lee was *his* for now. Maybe not in the sexual sense, but he was Kamran's protector, and with his hands on him, that felt almost like the same thing.

"Only a couple of months," Kamran said as Lee had apparently clammed up like a, well, clam. Maybe once he'd finished that glass of wine, he'd loosen up. "I was keeping my shnookums all to myself, but when he mentioned a big family reunion this morning, I just dropped *everything* to come. You all seemed so charming, the way he told it."

"Oh, isn't that the sweetest?" said Ginny. She had to be in her late fifties, and Kamran would have bet anything that the huge rock on her engagement ring finger was not her first. "What's he said? All bad, I bet." She gave him an over-exaggerated wink through her owlish glasses.

Kamran blinked, not letting his smile creep down one millimeter. "Oh, honeybunch," he said, digging his elbow into Lee's rock-hard side. "What was it you were telling me about your family the other day?"

Somewhat noisily, Lee swallowed his mouthful of mini quiche and hastily wiped his mouth. "Uh...my family?" he repeated to Kamran, who nodded back.

"You know, you were telling me about this week and how *fun* it sounded."

For a second, Lee looked like Kamran was talking Greek. But then he beamed a devastatingly handsome smile and nodded down at Kamran.

"Right, yeah." He turned to his aunt. "I was telling him all about the neat things that Mom had planned and who would like what best, y'know? Like how Uncle Max would take the paintballing too seriously, especially when Cousin Milly is going to annihilate us all anyway – she's in the army. This week was partly arranged around her leave."

"Oh, cool," said Kamran genuinely, then realized he was

supposed to have heard this all before. "Now I remember. I can't wait to meet them."

It occurred to him that he really wanted to know about this guy's crazy relatives. Perhaps that was because family was still such an alien concept to Kamran. Even when he'd been with Chaz, as he had cut ties with all his relatives, whereas Kamran hadn't really had a choice. This was a strange situation he'd found himself in, surrounded by people only connected by blood, but he was finding it kind of fascinating. He hadn't had that since he was a kid, and he'd always felt so threatened by everyone then. Aunt Ginny didn't seem particularly scary.

"There's also Cousin Steve, who is going to kill it at karaoke," Lee continued, "and Aunt Rebecca will probably nail the go-karting, but Cousin Angelica is literally going to run rings around us when we go ice skating—"

"Ice skating?" Kamran repeated. He might have shrieked. Only a little. He cleared his throat. "Uh, sorry, sugar lips. But I don't think you said anything about ice skating." His heart was going like a freight train in his chest, and he took a long, soothing gulp of Champagne to calm him down...which he immediately tried to hiccup back up.

Lee frowned at him, and Kamran couldn't blame him. He was acting like a crazy person.

"Yeah...at The Lodge...I'm sure I told you?" He blinked like he was trying to talk to Kamran with Morse code. "But... we don't have to go if you don't want to...?"

Kamran cleared his throat and shot his best smile at Aunt Ginny, who was watching them with her unnaturally large-looking eyes.

"Oh, maybe you did, scrumptious," said Kamran. "I'm just such a scatter-brain, you know? I didn't bring the right clothes for that, though. Perhaps we could go shopping for something like that tomorrow?"

Lee's eyes widened as if he finally understood. He probably thought that Kamran had been spinning a line to give them an alibi to go out for his essentials tomorrow. But the truth was, he'd only thought of that at the last second.

Ice skating. He hadn't done that since...

No. He wasn't going to go there. Not now, not ever. He wouldn't set foot on the rink. In fact, whenever Lee's enormous, crazy family was planning on descending on the ice, he was definitely going to come down with a mysterious stomach bug. Yep. That was definitely his best plan.

"Ah, there you are," an imposing voice drawled from behind them.

Kamran tried not to flinch as Lee's blunt fingers dug into his side. He'd hung his leather jacket on one of the fancy coat stands by the front door, so there wasn't much between Lee's firm grip and Kamran's skin. Ordinarily, he'd enjoy such a sensation, but as they turned away from the food table, Kamran braced himself for the worst.

If he'd been honest, he'd been expecting Lee's dad. That man had definitely clenched his jaw and given his son a look that had suggested they were *far* from done talking about the new boyfriend situation.

But Kamran and Lee were met with a guy who looked a bit older than them both. Kamran recognized Lee's startling blue eyes, but on this guy, they were narrowed and held none of Lee's warmth. And since when had Kamran considered Lee *warm*? He'd been the *enemy* not two hours ago. Whatever. The other difference between the two men was that while their height and size were similar, Lee's bulk came from muscle, whereas this guy...

Well. He smirked as he sauntered around them, cutting an enormous slab of chocolate cake and placing it on his plate as they watched. He ran his finger around the serving dish, swiping up all the frosting from the edge of the cake still left and then sucking it noisily from his finger.

Kamran tried not to flinch as he pressed himself closer to Lee.

"Mikey," Lee said with a smile, but Kamran was sure he caught a resigned sort of sigh in his tone. "You're looking well. This is my boyfriend, Kamran. Kamran, this is my older brother, Mikey. He works with our father in the family business."

Mikey sucked his pudgy finger again before offering his hand out to Kamran. Ordinarily, Kamran wouldn't have touched something that gross with a ten-foot pole. But he was here under Lee's protection, and the price of that was for him to be on his best behavior. So that meant shaking his brother's slightly sticky hand with a demure smile.

"Dad said you'd shown up late with a surprise boyfriend," Mikey said as he squeezed Kamran's hand just a little too hard. "Where'd you drag this one up from?"

Kamran fluttered his eyelashes and squeezed Mikey's hand right back, possibly even harder. "Oh, wouldn't you like to know, handsome?"

Just as he'd predicted, Mikey wasn't okay with that. He snatched his hand back, then brushed it on his very expensive-looking suit jacket like *he'd* been the one to have been subjected to an icky physical encounter.

"Mikey," said Lee tersely. "I'm sorry to have surprised you. But Kamran is my date, and he'll be joining us for the week. So I know you'll make him feel *welcome*."

Kamran tried to tell his heart not to flutter at the protective way Lee said the last word, but it was hopeless. It didn't matter that it was for a job – Kamran liked Lee looking out for him, even if it was just against his own judgmental family.

"He's going to come ice skating with us!" Aunt Ginny chimed in, and Kamran tried not to wince.

Mikey snorted and shook his head. "Well, *someone* will have to look after him, won't they? I give you three days before you scuttle off back to work, Leo. I'm honestly astonished you made it here tonight at all. Busy little bee that you are."

Kamran narrowed his eyes at Mikey as he took another sip of bubbly. He'd sort of slipped a backhanded compliment in there, but Kamran could smell shade a mile away.

"Oh, Lee *always* makes time for me," he said, aware that his words had a slightly challenging air to them.

Aunt Ginny sighed, twisting the rock on her left hand. "How romantic."

Kamran preened. Yes, it *was* romantic, even if it wasn't real. "And he's promised not to leave my side all week. Not that his work putting dangerous criminals behind bars isn't *really* important, but we've talked a lot about a good work-life balance. Remind me, what is it you do again?"

He smiled serenely, ignoring the way Lee's fingers dug into him. He probably intended it as a warning, but unfortunately for him, Kamran just hoped they'd bruise.

"I work in management with Dad," Mikey said, flashing Kamran a smile that made his skin crawl. "You know, all those hotels we own up and down the country. But enough about us. What do *you* do, Kamran? Leo's previous boyfriend had a very impressive job in IT. In fact—"

"I'm a NASCAR driver – regional short track,' Kamran said without any hesitation whatsoever. He'd been right. Lying to assholes like this was *fun.* "They're calling me the next big thing. I just got a sponsorship deal from Excalibur."

Lee almost choked on his crudité.

"Ooh, the condom people?" Ginny asked in earnest.

Kamran winked at Ginny, who tittered into her fishbowl.

Then he rubbed Lee's back as he was still coughing. "Are you all right there, shnookums?"

Lee managed a nod. "Uh, yeah. I just didn't realize *that* was who your new sponsor was."

He narrowed his eyes, probably telling Kamran to behave, but Kamran was having too much fun.

Mikey didn't seem impressed. In fact, he looked Kamran up and down, arching an eyebrow as he took in his jeans and T-shirt. "A fancy sponsor like that, and yet you seem to struggle with the meaning of 'black tie'? Huh."

Kamran gave him a tight smile. Superficial asshole. He plucked his T-shirt from his chest. "It's designer," he said dryly. It was from a thrift shop, but Daddy's Boy didn't need to know that.

"Oh yes," Ginny chimed in. "That probably cost young Kamran a pretty penny, Mikey. But you wouldn't know that. You've never been one much for fashion, have you?" She nodded sympathetically as Mikey scowled and Lee cleared his throat.

"Besides, Kamran decided to come last minute," he said, wrapping his arm around Kamran's waist and smiling at him. A shiver ran through Kamran, even though Lee might be mad at him for goading his brother.

Whatever. Mikey deserved it.

Kamran beamed and patted Lee's solid chest. "Luckily, I was able to take some time off so Lee and I could have a *real* vacation. Next, I'm going to convince him to go to Europe. But you know how it is – baby steps."

He waggled his eyebrows at Mikey, daring him to contradict him. Unfortunately, old Mikey obviously thought a lot of himself, as he scoffed and shook his head.

"Well, good luck to you. Billy thought he could make Leo see that there are more important things in life than dragging yourself to a fluorescent-lit office with stale coffee every day to chase after lowlifes. More important things like good old-fashioned marriage." He flashed a chubby finger at them and waggled a gold wedding band with his thumb. "And if he couldn't straighten old Leopold out, I'm not sure who can."

Kamran had only just met the man, but he was pretty sure Mikey was giving Lee a not-so-subtle homophobic dig. So much for the family being all welcoming and shit.

Kamran glanced at Lee, expecting him to roll his eyes or look pissed off. Instead, he looked wounded. Defeated. Oh no, Kamran wasn't having that. This was his tough FBI agent! His life depended on Lee's badassery. Besides…Kamran fucking hated bullies, and he much preferred Lee when he was all grumpy and in charge.

"Oh, where is your wife?" Kamran asked cheerfully. He took it as his turn to dig his fingernails into Lee's side to try and drum up some spite in him. But that comment about his ex really seemed to have popped his balloon. "Or husband?"

"Wife," Mikey spat, confirming that Lee's older brother was indeed one of the assholes who wasn't as comfortable with Lee's sexuality as the others, despite what Lee might have told him up on the Ridgeway. "And how should I know? She's around here somewhere."

Charming, Kamran thought as he hummed and smiled at the man, sipping more Champagne. *Yes, I can see that you have the superior relationship to Lee here.*

Instead of following up the comment, Kamran shrugged and went back to the ex thing. Lee had mentioned something briefly about how his family wasn't over it, and now he was starting to wonder in what way.

"Well, like I said, Lee and I have talked a lot about work-life balance. It's one of the reasons we're here." He fluttered his eyelashes as Mikey shoved a too-big bite of chocolate cake into his mouth, leaving crumbs scattered over his lips. "I don't know much about Lee's ex, but I do know that he doesn't hold a torch to me. Lee deserves someone amazing, like he is. Don't you agree?"

He smiled, warmth blossoming through his chest as he looked up and met his gaze with Lee's astonishing blue eyes. They were wide and curious, looking down at Kamran like he wasn't quite sure what he was saying.

"Yeah, amazing," he croaked, blinking at Kamran.

To his surprise, his blunt fingers stroked little firm circles against Kamran's side. It sent shivers up and down Kamran's spine, and he told himself that they were just roleplaying, but in that moment, he could have sworn he felt something *pulsing* between them.

"Ooh, yes," agreed Ginny eagerly. "I'll be honest, Leo, I never cared much for your last boyfriend. He was handsome enough, but I swear I caught his eyes wandering more than once. In fact—"

"Well, like I said – good luck," Mikey interrupted, sucking chocolate off his fingers and raising his eyebrows at Kamran. "If you're still around for Christmas, maybe I'll change my mind. But I think Leo's so desperate to prove to us that he didn't make a colossal mistake with his career that he's married to *that* first and foremost. Isn't that right, baby bro?"

He winked, but it wasn't friendly in the slightest.

Kamran bristled with overflowing rage. But he did what he was good at and covered up how he was feeling with a big smile. "Luckily, it's not you he has to impress, and I already think he's magnificent." He placed his plate down on the table and rubbed Lee's back. "Honey? Would you mind if we went and got some air? It's kind of hot in here."

He wasn't lying about that. With all these people crammed into this…was it a living room? It felt more like a hotel lounge with all the sofas arranged around coffee tables. But maybe rich people considered this kind of arrangement cozy. Anyway, there was an actual fire crackling in the mantelpiece, hot food, warm bodies, and after a couple of glasses of bubbly, Kamran was feeling lightheaded despite the food he'd eaten.

It probably had something to do with the windbag that had parked himself in front of them.

"Uh, yeah," said Lee with a nod, also putting his plate down. "Sure, whatever you want. See you, Mikey."

"Toodeloo," Ginny cried, saluting them with her fishbowl.

Kamran steered them away before he realized he didn't know where he was going. But Lee suddenly seemed to wake up as he took them down the hall and through another room with big French doors that led out to a patio.

"I'm sorry about that," he mumbled as they stepped out into the cold air. There were heaters out here, though, like there had been at Aquarium, so Kamran didn't feel too cold in his T-shirt.

Especially not with Lee's arm wrapped around him.

He blew a raspberry and took a big gulp of Champagne. "You said some of your family were assholes. I don't care. I'm sorry he talked to *you* like that. Why didn't you tell him to shut the fuck up?"

Lee shrugged and stepped away from Kamran. There wasn't currently anyone else out here, so Kamran figured they didn't have to pretend in that moment. But he still wanted to whimper, and not because he was suddenly much colder.

"He's right," Lee said dismissively. "Not about you, obviously. About me being a workaholic and incapable of keeping a relationship going."

Kamran narrowed his eyes and stepped in front of Lee, getting all up in his face. "Well," he said quietly, "this is our little make-believe undercover op, right? So I say we make it the best fucking relationship he's ever seen. We crank up the

PDA to eleven and act like we're so in love it makes him sick." Kamran had a suspicion that wouldn't be too difficult to do in Mikey's case.

A smile tweaked at the corner of Lee's mouth. "Why do you care?" he asked, sounding genuinely curious. "You're safe here. We don't need to impress anyone for the sake of your protection from Bolt."

Kamran smirked. "Oh, I know," he said cheerfully. "But I hate bullies, and I think it would be fun to make your brother eat his own words, wouldn't you? How long has he been talking shit like that at you?"

Lee huffed out a laugh. "My whole life," he said, just as Kamran had expected. Then he cleared his throat. "Aren't you glad you agreed to this cockamamie scheme? I bet you feel *super* safe with a spineless oaf who can't even tell his own brother to fuck off."

Kamran frowned at him, and before he could think about what he was doing, he placed a hand on Lee's chest over his heart. "I feel *incredibly* safe with you," he said softly.

Lee licked his lips as he held Kamran's gaze. A shiver ran all through Kamran's body, and he leaned in, just a fraction—

"—don't know *what* he's thinking," a voice floated out of the darkness, and Lee immediately froze. Kamran flicked his eyes around the patio, but he couldn't tell where the man was.

But he had a feeling he knew *who* it was.

Sure enough, Lee's mom's voice came drifting toward them next. "Now, now, Donald. They looked very sweet together."

"He's a bit old for a teenage rebellion phase, isn't he?" Donald snapped. "To drag someone like that here, unannounced, in front of the whole family. I'm just glad the Clements aren't here until next Saturday. Or the Levensons. The mortification of them seeing that scruffy, deadbeat man isn't worth thinking about. Maybe we can run him off before the ball?"

Kamran felt like he'd been pierced with an icicle. He'd promised himself that he wouldn't care what these people thought of him, that it would be funny.

But constantly being told you were a piece of shit was exhausting, and he couldn't stop the immense hurt that rushed through him, taking his breath. He knew he wasn't good enough for someone like Lee, but to hear that he was so lowly he was an *embarrassment?* That was too much to bear.

But what else could he do?

He *was* kind of an embarrassment.

7

LEE

"MAYBE I SHOULD JUST GO WAIT IN YOUR ROOM," KAMRAN SAID softly, looking down at the ground.

"What! No...why...?" Lee knew why.

A fire ignited inside him that burned from his heart all the way to his fingers and toes. His family could speak down to him like they always had. But as far as they knew, he was madly in love with Kamran Amir, and this was how they were treating him?

"Mom, Dad," he said, loud and clear as he hugged Kamran tightly to his side, making sure that he wasn't going anywhere. "Is that you? Kamran and I were just getting some air."

He took a mouthful of red wine to fortify himself as his parents finally came into the soft light being cast from the party inside. They'd probably been walking the garden paths. Mom often took Dad out there to calm him down when he was ready to blow. Lee had anticipated that his dad wouldn't be impressed with a surprise boyfriend for the reunion, but he'd gone too far calling Kamran names like that. Just because Kamran was exuberant didn't mean he was unworthy.

And – yeah – maybe Lee was feeling a tiny bit guilty over how judgmental *he'd* been when he'd first laid eyes on Kamran. He might be a loose cannon with a shady past and a completely different attitude toward sex than Lee, but he was also a person who was scared and in trouble. His folks didn't know that, but they shouldn't have to. It was so wrong that his dad was making snap judgments.

The melancholy brought on by Mikey's jibes about Billy vanished in an instant as Lee remembered all too clearly that his job was to protect Kamran from harm.

Even if that was from his own parents.

"Oh, uh, Leopold?" his mom said, sounding flustered. She had her hand on his dad's back, and she rubbed it as she smiled between him and Lee. As if that might make Lee's dad behave. "We were hoping to find you out here. We lost you in the party."

"We've been standing still for twenty minutes," said Lee pleasantly, hugging Kamran to him. "And it's Lee, remember?"

His dad scoffed and rolled his eyes, but his mom's expression softened.

"Sorry, Lee," she said purposefully. She and his dad came to a halt in front of them. Sounds of the party drifted out from the French doors, and Lee felt himself soften too.

"You've done a really great job with the welcome evening, Mom," he said genuinely. "The food is delicious, and everyone seems to be having a good time."

"Well," his mom said, waving her hand despite looking pleased as punch. "We used that caterer that we had...oh, never mind that. Are you both having fun? Kamran? We didn't really get a chance to speak much when you arrived. I hope you've helped yourself to food and drink. I want you to make yourself right at home while you're staying with us, okay?"

His dad still looked stony-faced, but his mom's anxiety was clear as she smiled at Kamran. Despite what other family members might think of Lee, his exes, or his career choices, he knew his mom just wanted him to be happy. So he thought of Kamran's words just now and decided he was right. If they were going to pretend and live in a fantasy for a few days, why not go all out and act like he was madly in love?

"That's what I told him," Lee said brightly, squeezing Kamran to him and kissing the top of his head. He smelled faintly of leather and a spicy cologne, and Lee resisted the urge to nuzzle his nose through that thick, dark hair in front of his parents. "But then we ran into Mikey, and that went about as well as you might expect, so I brought Kamran outside to reassure him."

"Oh, you boys," said his mom in exasperation, speaking of her sons.

"Leave your brother alone," his dad drawled, predictably taking Mikey's side.

Kamran cleared his throat, and Lee felt him come back to life by his side. "You have a lovely home, Mrs. Marshall," Kamran said, the picture of perfect manners. "And Lee's right. The food is amazing. If this is just the start of the celebrations, I can't wait to see what you have in store for the rest of the week."

His mom shot a look at his dad that Lee was sure said 'I told you so,' then placed her hand over her heart as she beamed at Kamran. "Why, thank you, sweetheart. But you call me Cheryl, okay? Why don't you join me in getting another drink? I left my glass somewhere, and yours is almost empty!"

Mom hated anyone with an empty glass. Lee couldn't

help but shake his head and smile a little as he watched her pry Kamran away from him so she could place her hand on his back and walk them both back inside toward the drink station. She barely came up to his shoulder, and Kamran smiled down at her as they went back inside.

Lee felt a pang for a second as he wished this were real, but then he reminded himself that he'd only known Kamran for a couple of hours. He shouldn't be so ridiculous.

Apparently, he wasn't the only one thinking that.

"Care to explain yourself?"

He turned to look at his dad, raising an eyebrow. If this *were* real, Lee would have every right to be pretty fucking pissed over what he and Kamran had accidentally just heard right now.

"Explain what?" Lee asked. "To Kamran as to why my dad is being a jackass?"

His dad narrowed his eyes. "That job has made you so crude," he said, looking out over the dark gardens.

Lee took a mouthful of wine, hoping it would help him keep his temper. "Yes, because my choice of language is really the issue here."

"That boy—" his dad began, but Lee cut him off.

"That *man* is very important to me." Technically, that wasn't a lie. He *was* important to the case. "And can you really blame me for not telling anyone about him when that's the way you're going to talk about him?"

His dad fixed Lee with a stare, then shook his head. "You should have tried harder with Billy."

That cut like a knife, and Lee was sure his dad knew it. But rather than show his pain, he swirled the last of his wine in the glass. "Probably," he said in resignation. "But that's done now. There's no turning back the clock. Kamran and I have talked about a better work-life balance, so maybe I'll have better luck with this relationship," he said, playing off what they'd mentioned before. "In *which* case, I'll respectfully ask you again to stop being a jackass. Kamran isn't going away because you don't think his credentials are good enough."

No, he'll go away because this is all a lie and he's not the kind of guy who I'd ever date – or that would date me.

That was an issue for future Lee. Right now, he was sick of his dad treating him like the black sheep of the family just because he'd had his own ideas of what he wanted to do with his life – both his work life and love life.

"If you're trying to prove some kind of point, I'm afraid I'm at a loss as to what it could be," said his dad, skirting around Lee's request to behave, unsurprisingly.

Lee just sighed. He hadn't been home even an hour, and they were already fighting. "I'm not trying to prove anything or score points, Dad," he said softly. "I like Kamran. I wanted you all to meet him. That's it. Please don't be cruel to him to get to me."

His dad scowled. "Cruel? I'm simply being honest. I've seen enough gold-diggers in my time to spot one a mile off."

Lee laughed. He couldn't help it. He knocked the rest of his wine back, then fixed his old man with a stare. "Is that what you think is happening here? One, Kamran does just fine for money. At this level of racing, he's responsible for his own car. He lives a little on the frugal side because he's pouring every penny into each race and the maintenance of his car." Lee mentally thanked the tech guy who had slipped him that nugget of information. "And two," Lee continued, "Kamran didn't even know my situation or who my family was until today, so he's not sniffing around for money, okay?"

Obviously, Kamran wasn't a gold-digger, because they weren't really dating. But Lee suspected that even before Bolt's crew had trashed Kamran's place, he had been struggling financially. He'd looked stricken when he realized he had almost nothing to his name but his car and the clothes he was wearing.

Lee could go some way to fixing Kamran's situation tomorrow with his credit card for his family trust fund. His pay from work was all right, so he hardly ever touched his family money, wanting to prove that he was doing just fine out on his own. But if he could use those funds to take care of Kamran, he'd do so in a heartbeat.

He was aware that he'd only known Kamran a few hours, but that didn't seem to make a difference to him in that moment.

"I know this might shock you, Dad," Lee continued, "but Kamran likes me for who I am. And I like him for who *he* is, not his parents nor his bank balance. Now, if you'll excuse me, I'm going to go find him and make sure he's okay and introduce him to a few more people. Because he's going to be with us all week, and I don't want anyone else making snap judgments."

He waited a beat, but his dad just harrumphed, then looked away. Fine. Lee didn't need his approval anyway, just for him not to be so openly hostile. So Lee shrugged and turned, making his way back into the party and trying not to muse too hard on how he'd very much like those last few things he'd said to his dad to be true as well. About being with someone regardless of their wealth or connections.

Not that he meant Kamran, of course. That was crazy. They were far too different, and besides, Kamran was a witness under Lee's *protection*. But Lee could hope that maybe someday he'd have that kind of relationship with someone. One based on mutual respect and love, not money and power.

It wouldn't hurt if that guy could be as fucking *hot* as Kamran, though. Lee's breath hitched in his throat as he scanned the reception room for him and discovered him talking with his mom and his sister, Florence. His white T-shirt clung to his body, shifting over his slim frame as he moved his hands animatedly as he talked.

Lee paused for a moment, simply admiring Kamran looking happy and confident once again. Lee had been worried that a verbal assault from Mikey followed by his dad would crush him, but he looked like he'd bounced back. There was that sparkle in his eyes again as he told his story, and his smile...

God, Lee wanted to kiss that mouth.

He shook himself. Nope. That was a totally out-of-bounds thought. Kamran was under his protection. They were trying to bring down a dangerous criminal. Lee should be grateful that Kamran was able to play his part so well, and not be sucked in by the performance.

But it wasn't the big smiles and small talk that were tugging at Lee's heart, and he knew it. It was how fast Kamran had assumed that Lee would want him to go hide away in his room. How quickly he'd believed Lee's dad's words about him being an embarrassment.

It suddenly occurred to Lee that he kind of wanted to protect Kamran from *himself* as well. He shouldn't be so fast to put himself down like that, to assume the worst of himself. He'd been willing to fight for Lee, but not himself. That wouldn't do.

When Kamran met the right man – someone he was truly compatible with – he would make that guy incredibly happy. But he'd never fit in with Lee's lifestyle, he was sure. His family was kind of right calling him out on that. He needed someone steady and quiet and sweet.

So why did he *want* Kamran?

"Someone's in love."

Lee whirled around and found himself face-to-face with a

man in an expensive suit, even by this crowd's standards. He also wore a big, warm smile and handed Lee a fresh glass full of red wine.

"Graham," Lee said with a sigh. He placed his empty glass on a nearby table, then gave his cousin a one-armed hug. "Oh, it's good to see you."

Graham's laugh was a deep rumble, and he patted Lee's back. "That bad already?" he asked as they separated. Graham clinked his own glass of red with Lee's and took a sip. "Let me guess. Mikey…or your dad."

"Both," said Lee, rolling his eyes, then taking a drink. The buzz was helping him shake off his anger at certain family members, but it was also making Kamran look even more delectable. Lee cleared his throat and turned back to Graham. "I didn't think you'd make it until tomorrow."

Graham smiled. Objectively speaking, he was devastatingly handsome with a sharp, square jaw, dark hair, and startling green eyes. He was about as lucky in love as Lee, though, and if Lee didn't know first-hand how annoying it was to have people hounding you about settling down, he might have asked why that was. But if Graham wanted to keep his love life – or lack thereof – private, Lee would respect that.

"My meeting got canceled so I scheduled an earlier flight with my pilot. I knew it would make Mother happy, seeing as I have to return to the office by Monday morning."

Lee chuckled and nodded at his favorite cousin. Of course the other thing that made Graham so attractive was that he was an actual *billionaire*, but from what Lee knew of his own money issues, that was probably a factor as to *why* Graham was single, too. His dad wasn't entirely wrong about gold-diggers being a blight for their family. They'd been almost swindled more than once.

"So, who is he?" Graham asked pointedly. Lee blinked at

him until he jutted his chin in the direction of Kamran. "Your charming guest. You seem besotted."

"Oh, no," said Lee, not remembering for a second that he was *supposed* to be besotted. "I mean, he's gorgeous, obviously. But I don't know. It's not serious. It's just…it's all quite new."

If he squinted really hard, he could tell himself that was all technically true, too.

Graham hummed at him and quirked an eyebrow. "New doesn't mean it's not serious – or won't be soon. I saw you. You haven't looked like that in a very long time. In fact, I don't think you ever looked at Billy like that."

Lee opened and closed his mouth. He wanted to tell Graham that he was talking nonsense. Of course Lee had looked at Billy like that. He'd been totally in love with him once upon a time.

Hadn't he?

"Dad doesn't like him," he said instead.

Graham scoffed. "Who *does* Uncle Donald like?"

"You," Lee said bluntly. "You're the son he wishes he'd had. And the man Mikey thinks he is. We were definitely swapped at birth."

Graham laughed and bumped their shoulders together. "I just sit in fancy offices all day. You're the one with an exciting career."

"Tell that to my dad," Lee grumbled.

"I'd rather have some more wine," Graham said with a smirk. "Come on. Introduce me to your man. Let me be deliciously jealous of you."

Lee bit his lip as they began walking across the room. "You don't have a special someone on the horizon, then?" he couldn't help but ask.

Graham didn't seem put out, though. "No. But I'm okay. I was just teasing."

Lee would have pressed a little further – just to make sure Graham *was* okay, but Lee's mother and sister spotted them, and both women started waving frantically, like Lee wasn't just ten feet away.

"Leo – Lee!" his mom called, in case he'd missed their frenzied display. "We've just been talking to your lovely Kamran. He's a hoot! He was just telling us how he met Bella Dalton and Sabina Max not long ago! Apparently, his friend worked on their new movie! Isn't that exciting?"

Lee cast his eyes to Kamran, whose grin told him nothing about whether he was telling the truth or not. Probably not. He was supposed to be an up-and-coming face of NASCAR, so famous connections were probably a good way to make that seem convincing.

Lee told himself he was impressed with Kamran spinning tall tales and not irked at the reminder that none of this was real.

"He's just full of surprises," Lee said as he slipped his arm around Kamran's waist like he would if it had been Billy back in the day. Except...had Graham been right? Billy had been very cagey about public displays of affection. But this felt totally natural with Kamran. "I see you've met my sister."

Florence winked at them both. She was a curvy woman poured into a stunning green wrap-around dress with black stilettos that looked like they could kill a man. Sure enough, though, Lee glanced at her head, and the impressive ensemble was offset by dangly frog earrings. She worked hard for the family business, but she'd always kept that sense of fun about her. Lee knew she never wanted her kids to think she was unapproachable like their dad had been.

Even though she was talking with Lee and the others, he just knew she was fully aware of where her half a dozen children were at all times. She had a sixth sense when it came to that. Also when it came to teasing her baby brother. She grinned devilishly at him, taking a sip of her white wine.

"Well, when I heard you'd brought a real, live man home, I simply had to investigate for myself. But the rumors were true! But I didn't expect him to be quite so exciting. Friends with Bella Dalton *and* Sabina Max." She whistled and raised her eyebrows.

"Sabina Max, what?" a breathless voice cried out. A teenage girl appeared as if by magic at Florence's side. She had long brown hair and was wearing a glittery rainbow Below Zero T-shirt, whatever that was. "Who knows Sabina Max?"

"I do," said Kamran, raising his hand with a proud grin. "I worked – I mean, I have friends who worked on the new Fallen Angels Club movie with her. She's amazing."

"Of course she is!" the girl cried, dancing on her toes. "Holy moly, I'm so jealous!"

Suddenly, Lee realized with a jolt who this young woman was. *"Mia?"* he spluttered, making everyone look at him. "But – you – how *old* are you?" She couldn't be eight or nine like he'd thought – could she? How out of touch with kids was he?

She blinked and raised her eyebrows. "I'm thirteen, Uncle Lee. You know that. You got me concert tickets for the reunion tour for my last birthday, remember?"

She held out her T-shirt, and Lee vaguely recalled that Below Zero was a boy band that were all gay or something, but he certainly hadn't ever bought his almost grown-up *(WTF, when had that happened?)* niece tickets of any kind…

He was frowning, about to say something, when he caught his sister shaking her head violently behind Mia's back. He felt a warm rush of affection for her. Lee often didn't know how to spoil his niblings, so he just gave Florence a lump sum and told her to go nuts. If she wanted to pretend that the tickets had been Lee's idea to save face, he'd play along gratefully.

He wished he didn't have to, but perhaps he should actually *pay attention* to his family a little more in the future so that pretending wouldn't be necessary.

"Of course," he said with a smile. "How was the show?"

"Ah-MAY-zing," said Mia, throwing up her hands. "I like their new album even better than their old ones."

"Oh, I don't know," said Kamran. "I'll always have a soft spot for that one that goes *'Oh oh oohh!'*"

"Hearts Bound!" Mia squeaked, clapping her hands together. "That was their first big hit! Did you know—"

"Okay!" said Florence loudly. "I love you, sweetie, but I do not need to hear your BZ trivia for the third time today. Maybe you can chat with Lee's new guy later? For now, why don't you go find the twins and make sure they haven't broken anything…else."

She sighed. "Okay, Mom." Then she pointed at Kamran. "I'll find you later. Don't go far."

"Uh, sure thing." Kamran raised his eyebrows at Lee, who nodded to show that Mia was probably very serious as she beamed, then scampered off. She'd always been an enthusiastic little thing. Or…not so little anymore.

Lee had missed so much. Well, now was the time to start fixing that. He was here now, and he had the perfect excuse to talk to everyone standing right by his side.

Lee angled himself and Kamran so they included Graham in the circle. "Hon, this is my cousin Graham. He's more like a brother, though."

Kamran wrinkled his nose. "He better be nicer than the actual brother you introduced me to," he hissed in a not-that-quiet whisper.

Lee felt his eyes widen, but his mom and sister giggle-snorted, and Graham beamed.

"Much nicer," he assured him, extending his hand out to shake with Kamran. "It's a pleasure to meet you, Kamran. Anyone who makes Lee all glowy like this is more than welcome at family gatherings from now on as far as I'm concerned."

"Hear, hear!" agreed Florence.

"I am not 'glowy,'" Lee grumbled.

Kamran laughed as he let go of Graham's hand and actually *pinched* Lee's cheek. "Yes, you are, shnookums! See, I told you a little R and R was all that was needed. You'll be chilled out in no time."

Lee took it all back. The man was a menace. Lee was never going to live this down.

"Shnookums?" Florence repeated, looking like a shark that had just sensed blood in the water.

"I thought we'd agreed *not* to go with 'shnookums,' hon?" said Lee through gritted teeth.

Kamran smirked and winked at him. "Whatever you say, honeybunch. It's lovely to meet you too, Graham."

"So how did you crazy kids meet?" Florence asked, looking between them and sipping her own Champagne.

"Oh, yes," chimed in Lee's mom. "I want to hear the story!"

"Oh, um, through work," Lee said.

Just as Kamran said, "At the gym!"

They looked at each other as Kamran's eyes widened and his brows crawled up his head.

Oh – fuck! They'd gone over this! They'd worked out a story and Lee had completely blown it. "Uh, I meant Kamran's work – he works at the gym."

Kamran's eyebrows practically disappeared into his hair.

"I thought he drove for NASCAR," said Florence, sounded confused.

She wasn't the only one.

All those years on the job and one hot guy had thrown all of Lee's training out the window. He was a mess. "Uhh…"

"I *used* to work at that gym before my driving took off," Kamran said with a laugh, shaking his head. "They're so adorable, though. They still give me a discount because they like to tell people someone famous works out there. Isn't that too cute?"

"Very," agreed Graham, his voice warm with mirth.

"Anyway," Kamran continued, patting Lee's chest. "This one here kept staring at me, but he was too chicken to say hello. Naturally, *I* had to make the first move. And now here we are, all loved up."

He moved and put his hand on Lee's back…then promptly slid it down to cup his ass.

Lee jumped so hard that he almost sloshed red wine down himself. Obviously, that made his family laugh and go "aww." But Lee leaned in to hiss in Kamran's ear.

"We said *no* PDA. You're skating on thin ice."

But Kamran just giggled, apparently thoroughly enjoying himself. How quickly he'd bounced back from his upset outside. It was making Lee's head spin. Could he trust *anything* this guy said? Or was it all just an act?

Kamran winked. "Of course, baby bear. Whatever you say."

Lee wasn't sure if he was pissed off or aroused.

It was Kamran's turn to whisper in his ear. *"If you remembered your lines, I wouldn't have to improvise."*

He sort of had a point, but Lee was still fuming.

His mom, however, was beaming. "Oh, you two are so sweet together."

Lee hummed. "Actually, I'm feeling kind of beat. It's been a crazy day, and it's getting late. If Kamran doesn't mind, we might just head over to the guesthouse—"

"Oh, don't be ridiculous, Leopold," said his mom sharply.

"I made up your room for you. It will *always* be your room. Come on, let me show you, Kamran."

She took his hand and began dragging him across the room toward the stairs. Lee sighed and handed his wine glass to Graham. "See you guys in the morning," he said with some trepidation.

Kamran was going to be sleeping in Lee's room? In his *bed?* The place he'd spent hours upon hours when he'd been growing up? Where he'd mused over his hopes and dreams? The place where he'd jerked off countless times as a teenager?

This was all a little too real. It had taken almost a year before Lee had felt comfortable letting Billy see his old room, and now his mother was marching Kamran into it, mere hours after they'd met.

Lee shook his head as he grabbed his bags from the sunroom by the foot of the stairs. "You made this bed. Now you have to lie in it," he said, using the eerily apt metaphor. But he was right. This mess was of his own doing. He'd agreed to this ridiculous scheme in order to increase his chances of convicting Bolt. Now he had to deal with the consequences.

Which apparently included spending the night with a man he was becoming increasingly attracted to, but who was completely inappropriate for him.

Lee sighed and pinched the bridge of his nose with his free hand. He hadn't even said hello to most of his family members yet, and he could still feel the drama brewing. Maybe they shouldn't have abandoned the hotel idea so quickly. After all, what was the point of Lee taking this vacation if he wasn't actually going to relax? And with Kamran by his side twenty-four seven, it wasn't like he was leaving work behind at all.

As everyone else was down at the party below, Lee could

hear his mom and Kamran walking up ahead. He couldn't tell exactly what they were saying, but from the soft murmur of her voice, he figured his mom was probably giving Kamran a running commentary of the house.

He looked around, yet again finding himself wishing he knew what Kamran was thinking, trying to see the framed paintings and chandeliers through his eyes. The stormy gray plush carpets and cream walls were so familiar to Lee, but a part of him knew they weren't like most family homes. The antiques in glass cases were more suited to museums and the chrome-framed mirrors to corporate hallways.

His whole family was so concerned with appearances it made them sterile. Lee could never imagine his parents hanging any of their kids' paintings on the fridge or letting their toys spill out beyond their bedrooms. Lee used to find that kind of thing so alien to see on TV when he'd been growing up.

What had Kamran's childhood been like? Would it be inappropriate to ask? Lee chewed his lip as he made his way up the second flight of stairs. Where was the line between asking research questions for this week of undercover subterfuge and just wanting to know more about the man?

Lee was too tired to try and work that out tonight. But the fact that he wasn't sure unsettled him. There was no denying his instant, strong attraction to Kamran, despite how much his head tried to tell him this was a bad idea for several reasons.

His heart – and his cock – weren't really listening.

"Just get through the night," Lee told himself through gritted teeth. "This will all be better in the morning."

If he told himself that enough, he might believe it.

"...of course, back then, all these walls were covered with Seahawks posters," he heard his mom saying from within as he approached his room. "He was such a tidy boy, but if you ever looked under the bed—"

Lee ran the last few steps and burst into his room. "Let's not give Kamran my life history on the first night," he said with a bit too much forced laughter.

He glanced around the room. It hadn't changed at all since he'd last seen it a couple of years ago, and not much since his college days when he'd come home for the vacations. A huge double bed with a hand-carved wooden base. Blue-and-gray bedspread and curtains. A framed map of America with pins stuck in all the places he'd wanted to visit but had never gone to. A pair of binoculars that hadn't ever been used to his knowledge. They were just for decoration.

God, it was soulless.

But then...his apartment back in Seattle wasn't much better. All sleek and mature and devoid of any real character. He'd turned into his parents without even realizing it.

He flicked his gaze to Kamran, desperately wondering what he was thinking. It was as if Lee was revaluating his entire life through this stranger's eyes. Suddenly it became very obvious to Lee why he couldn't maintain a relationship.

He'd mistaken work for a personality, and now outside of the office, he had nothing to show for it.

"So this is where my honeybun grew up?" Kamran said. He raised his eyebrows, then winked at Lee. "I bet you got up to all kinds of trouble in here."

"Oh, yes," said Lee's mom. "This one time, I walked in and caught him—"

"Okay!" Lee cried, steering her toward the door. "That's enough! Thank you, Mom!"

"But, hon, I was just talking about the model planes and all that glue—!"

Lee slammed the door and pressed his back to it, raising

his eyebrows at Kamran, who had folded his arms across his chest and had a playful half-smile on his face.

"So, uh," said Lee, licking his lips and looking anywhere but at Kamran because having him in his room was making Lee feel like a teenager who'd snuck his high school crush over. "This is one way to get to know someone."

"It's certainly a crash course," Kamran said, sounding amused. Then he dropped his arms and began slinking over to where Lee was pressed against the door. "Do you know what's another good way to get to know someone?"

Lee forgot how to breathe as Kamran stopped right in front of him and ran a single finger down the middle of his chest.

"I-I…" Lee uttered.

It would be so *easy.* No one would ever have to know.

Except…that wasn't who Lee was. This would just be a fuck for Kamran. But Lee knew what he was like. If he gave in to these urges, his feelings were only going to get stronger, and he'd end up crushed when Kamran moved on to the next guy without a second thought. Besides – he was a *witness!* Lee had to *protect him!*

He shook himself and managed to retain just an ounce of professionalism. "I said no flirting," he said, brushing Kamran's hand away and moving aside.

Kamran huffed. "Then stop giving me come-to-bed eyes," he said peevishly. "Speaking of which, there's only one bed in here. However will we—"

"I'll sleep on the floor," Lee interrupted him. He moved to the closet, where, sure enough, there were several spare blankets.

"W-what?" Kamran spluttered. "Oh, now, come on. Don't be like that. I'm sorry, really. I'll behave. That bed is *huge.* I'll practically be in a different time zone. You can't sleep on the floor. That's awful."

"It's fine," Lee said, determinedly not looking at the other man as he collected two of the pillows from the many positioned at the head of the bed. It wasn't really fine. After a day at work, all that driving, the drama of the evening, then the disagreements with his father and brother, he really could have done with a decent night's sleep. But if Kamran said he was giving him 'come-to-bed eyes,' Lee needed to nip that right in the bud.

And that did not include sharing a bed and sleeping right next to the biggest temptation that had ever tempted.

At least the floor was carpeted, so his back would have a tiny bit of padding. He dropped the blankets and pillows, then crossed the room to where he'd left his bags. "Um, you can use the en suite. If you look in the cabinet, there should be some new toothbrushes." That was the kind of thing his parents stocked up on, being in the hotel business. "You can borrow these."

He practically threw a T-shirt and a pair of sweatpants at Kamran that he'd brought with him for running in. Usually, Lee slept in the nude, but he was very sure that the both of them should be clothed, so he got out a similar ensemble for himself as well.

Kamran looked between the clothes in his arms and Lee, then wordlessly stalked into the bathroom joined to Lee's room.

Lee tried to tell himself as he hastily got changed that he didn't care if Kamran was annoyed at him or not. They were doing this to keep Kamran safe from Charles Bolt, not to become best buddies.

Rather than wait around, Lee grabbed his toiletry bag and nipped across the hall to his sister's old room. He checked to see if anyone had their stuff in there, but it was empty of luggage. Lee knew that she and her family had chosen to stay at a hotel in town rather than have all of them take over the house, but it appeared no one was staying in her room tonight. Or if they were, they were still downstairs enjoying the party.

So Lee quickly made the most of her en suite, using the toilet and then scrubbing all that red wine off his teeth. He scooped up several handfuls of water and gulped them down, then padded back through her room and across the hall to his own room.

The lights were already off as he stepped back inside. From the hallway light, Lee could see a lump under the bedsheets, but from the tuft of dark hair poking out the top, it looked like Kamran had his back turned to him.

Lee pursed his lips and resisted the urge to ask if Kamran was okay. He could see he was still breathing, so professionally speaking, that was all that mattered. He left the door ajar as he moved to pull the curtains, then set up his bed on the floor. Once it was slightly less pitiful than just a pile of blankets, he closed the door and plunged them into mostly darkness.

He fumbled his way back to his little nest at the foot of his actual bed and tried to get as comfortable as he could. At least the pillows were memory foam. But as he stared at the ceiling in the gloom, it wasn't so much his back that was bothering him.

The silence in the room felt as heavy as a ton of bricks.

"Good night, Kamran," Lee said eventually.

He got nothing back in return.

8

KAMRAN

BEING TOLD 'NO' WASN'T EXACTLY A NEW CONCEPT FOR Kamran. He'd been denied a lot throughout his life. And when he heard it from people he was trying to hit on, he backed off immediately.

But Lee had been giving Kamran so many mixed signals all evening he'd been certain that there was at least a little bit of interest. So like a total jackass, he'd pushed things too far.

Now Lee had preferred to sleep on the goddamned floor rather than be anywhere near Kamran.

He felt like shit. And he deserved to.

He was buzzing from the alcohol and residual adrenaline of the day, not to mention all the thoughts that were whirring around in his head. So despite being exhausted, he'd found himself staring into the darkness for the past couple of hours, replaying everything that he'd done wrong that evening.

He'd been so determined to put a mask on and be his usual fun-loving self that he'd probably seemed like a lunatic. But that was how he functioned. Lee's brother made sly jabs at him, so Kamran laughed it off and told Lee to fight back.

Lee's dad called him an embarrassment and made him feel like shit, so he took all of three seconds to really feel the pain of that before bouncing back harder than before, charming everyone and Lee, just to get a rise out of him.

And now the poor man was sleeping on the floor.

Kamran had debated several times whether he should get out of bed and insist they swap places, but he had a feeling that would just make things worse. He didn't want Lee to think he was trying to give him the come-on again. So he'd been lying there stewing for goodness knew how long.

He should have just said good night back.

But he'd been too hurt. Lee would honestly rather subject himself to the floor than be anywhere near Kamran. Usually, he couldn't keep men, women, and anyone in between off him.

It was typical that the one person he wanted the most refused to get anywhere near him.

But only in the bedroom. Downstairs, Lee had kept his arm around Kamran like a vise, far more than Kamran had felt was necessary for their charade. No other couple had been that clingy. So Kamran had convinced himself like an idiot that it *had* to have meant something. That Lee wouldn't kiss Kamran's hair in front of his parents unless he felt *something*.

But he'd been wrong. Totally wrong.

Kamran knew this coming into the situation. They weren't compatible. It was clear from the start that he was a big old ho, whereas Lee was clearly built for monogamy and long-term commitment.

The only long-term commitment Kamran had was to his car.

Did he really want Lee that badly? Once this Chaz thing blew over, Kamran could go back to his usual ways and have any number of people in his bed – several at the same time if he wanted, which he probably would. Because he loved sex, not relationships. Relationships led to pain and suffering. Sex just led to orgasms. And orgasms were great.

He scratched his chest and frowned into the darkness, listening to Lee's breathing. It was steady enough, but Kamran couldn't tell if he was asleep or not. Was he lying there thinking about Kamran?

Oh holy hell, what did Kamran care? They were completely mismatched. Lee had said 'no,' and Kamran would respect that from now on. No matter how many mixed signals he got after this – if there were any. He was *not* a sleaze who couldn't accept a rejection. He hated guys like that.

So what that he desperately wanted to climb Lee like the mountain he was? So what Kamran hadn't been fascinated by anyone this badly in a very long time? It hurt that Lee didn't want him, but that was life. Kamran would replace him with thoughts of a dozen other people before the month was through.

Right?

Angrily, Kamran turned over yet again and tried to get comfortable. He'd only just met Mr. FBI Agent, and they barely knew each other. So why did it feel like Kamran was going to have to fuck a lot of people before he got this particular mountain of a man out of his system?

It was going to be an even longer night than it had been already.

SOMETIME BEFORE THE sun started rising, he must have finally drifted off. He awoke to an empty room and bright light streaming around the pulled curtains. His neck was stiff, and so was his cock. He groaned as he peeked at the end of the bed, but Lee was definitely gone.

Kamran flopped back against the pillows and briefly debated jerking one out to alleviate his frustration, but he wasn't sure where Lee had gone or if he'd be back soon. He went to check the time on his phone, which was resting on the nightstand...then paused as he realized it had been plugged into a charger attached to the wall that definitely hadn't been there the night before.

He bit his lip as a strange sensation blossomed in his chest. Had Lee done that? Sneakily moved his own charger next to the bed so Kamran's phone could be plugged in while he was still sleeping? He must have. That was...

Well, that was one of the sweetest things anyone had ever done for him.

"You're pathetic," Kamran grumbled to himself as he rubbed his forehead. But the bubble of happiness refused to burst in his chest.

Maybe Lee wasn't interested in sleeping with him. But he definitely cared about Kamran in *some* way. And not just in a 'this is my key witness' kind of way. Kamran bit his lip and touched the phone, feeling kind of tingly all over, even though he knew he was being totally ridiculous.

As he pressed his fingers to the screen, it flashed to life, and Kamran could see all the many, *many* notifications he'd received. He had several messages from the husbands asking if he'd changed his mind. Usually, that would have bolstered Kamran's ego right up, but seeing them desperate for his ass left him feeling kind of cold.

He dismissed those, then quickly read through the few messages he'd gotten from his friends. Scout and Emery had asked for a follow-up on 'Mr. Tall Dark & Handsome' in their group chat, so naturally, everyone was interested in what Kamran was doing – or *who*. Kamran wasn't sure how they knew about Lee, but Emery and Scout had been at the bar last night, so maybe they'd seen something.

Kamran groaned, trying not to worry about them judging his questionable life choices. They had that big party for Angel at the Coal family house today to keep them preoccupied, so Kamran hoped they'd forget about his drama soon enough. His heart panged a little that he'd be missing it, but he'd been missing a lot recently since Chaz had found him again. It was difficult to be around couples when Kamran felt like the most unlovable slug on the planet. He was sure the gang had noticed his absences lately, but he had his own problems to deal with today. Hopefully, they'd forgive him.

If he made it through this whole investigation unscathed.

He typed out a vague 'I'm fine' to them and put the group conversation notifications on mute for the foreseeable future. He adored his friends, but he really didn't know how to explain what was going on with him right now. Not with Chaz and his past nor Lee and his present. He definitely had no clue about what the future might hold.

At least catching up on his various phone apps had allowed his morning wood to calm down, but there was still no sign of Lee. It was just after ten in the morning, so Kamran wasn't sure what to do. He *did* know that he was hungry and needed coffee.

Throwing the bedcovers back, he hopped out of the bed and padded across the room to ease the door open a crack.

There weren't any signs of life out in the hall. Kamran sighed, then decided he had no reason to hide or creep around. Just because he had no experience of staying over at a partner's family's house didn't mean he hadn't watched TV. The fact that Lee's mom hadn't insisted they sleep in separate bedrooms had already discarded that particular sitcom trope, so he figured no one was going to freak out if he got caught coming out of Lee's bedroom.

He closed the door again, then moved back into the en suite bathroom to freshen up for the morning. As there were products on the shelf, Kamran made the spontaneous decision to grab a thirty-second shower, rinsing his hair and body as fast as possible. He didn't want to come across as greedy or anything to Lee's family by using too much hot water, but he didn't want to smell like yesterday, either.

He peeked back into Lee's room with a towel wrapped around his waist, but there was still no sign of the man himself. However, Kamran was done hanging around and needed to go in search of breakfast.

And Lee.

So much for not leaving Kamran's side.

He refused to feel hurt. Or at least he tried to. Instead, he pulled his jeans on commando and then slipped Lee's T-shirt back on. Kamran told himself that was because it was less suspicious than wearing the same thing from the night before and definitely not because it smelled of whatever fabric softener it was that Lee used.

The house was very quiet as Kamran retraced the route back downstairs. Had the whole family gone out without him? Why hadn't Lee woken him?

"Because you're not really his boyfriend. You're just here under witness protection," he muttered to himself as he crossed the second landing. "Get a grip."

He soon cheered up as he reached the first floor and the smell of bacon greeted him, calling like a siren, beckoning him to the kitchen. Well, *someone* had to be around in that case.

He'd only seen this part of the house briefly since last night, but it was so immaculate that Kamran figured someone must have cleaned it since the guests had departed.

Damn, that was efficient. He could barely manage to remember to wash his dishes once a week.

Oh, duh. Lee's folks had probably had professionals come in first thing and deal with all the party mess. Having money was a whole different life.

The kitchen was a ridiculously big open space. Kamran stepped from one of the living rooms through an archway into a chrome-and-black-tile dream with a huge square island occupying the middle of the room. The appliances had a kitsch, fifties sort of feel to them, even though they were undoubtedly state-of-the-art and all probably cost hundreds, if not thousands of dollars. But Kamran only got to study them briefly before his attention was diverted.

Because at the island, an elderly woman was sitting with a puff of snowy white hair, a multicolored vest over her blouse that looked like it had been made out of carpet from the seventies, and reading glasses perched on the tip of her button nose that were about an inch thick. She was studying a tablet in her hands that was emitting quiet voices in conversation, jabbing at it with a crooked finger and her tongue between her teeth. Next to her on the island, a rat (okay, it was probably a small dog) was lapping something out of a big round mug.

Whoever this woman was, she hadn't been at the party last night, Kamran was sure.

A coffee machine was gurgling on one of the countertops, the smell of it reaching out to greet Kamran like an old friend. There were several pans on the stove, but he wasn't sure if anything was actually cooking, although he could definitely still smell bacon.

The elderly lady huffed at the screen, then looked up at Kamran, shaking her head. "No matter how many years this show runs, there's always some bitch that can't sew. Every time!"

Kamran blinked, not quite sure he'd just heard what he thought he'd heard the sweet old lady say. "I-I'm sorry?" he stuttered.

He'd been expecting a 'Can I help you, dear' or something of that ilk. He looked behind him to see if there was someone else who'd previously been having a conversation with this lady, which might make her words make sense. But they were alone.

Kamran stepped closer. "Are you...watching a show?" he guessed, jutting his chin toward the tablet in her hand. The little black, tan, and white dog looked up from their mug, licking their lips as they stared at Kamran as he approached the kitchen island.

The woman waved the tablet at him and shook her head with a faint air of incredulity. "The one where the boys dress up as the ladies. Half an hour with a sewing machine, I'd set them right! But no – now I have to watch them hot glue aluminum foil to tennis balls and call it a skirt. It's all going to end in tears," she added with a sigh.

Her gaze was just flicking back to the tablet when it suddenly snapped to Kamran. She tilted her head, then lifted her glasses to peer through them without actually putting them on.

"Oh. You're not one of mine, are you?" She tapped on the screen, and the low-level noise stopped altogether. She smiled to show a perfectly straight set of white teeth, then slapped the barstool next to the one she was perched on. "Come over here and say hi to me and Sugar. She doesn't bite, but I might." She chuckled at her own joke and banged the stool again.

Kamran was wary as he moved around the island. "Are you...?" he began. "I mean...do you know Lee? Leopold?"

The lady's eyes went wide, and she sat up straight, staring at Kamran. It made him pause before he got to the seat.

"Oh, don't tell me my little Lee has a young man?" she asked, her eyes suddenly brimming with tears.

Shit. Kamran had *not* signed on to string along adorable old ladies who swore at Drag Race. But what could he do?

"Uh…yeah," he croaked, licking his lips. "I'm his…Lee's boyfriend. Kamran."

The lady sniffed and clasped her hands to her chest. Sugar wagged her tail and did a little dance, her claws going *tappity-tap* on the kitchen island.

"Oh!" the lady cried, springing to her feet with surprising bounciness for a woman of her years. She dashed around her stool and flung her arms around Kamran's middle, her head coming up to his shoulder. "It's so nice to meet you, Kamran! I'm Lee's gamma, but you feel free to call me Joy or Gams or Gamma, whatever you're comfortable with."

She pulled back and looked Kamran over before nodding.

"You're so handsome! I bet my Lee is smitten with you. Would you like some waffles and bacon? And eggs. Or maybe pancakes or French toast?" Joy waved her hand dismissively. "What am I talking about? Lee will be back in any minute. I'll just cook everything for you boys."

"Lee's here?" Kamran said, looking around. Nerves fluttered in his belly, but he couldn't see his fake boyfriend anywhere.

Joy chuckled. "Well, *you're* certainly smitten with my Lee, so I know you have sense." She cupped the side of Kamran's face and studied him with watery eyes. "Yes. I can tell you're a nice boy," she said confidently. "I think Lee chose better this time. Right, Kamran. Is there anything I should know?"

"K-know?" he asked, practically breaking out in a sweat.

But Joy just continued beaming at him and nodded. "Yes. Like are you vegan or gluten intolerant? That sort of thing. No sense cooking up a storm if you can't satisfy your belly."

She chuckled to herself again as she began fussing with the pots and pans on the stove.

"Oh, right," Kamran uttered. He took a breath and assured himself that sweet Joy was not questioning the legitimacy of their relationship. "Uh, no. Thank you for asking. ma'am, but I'll eat just about anything."

Joy shoved a couple of pans into the sink, then waved a wooden spoon at him. "Don't you 'ma'am' me," she said with an arched white eyebrow and a grin. "I know I said to call me whatever you like, but anything but that, please."

Kamran managed a weak laugh as he finally sat down at the kitchen island. "Okay," he said meekly.

"Excellent."

Joy puttered over the enormous fridge and began emptying half of it. Sugar trotted over to Kamran and started sniffing at him. He'd learned from his friend Jay's corgi to let dogs inspect your hand first, so he held out his fingers. Sugar's little black nose twitched as she read whatever his hand was telling her, then her tongue lolled out as she gave him a doggy smile and wagged her butt happily.

"Hey there, little one," he said softly as he stroked her short fur. She was actually much cuter than he'd first thought. "So, um...Lee's gone out with his family?" he probed.

But Joy shook her head as she began cracking eggs into a bowl. "Oh, no, honey. They all went out hunting rabbits at the crack of dawn. He came down about twenty minutes before you did, but then his dang phone went off, so he took himself walking around the gardens to answer it. He said it was work."

She shook her head and sighed as relief washed over Kamran that Lee hadn't ditched him after their awkward end of the evening. Kamran wondered if Joy also thought that Lee worked too much and needed more of a life.

For half a second, Kamran allowed himself to indulge in a fantasy where *he* was the reason that Lee actually did spend more time at home and less time at the office. But that was silly, so he shook it off.

"Oh, okay," said Kamran. "I hope he's okay." His boss had agreed to this plan, but still, Kamran worried irrationally that he was going to get Lee into trouble.

He also felt a bit safer knowing that Lee was still on the premises. Not that Chaz should have any idea that Kamran was here. But until Chaz was in FBI custody, Kamran would feel best by Lee's side.

In more ways than one.

No, he scolded himself. *Behave!*

But how was he supposed to do that when Lee chose to walk into the kitchen at that very moment, looking like a wet dream in the softest dove-gray cashmere sweater and light blue jeans that gripped every muscle on his sculpted body like they were shipwreck survivors clinging to driftwood for dear life.

Kamran cleared his throat. "Hi," he said. Well, he sort of squeaked it, actually, but he hoped if he ignored that, so would everyone else.

Lee looked up from his phone, and his blue eyes widened as he realized Kamran was in the kitchen with his grandmother. "Hi," he said faintly back. "You're awake. Did you, uh, sleep well? I didn't want to disturb you."

He waved his phone guiltily. Kamran was about to tell him that it was absolutely fine and that of course he needed to report in, when he remembered what role he was supposed to be playing.

"It's okay, shnookums," he said, sounding patiently annoyed as he slipped off his barstool and made his way over to where Lee was hovering. "But that's it now, all right? No more work. You promised. *Especially* not over the weekend."

Aware that Joy had stopped beating eggs and was watching them, Kamran slipped his arms around Lee's tree trunk waist and batted his eyelashes up at him.

Was it his imagination, or did Lee's breath hitch?

"Okay, baby," he murmured, pressing his lips to Kamran's cheek.

For a second, it was almost a perfect moment. But then the word 'baby' registered, and Kamran jumped away from Lee like he'd gotten an electric shock.

That was what Chaz used to call him, making Kamran believe that he loved him when really he was using him all along. That word was *poison*.

Of course, to most people, it was totally fine. Kamran felt his cheeks heat up as Lee and Joy both stared at him.

"Oh, hey," he said awkwardly, skipping back to Sugar, petting her affectionately. As she got into his ploy by dropping dramatically onto her back and wriggling as he petted her, Kamran decided that she was not, in fact, a rat but an angel and the best accomplice ever. "Breakfast smells *amazing*, Joy. Hey, Lee – your gamma is making us a huge breakfast, even though everyone else already ate earlier. Isn't that the nicest?"

Lee definitely had questions about Kamran's behavior, but at the praise for his grandmother, he melted into a sweet smile and sat himself on the stool beside Kamran. "Thanks, Gamma," he said genuinely. "I'm starving, and I bet Kamran is too. We only got a bit of the buffet last night."

Kamran had thought they'd eaten quite a bit, but Lee's remark supported his four-thousand-calories-a-day theory.

"What do you boys have planned for today, then?" Joy asked as she opened a package of bacon. Sugar's nose jumped, and the little dog suddenly abandoned Kamran in favor of chasing the smell.

He couldn't say he blamed her.

Surprisingly – considering how he'd just yeeted himself from Lee's side – Lee smiled warmly at Kamran, then rubbed his back. "We're going to go shopping," he announced. "Kamran decided to come on this vacation at the last minute but didn't really know what he'd need. So I'm going to help him pick out the perfect wardrobe for the week."

"Aww, that's lovely," said Joy as she dropped a full stick of butter into a pan where it immediately started sizzling like crazy.

However, Kamran got a case of cold feet. "Are you sure?" he whispered, looking into Lee's eyes. "I wasn't…I was a dick last night. I'm sorry."

But all he saw in those ocean blues was sincerity.

Lee licked his lips and nodded. "I'm sorry too," he murmured. "But yes. Let me do this for you."

A shiver ran the full length of Kamran's spine.

With a request like that, how could he refuse?

9

LEE

"HOW DO YOU FEEL?" LEE ASKED AS HE WATCHED KAMRAN taking in his reflection in the mirror.

Lee asked how Kamran was feeling because he already knew how he looked.

Fucking *gorgeous.*

Lee had insisted on getting Kamran a full wardrobe for the week – a pair of jeans and some khakis, as well as several T-shirts, sweaters, and formal shirts, underwear, and both a pair of sneakers and some dress shoes. Kamran had been wearing what he called his 'fancy shoes' the night before, but Lee had taken the opportunity to upgrade him.

Right now, they were in the formalwear store of the Penny Falls mall (where they were less likely to be recognized than in Pine Cove), trying on a classic tuxedo for the big formal farewell ball next Saturday.

Lee was having trouble sitting straight. Kamran looked so delectable. The clean line of the suit cut his slim but muscular figure in the most sinful ways. They didn't even need to get the damn thing tailored. He looked like the fabric was dripping off him. Like it was already made for him.

But Kamran was pulling a face at his reflection that bordered on a grimace. He looked around the store, then fixed his gaze on Lee. "This is too much!" he hissed, his beautiful brown eyes wide and panicky.

Lee licked his lips and stood from the chair he'd parked his ass in by the changing room mirror. There weren't any other customers there at present, so he and Kamran were alone. As dangerous as that was for Lee's more animalistic impulses, it probably worked to his advantage right then for giving Kamran a quick pep talk.

"Kamran," he said gently, holding his arm and squeezing it. Kamran looked up at him and blinked, his mouth open and his lips plump and wet from where he'd obviously been worrying them.

Lee ignored how kissable they looked. Mostly.

"Dude, this is crazy," Kamran said before Lee could keep talking. "I thought you were going to get me a couple of shirts. You've already spent hundreds on me, and this thing here will take us into the thousands!"

Lee narrowed his eyes. "I explained that we're having a black-tie event a week from today, yes?"

"Yes," Kamran grumbled.

"And what do you think you'd wear to that if not a suit?"

Kamran scoffed. "Exactly! A suit! I thought I'd just add a tie to one of those shirts you got me! This is...I can't..."

He blinked his eyes, and Lee felt like he'd been physically punched when he realized there were tears about to fall.

No. No. That wouldn't do. He couldn't kiss or hold this beautiful man, so he would do what he could to make him understand that he was *completely* worthy of this extravagance, as Kamran saw it.

Lee took his chin between his thumb and index finger, tilting his head to make him meet Lee's gaze. "And do you think I would let my man face my family feeling anything less than a million bucks? Tell me you don't like this and would rather wear a button-down and jeans, and that's what you'll wear. But *I* think you look fucking astonishing in this tux, and if you like it, that's what you'll get."

Kamran's mouth opened and closed a couple of times. "But...I'm not your man?" he whispered.

"You are for this week," Lee growled, aware he sounded like a caveman.

But he was sick of Kamran being his own worst enemy and acting like he didn't deserve anything. These here were his truest moments that Lee couldn't resist. When Kamran was vulnerable and pure. Not a larger-than-life cheeky party boy with all the answers.

This was the guy Lee was falling for.

And goddamn it, he was going to look his best for the grand finale of the family reunion so he'd feel his best. Lee would walk out of this store right now and buy him a glittery shirt – a Stetson, a hoodie, a fucking *ballgown* – so long as it made Kamran shine from within.

But it had become increasingly obvious that Kamran needed permission to enjoy being spoiled.

For fuck's sake, if Lee's money was good for anything, surely it was this?

Kamran's breath hitched, and Lee rubbed his shoulders. "Let me give you this, please," he said softly. "Not because I have to, but because I want to. Okay?"

Kamran swallowed, studying Lee's face. "I don't get you," he said. "You tell me to stop flirting with you, and I'm doing my best. But then you say things like that to me and look at me like that and touch me like this and...and...you plugged in my goddamned phone."

Lee raised his eyebrows. He'd quite forgotten that he'd put Kamran's cell on to charge before he'd snuck out of the room that morning. It had just seemed the polite thing to do, but Kamran bit his lip and looked up at him with such sincerity Lee realized what a caring act it really had been.

It just felt natural to be like that with Kamran, though.

He sighed and dropped his head, rubbing his thumbs against Kamran's shoulders. "I'm sorry," he said. "I know I'm being hypocritical. I don't mean to confuse you."

"I just want to know where I stand," Kamran said, his breath ghosting over Lee's lips. "I was an asshole last night, pushing after you'd said 'no.' But I gotta admit all this here doesn't *feel* like 'no.'" Lee looked up to see him lick his lips, his eyes flitting over Lee's face. "Because I'll be totally honest – no games. I want you."

"I…" *Urgh!* Why was this so complicated?

If Lee was also being totally honest, he knew he'd throw his no hookups rule out the window for Kamran. He'd do anything to have a taste of him, if just for one night. But there were other factors at play here.

"I think you're remarkable," he managed to say. "I am…*deeply* attracted to you. But you are under my protection and part of my investigation. It wouldn't be ethical."

Kamran dropped his head as he nodded, stepping away from Lee. Lee wanted to protest as his hands fell to his sides, but he knew Kamran was doing the right thing.

"Unethical, yes," Kamran said. Then a ghost of a smile tugged at his lips as he looked at Lee through his long, dark lashes. "But just so we're clear – if it weren't for the investigation, you'd let me climb you like the Rockies, yeah?"

Lee couldn't help but laugh. "Yes, I think I would," he admitted softly. "But seeing as I can't, will you allow me to buy you these gifts?"

He wanted to add that it wasn't just because Kamran needed them for the week with his family. But because Lee just wanted to do something nice for him. He got the feeling that not a lot of people had been nice to Kamran in his past, and Lee wanted to show him what it was like to be spoiled, even if it was just for a brief moment.

Maybe then Kamran might demand better of his next relationship and not fall for someone like Chaz Bolt ever again.

Except Kamran didn't do relationships. Otherwise, Lee would seriously consider throwing himself at Kamran's feet and begging for a chance once this case was over. He'd never met anyone like Kamran in his life, and the thought of losing him, even after only such a short amount of time, was already painful.

But some people just weren't meant to be together. Like two puzzle pieces that didn't fit.

Kamran was looking at his reflection again, smoothing down the jacket sleeves. "Okay," he said quietly. "I'll let you buy me this. If it'll make you happy."

Lee quirked an eyebrow. "Would it make *you* happy?"

Kamran opened his mouth, and Lee would have bet any money that he was going to come out with something dismissive. But instead, he glanced at the mirror again, then gave Lee a grin. "I do look pretty hot, don't I?"

Lee bit his lower lip and tried not to grin back too much. "You do," he agreed.

"Then that makes me happy," Kamran told him with a wink.

Lee rubbed his hands together and stepped back to where he'd left their other bags. "Okay, then. We'll take it. Get dressed, and then we'll have a look at the outdoors store across the way."

Lee was looking forward to seeing Kamran back in the T-shirt he'd borrowed from him. Lee was pretty sure he was going to let him keep it, even though he had all this new stuff. It looked good on him. But it also made Lee feel in a small way like he'd been able to stake a claim on Kamran after all.

Kamran frowned. "What do I need from the outdoors store? I already have my leather jacket. I really don't need another coat."

Lee had to agree with him on that. Not only did that jacket fit him sinfully well, but Lee loved the smell on him.

"No, not for a coat," he agreed. "You need gloves, a hat, and a scarf. For going ice skating later."

"Ice skating?" Kamran repeated, snapping his head around. "I...um, okay," he said, then disappeared into his cubicle to change.

"I THINK I'll probably just watch, you know?" Kamran said as they pulled up to the ice rink parking lot an hour later. "You said your family is already there, so by the time we rent skates and stuff they'll probably want to leave, right? So, uh..."

Lee looked over at the passenger seat, crooking an eyebrow. Kamran had been unusually quiet since they'd left the formalwear store. There was definitely something hinky going on around the skating, but Lee couldn't for the life of him work out what it was.

"We can go home if you want?" Lee said. He honestly wouldn't mind if they did. He liked skating, and this rink was particularly charming, but he wasn't dead set on it. If they went home, he could catch up on some emails and—

Nope. No work. He could get his e-reader out and maybe finally start that thriller he'd been meaning to read for months. In fact, the idea of him and Kamran snuggled up by the fire, reading or doing sudoku or something sounded really—

Dangerous. If Lee thought that wouldn't end in making out, he was deranged.

Maybe they shouldn't be at home alone.

Kamran was staring at the building as Lee found a parking spot. Most ice rinks Lee had been to were gray and practical looking – like gyms – usually places where hockey teams trained and the like. But The Lodge looked like exactly its name. A huge wooden cabin with fake snow on the triangular roof. It was a cozy Bavarian dream that Lee had spent half his childhood at. Having not been for a few years, he had to say he was really looking forward to showing it off to Kamran, who obviously hadn't been there before.

It was lucky because the place was closed next week for renovations. His parents had specifically timed the family's visit here today before the season changeover that The Lodge had every year. So Lee really didn't want to miss the chance for Kamran to see it at its most wintery and, therefore, most magical in Lee's opinion.

But from the look of trepidation on Kamran's face, maybe that wasn't such a good idea after all.

Kamran licked his lips, then turned to face Lee. "Uh, what? Oh, home? No, no, we can't do that. You've already missed hunting and walking with your family this morning. This is your vacation. The idea is to actually spend time with the people you came to see." He chuckled, but then he looked back at The Lodge and nibbled on his lip.

Lee frowned. "Can't you skate?"

He hadn't thought of that until this second, but it was an obvious answer as to why Kamran was less than enthusiastic. Lee cursed himself for not thinking of it earlier. Just because his whole family loved skating didn't mean everyone could.

"Because that's totally fine if you can't!" he added. "There are loads of food and craft stalls in there. It's like a German Christmas market all year round. We could get soft pretzels and hot chocolate and sit on the picnic benches they have in the fake pine forest that's set up by the rink. They actually pump pine scent into the air, so you feel like you're in a real forest and…"

He realized he was rambling. But he felt like he'd only just made Kamran a little more comfortable back at the suit place, only to drag his mood down again by mentioning skating.

However, Kamran surprised him again. "No, I can skate," he said with a sigh. "Okay, come on. You're making this place sound so damn magical. Now I have to see it." He threw Lee a sheepish smile as they undid their seat belts and exited the car.

"I think you'll like it," Lee said earnestly as he locked the Jeep. "But honestly, you don't have to skate if you don't want to."

Truth be told, since Lee had gotten older and much bulkier, he wasn't nearly as zippy as he'd been on the ice as a kid. He'd enjoy puttering around, but he kind of liked the idea of sitting with Kamran more. Maybe they could get to know each other a little better?

Kamran just hummed as they walked up the steps to go inside. But Lee smiled as he watched his expression change as they pushed through the doors. It reminded Lee of Disneyland or a Vegas hotel. Even though there were plenty of actual pine forests around this part of the world, this was like stepping into what Lee imagined Germany or Switzerland was like. As if they'd been transported to another land.

"How come I never knew this place existed?" Kamran marveled, turning slowly in a circle and blinking as he looked at all the fake snow and wooden stalls. The scent of pine, cinnamon, and other spices drifted through the air along with the smell of sweet chocolate and warm, salty pretzels. A functioning ski lift trundled overhead that people could ride on, and music could be heard from the carousel over the other side of the rink. Above them, the ceiling was dark but covered in hundreds of tiny lights to simulate a night's sky.

It was just as mesmerizing as Lee had remembered it to be.

"I've been coming here since I could walk," Lee admitted. He glanced around the crowd, but he couldn't see his family. They were all probably on the ice or shopping. Damn. Lee was hoping for an excuse to hold Kamran's hand, but maybe...

He slipped his fingers against Kamran's. Both their hands were gloved, but the intimacy of it still sent shivers down his spine.

"Is this okay?" he asked.

Kamran smiled at him. It was warm and gentle. "Yeah," he said.

"They'll close it all next week and give it the springtime makeover," Lee explained, wanting to impress Kamran like a schoolboy with a crush. *Damn.* Kamran had a way of breaking down all his defenses. "I prefer it like this, though. It's like getting Christmas for a few extra months."

Kamran hummed, and Lee wondered what Christmas was like for someone with no family. But then Kamran inhaled deeply and turned his head to smile at Lee. "I love it. I'm glad we got to see it before it shut down for the week."

"Me, too," Lee agreed.

Lee began walking them toward the skate rental booth, hoping they'd have a pair big enough to fit his boat-sized feet. Sometimes he had to wait, and he didn't want Kamran having to hang around if he didn't feel confident on the ice by himself. But he was in luck, and once they'd handed over their shoes, they made their way to the seated area to lace up.

"Hello, boys!"

Lee looked up to see Gamma waving from a table that was surrounded by a mountain of bags and coats, presumably from Lee's family members who were already skating. Sugar was in the special purse Gamma had to carry her around in and was happily licking at a candy apple Gamma had propped up in front of her.

"Joy," Kamran said, sounding genuinely delighted as they walked over to her in their socks. "You're not out there doing a triple axel?"

Gamma chuckled and waved her trusty iPad at him. Lee loved seeing them interact, he had to admit. "With these hips? Not on your life. Besides, it's Snatch Game!"

Kamran nodded as if she'd said something wise. "Well, you can't interrupt that," he agreed. Lee had never watched Drag Race, but he loved how much Gamma had gotten into it, and he liked that Kamran seemed to know what she was talking about.

"Did you boys have fun shopping?" she asked as they found seats and began the long process of tightening up their laces on the borrowed skates.

"We did," said Kamran, like he was surprised. "But did you know that you have a very bossy grandson?"

He winked at Lee, who couldn't help but wink back. His insides felt all bubbly. Like for a moment in this make-believe Bavarian getaway, he could pretend that he and Kamran were really a couple.

"I did know that, and I love him for it," said Gamma firmly. "Someone in this family needs to stand up to my son-in-law, god love him. He's a peach, but he's also stubborn as a mule." She meant Lee's dad, and he winced. She wagged a crooked finger at Lee. "Being bossy is what got you your career. Don't you let anyone tell you otherwise."

Lee wasn't sure why, but he glanced at Kamran. He

wondered if he might look put out at being told that bossy was a good thing. But instead, he was beaming at Lee, like he was proud.

Lee cleared his throat, trying not to bask too much. "I won't," he promised his gamma.

When their skates were secure, Lee offered Kamran his hand again to walk him over to the rink entrance. Kamran took it with a smile, but he had no trouble walking on the blades like Lee had expected. In fact, he strode so fast Lee had a little trouble keeping up. When they stepped on the ice, Kamran didn't slip or seem unsteady at all. Huh. Apparently, he could skate, just like he'd said.

Then why the hesitation before?

Lee shook his head and decided not to worry about it. "You want to do a lap?" he asked, waving at his sister, who was wrangling several of her children with her husband up ahead. The rink was like a lazy river in a water park, constructed in an imperfect circle around several dozen trees in an area of fake forest in the center. Lee remembered when it had been a standard rectangular rink before they'd totally remodeled it one summer in the early nineties. Apparently, it had inspired several other rinks across the country.

He felt so at home here it took him a second to realize that he and Kamran were already slowly gliding forward. They were also still holding hands, and Lee allowed himself a moment to enjoy the guilty pleasure of that.

"You *can* skate," he said without thinking, watching Kamran's feet glide in perfect Vs. He seemed totally at ease on the ice. In fact, Lee only just noticed that Kamran had gotten figure skates, not the standard hockey skates they usually gave guys. He must have asked for them specifically.

Lee looked up to see Kamran give him a funny look.

"I told you I could skate," he said.

Lee shrugged. "But then you wanted to go home. I figured there had to be a reason."

Kamran sighed and looked out ahead for a while. "I used to skate," he said eventually. "As a kid back in Arizona. I'd tell my folks I was going to play basketball with my friends or to the library to study, but I'd go to the rink instead."

Lee frowned. "Why did you lie about it?"

Kamran's laugh was hollow. "Because my dad said skating was for sissies, and my brother would have beaten the shit out of me if he'd found out just in case he was called gay by association. I mean, beat me up more than he already did."

Lee felt like he'd been doused in cold water. "I'm so sorry they treated you like that."

Kamran was the one to shrug this time. "It was all kind of normal back then. You don't know any different as a kid, do you? Anyway, of course my dad eventually found out what I was doing when I was fifteen, and basically grounded me until I left home not long after. I haven't been skating again since, which was kind of okay because I discovered driving, but…" He looked around at the fake trees and all the stalls around the ice, smiling. "I thought I'd feel sad, but…well, it's kind of nice."

Lee squeezed his hand, then rubbed it between both of his. "I'm sorry. I wouldn't have pushed if I'd have known."

But Kamran grinned at him. "No, I'm glad we did this. Hey – you wanna see a trick? I mean, I'll probably fall flat on my ass, but muscle memory's gotta count for something, right?"

"Sure," said Lee, not sure what to expect.

Kamran beamed at him, his melancholy completely gone, leaving an excitement in its wake that made Lee's chest hurt with happiness. Kamran nodded, then let go of Lee's hand, skating off ahead at an alarming rate. Wow, he could really move.

"What's he doing?" Lee looked to see that Florence and Mia had appeared at his shoulder. The three of them moved slowly together as Kamran sped up to a gap in the crowd.

"I'm not sure—" Lee began saying, then suddenly stopped as he gasped.

Kamran leaped through the air, turning and landing on one foot. Then he started spinning on the spot on that leg, the other leg stuck out behind him, both arms reaching toward it. People skated around him, their jaws hanging open as he got faster and faster. Suddenly he brought his leg back down and held his arms in front of him, spinning so fast he was a blur. Then he gracefully skated his way out of the turn in a circle.

People around him whooped and clapped as he extended his arms and gave them little bows.

However, his eyes quickly found Lee's. They sparkled with happiness and pride, but there was a slight wideness to them as well, like he was asking Lee what he thought.

What did Lee think? He thought Kamran was astonishing. A beautiful man who had been sorely lacking in anyone to believe in him, to support him. If that was his 'rusty' skating, Lee wondered just how good he'd been as a teenager. He boggled that any parent could ignore such a talent and deny their kid something they loved so much.

Lee also thought as he skated to greet Kamran that he was in trouble.

Big trouble.

Because he wanted to be the one to applaud Kamran's success. He wanted to take him skating anytime he liked and tell him how incredible he was. He wanted to buy him yummy treats and ride the ski lift with him, snuggled together, trading sweet kisses.

He wanted *Kamran*.

But he couldn't have him. Not like that.

So instead, he, Florence, and Mia caught up with him and patted his back, gushing about how insane his stunt had been, asking him what else he could do as he grinned at them and skated backward like it was the easiest thing in the world.

Lee tried to enjoy the moment and not worry about the heartache he was going to feel when he inevitably lost Kamran for good.

KAMRAN

"AND THEN KAMRAN DID ANOTHER SPINNING THING. DID YOU see it, Mom?" Mia gushed, waving her hands as she skipped around the kitchen island. "He was like *slam* and then *whoosh* and then *skrit!* It was so cool."

Kamran tried not to blush or shrink away from the praise Lee's teenage niece was giving him. The family was back from their afternoon at The Lodge, and Kamran had to say he couldn't remember the last time he'd had so much fun with something that didn't include orgasms.

After an hour on the ice, Lee had taken him around the cute wooden stalls and bought them both hot chocolates like he'd promised. They'd sipped their drinks while strolling around, looking at the crafty things. Oh, and Lee had held Kamran's hand the entire time – just in case his family saw them, of course.

Now they were back at Lee's parents' house, and Donald was in charge of the grill outside, barbecuing heaps of meat and veggies that Kamran was very much looking forward to. His body ached pleasantly from using muscles he hadn't even thought about in years, and despite Joy's enormous breakfast that morning, he'd definitely worked up an appetite again.

Joy, Cheryl, and Florence were currently busy in the kitchen with a salad bar operation that Kamran had to say he found really endearing. With Mia occasionally stirring or chopping something as well, it was pretty cool to see four generations of Lee's family all working together.

This was what family was supposed to be like.

Lee had tried to help, but he'd been banished back to the kitchen island by Joy and told to open a bottle of red wine for them all to share. "You're on *vacation*," Joy insisted.

"So's everyone else," Lee protested.

But Joy had waved her trusty wooden spoon at him. "Yes, but no one else has a brand-new boyfriend who needs fussing over. You boys relax and get that merlot into some glasses."

Kamran couldn't say he was complaining as he sat and sipped the rich wine, his and Lee's knees almost brushing. Most people were outside, enjoying the ambiance with the heaters and fairy lights that someone had set up. A lot of the sofas from the reception room had been moved onto the patio, and there were blankets everywhere for people to snuggle with. Music played from a sound system that appeared to be hooked up to every room on the ground floor of the house that Cheryl controlled from her phone.

It was extravagant but also kind of cozy. It was nuts how fast Kamran was getting used to the Marshall way of life. He caught himself feeling guilty, like he was somehow betraying himself by having a good time, but that was ridiculous. He was only here because Chaz had threatened him. It wasn't his fault. He was allowed to have a little fun while he was hiding out, for heaven's sake.

He looked at Lee. "What?" Lee asked, his lips quirking into a smile.

Kamran shook his head. "Nothing," he said, but then he changed his mind. "No, I mean thank you – for today. For not giving up on me."

Lee glanced at his family, but they were busy dicing and mixing things. Mia twirled around, singing along reasonably tunefully to a Glittergasm song.

"I'm not giving up on you," Lee said with such sincerity it almost made Kamran want to squirm. But he forced himself to keep looking into Lee's blue eyes. "I'm glad you had a nice day."

"It was…" *Everything? Spectacular? More meaningful than you'll probably ever know?* "Memorable," Kamran said finally.

Lee licked his lips and looked down. He briefly touched Kamran's thigh with the backs of his fingers. "You were absolutely incredible on the ice," he said as he looked back up. "You should keep at it."

Kamran laughed softly and rolled his eyes. "I don't know. What would be the point?"

"The point would be that you looked so happy," Lee said. He raised his eyebrows a little. "I don't think you let yourself be happy enough. But you deserve to be."

Kamran almost asked him why. Things that made him happy were taken away from him.

Like the skating. He'd been approached by more than one coach to train him to compete, but Kamran had known his dad would never allow it. Then his dad had stopped him skating anyway before finally kicking him out.

Like Chaz, who Kamran was so convinced had been in love with him. He'd taken all that away in an instant, leaving Kamran on his own.

He loved his driving, but he often wondered how long it would be before he had an accident and totaled his beloved Mustang, or worse – injured himself so badly he couldn't drive anymore. His friend Angel's accident a few months ago had proved how easily it could happen.

But then he took a second and looked back into Lee's eyes. They shone with sincerity. Kamran could see that Lee believed wholeheartedly that Kamran deserved happiness. That he deserved things he enjoyed.

For some reason, if Lee believed it, Kamran felt like it was easier for him to believe, too.

But Lee was practically a stranger. Why was his opinion so important to Kamran when his friends had been trying to take care of him for the last couple of years here in Pine Cove?

It just was. It might not make much sense, but Kamran was tired of fighting this undeniable pull that Lee had over him. It was as if he was the earth and Kamran was the moon, caught helplessly in his orbit.

"Thank you," he said softly.

"Kamran, Kamran," Mia cried, popping out of nowhere and tapping his shoulder. It was the wake-up call Kamran needed to pull away from Lee before he did something monumentally stupid, like kiss him.

"Yeah, hi," he said, laughing at her enthusiasm as she hopped around, waving a stick of carrot like a conductor's baton.

"What was that thing called where you spun around like this?" she asked before leaning forward and sticking her leg out in the air behind her to make her body into a T-shape.

"Careful there, Miss Ice Capades," her mom protested, tapping her leg as she tried to get to the fridge. "Don't be bothering Kamran now."

"No, it's okay," Kamran insisted. No one had *ever* asked him about skating stuff before. It was pretty cool. "That's called a camel spin."

Mia wrinkled her nose as she stood on two feet again. "That's a dumb name. Why's it called that?"

Kamran shrugged. "I don't know. I never asked. That's just its name."

"Huh," said Mia, thinking his answer over. "Well, I loved when you did that. And the jumps that turned into spins. And—"

"We're not still talking about skating, are we? Jeez…"

Kamran flinched as Mikey swaggered into the kitchen, heading straight to the fridge for a fresh beer.

"Michelangelo, be nice," Cheryl said pointedly.

Kamran almost spat out his wine. "Were your parents going for a full set of Ninja Turtles when they were naming you?" he asked Lee in a murmur once he safely swallowed his drink. He knew technically Lee should have been Leonardo, not Leopold, but still.

Lee grinned back at him. "Quite possibly," he agreed.

"Here he is, the star of the hour," Mikey said, coming and standing beside where Kamran and Lee were sitting. He grinned as he slapped Kamran on the back, but his eyes were cold as he looked between them. "Apparently, I missed quite the show. Lots of twirling." He waggled his fingers in jazz hands and smirked.

Kamran tried not to flinch. For a second there, he'd managed to forget that figure skating was for sissies. No matter how much he loved his proudly effeminate friends, there was something lodged so deeply within him that told him that was fine for other people, like Emery, who were empowered by their femininity. But not Kamran. Kamran couldn't be like that. Because that was seriously bad and people kicked you out of their lives when you behaved like that.

Lee sighed and shook his head at Mikey. "Fuck off, would

you, Mikey," he said pleasantly with a smile. "Haven't you got your own wife to bother?"

"She's out there talking about tanning products with Aunt Rebecca," Mikey said dismissively, swigging his beer. "She's fine. So – how many emails did you answer today?"

"None," Lee replied, which Kamran was pretty sure was the truth. He'd just answered that one call, but apart from that, he hadn't been on his phone all day.

He'd been with Kamran, giving him his undivided attention.

"You know," Mikey continued, shaking his head incredulously, "I might be able to understand it if you were catching serial killers or something. But bank robbery? Is that even a thing anymore? Dudes in ski masks with shotguns crying 'stick 'em up!'" He laughed like he'd told a hilarious joke, but Kamran didn't see what was particularly funny about it.

"I assure you it's very real, and Lee is brilliant at his job," he said hotly. It was possible that the red wine on an empty stomach had given him some false confidence. "At least *he* didn't get his job because of who his daddy is."

He could see Lee shaking his head from the corner of his eye, but rage had given him tunnel vision, and he was just focused on Mikey.

"Your brother is one of the kindest, most selfless people I've ever met," he continued, "and I'm not sure why the hell you look down on him like you do."

Mikey stared at him a second, then laughed. "Oh, that's right. I'm sorry. I forgot I needed to ask the opinion of someone who drives *cars* for a living."

"Mikey," Florence snapped from where she was mashing potatoes in a huge ceramic bowl. "Can you try not being a jackass for two minutes?"

"Ooh, Mom swore," said Mia in delight.

"Don't tell your dad," Florence said to her with a raised eyebrow.

"Now, now, boys," said Cheryl with a tinkling laugh. "No fighting please. This is my and your dad's special celebration. Don't spoil it."

"Can it before I set Sugar on you," Joy added. Sugar growled obediently by her feet.

"Yeah, Mikey," said Lee with a vicious smile. "How about you apologize to Kamran right the hell now? I know you can't resist tearing me down, but he's done nothing to you."

"I don't know about that," Mikey said, looking Kamran up and down, making him feel about three inches tall. "It's not my fault he can't take a joke. How about *he* apologizes to *me* for jumping down my throat?"

Shame washed over Kamran. He was supposed to be playing a role and being as nice as he could to Lee's family. And here he was, starting fights.

But Lee reached over and squeezed Kamran's thigh firmly. Then he left his hand on Kamran's leg, stroking comforting circles with his thumb. "Get lost," he said to Mikey in a growly voice that made Kamran shiver.

Usually, he was fiercely independent. The only way to make sure people didn't hurt you was to not rely on anyone for anything. But *damn*, he liked the way Lee was getting all protective and caveman over him.

But he shouldn't have to. In fact, if Kamran hadn't been there, maybe his brother wouldn't be acting like such a dick toward him.

Again, Mikey scoffed. "Why don't *you* get lost? Out of the two of us, which is the son who's actually around when this family needs him, hmm? Me. You're not here to the point that you forgot how old your own niece is!"

"Hey, don't bring me into this," Mia cried, folding her arms.

"Boys, I mean it," snapped Cheryl. "Cool it. Honestly, can't we have one night without you bickering?"

All of Kamran's euphoria from skating had melted away. This was all a charade and not worth causing problems for Lee's family over.

"Excuse me," Kamran said, slipping off the stool and walking out of the kitchen.

"Kamran, no," Lee cried as all his family aside from Mikey equally called for him to stay. But Kamran didn't belong with them.

He didn't belong anywhere.

He was halfway up the stairs before Lee caught up with him. "Hey, stop," he said kindly, reaching out to put his hand on Kamran's arm. "Don't listen to Mikey. He's a jumped-up prick. His reaction to anything that makes me happy is to attack it."

"But I don't *really* make you happy," Kamran said. He didn't pause in his stride, shrugging off Lee's hand. "Mikey might think we've been dating a couple of months and that we're in love or whatever, but that's all fake. I'm your *witness,* not your boyfriend. You're arguing with him over nothing."

"Shh, keep your voice down," Lee warned, matching Kamran's pace as he crossed the landing and began ascending the next set of stairs. "He was rude to both of us. That's not 'nothing.' And you know what? You *do* make me happy. Maybe not in the way he or any of them think, but you do, okay?"

Kamran scoffed and shook his head as he wrapped his arms around himself. He thought they'd had a pretty good conversation when they'd been getting him his tux, but Kamran had hoped he could sit in a sort of neutral position with Lee. One where he didn't have to be tempted by Lee saying nice things all the time, but also where he didn't have to put up with shit from his judgmental relatives.

Especially because nasty family stuff then *caused* Lee to say nice things and confuse the situation even more.

All in all, Kamran was feeling like crap as he marched into Lee's bedroom, but then he realized he didn't have anywhere else to go.

"Uh…I was kind of storming off to be alone," he mumbled as he turned and stood in the middle of the room.

But Lee followed him in anyway and shoved the door closed after him. "Well, tough," he said. "I'm not abandoning you. I'm supposed to look after you."

Kamran couldn't help but laugh. "You're *supposed* to keep me safe from Chaz. You don't have to worry about my feelings getting hurt. I'll just…I don't know, stew it off, then come down for some food later, all right? You can tell people I have a headache if you want."

Lee shook his head. "No, I don't want to do that. You're upset, and you shouldn't be. My brother is a dick, and I need to make this better!"

Kamran bit his lip and was ashamed to realize that his eyes were burning with tears. He stubbornly blinked them back.

"Why?" he asked.

Lee frowned at him. "Why what?"

"Why do you need to make it better?" Kamran expanded. "I'm not anything to you other than a work project."

Lee took a step back and frowned. "I thought I'd made it clear to you that I care about you, Kamran. I know we're not compatible, and you being my witness makes it complicated, but I—"

"Not compatible?" Kamran repeated. There was a sinking

sensation in his gut. Lee had a point. Kamran was so beneath him it was a joke. He was just embarrassing himself.

"Yeah," Lee said sadly. "You don't do relationships, and I don't do hookups."

Kamran laughed, dropping his head back as his self-pity tears threatened to turn to angry ones. "That's right. I'm just good for sex, nothing else."

"What? I didn't say that," Lee shot back hotly. "Those are your words. I'm just saying I'm looking for something long term, and I don't want to get my heart broken."

Kamran scoffed. "As if I could break your heart. You'd forget me in a minute. No, you're just looking for someone to slot into your life and wait for you at home while you spend all your hours at the office!" He jabbed a finger at Lee, his anger at this whole ridiculous situation bubbling over. "You use your job like I use sex – to keep people at arm's length to try and stop you from getting hurt. Well, guess what? It's not working – for either of us. Maybe *you* should consider working less and changing your life to fit in with a balanced relationship, not expecting some little house husband to fit into a 1950s fantasy for you."

Lee gritted his teeth, then swallowed. "Okay," he said, totally unexpectedly. "That's fair."

Kamran blinked at him. "It is?"

Lee nodded. "I've been wondering the same thing lately. Like how it didn't work out with Billy because I was expecting him to change for me. I told myself my work was the most important thing, so it was worth it. But then he left and I was so angry at him. But maybe… he was right."

Kamran deflated. He hadn't been expecting Lee to agree with him. He could only sustain his anger if they were both selfish fuckups. Now he was quickly sliding back to self-pity for the way he was living his crappy life.

"But what about you?" Lee asked, his eyebrows raised.

Kamran threw out his hands. "What about me?"

"Are you going to stop using sex as an excuse to hide from a real relationship with someone who actually likes you for *you?*" Lee demanded. "Are you going to accept that someone could love you as a person and not just as a quick fuck?"

Kamran angrily rubbed his eyes. Fucking dick. His brother had already made him feel cheap and worthless. He thought Lee was supposed to be trying to look after him? Wasn't that what he'd said?

"I hate to break it to you, but there isn't exactly a line of people wanting a relationship with me, Lee," he spat out. "I'm a nobody, a nothing, only good for a short time before they figure that out."

Lee shook his head and took a step forward. "Because you don't let anyone close to you! You run them off before they even get the chance! Besides, you don't need a line. You just need *one* person who loves you, who believes in you. But you're never going to find them if you don't try."

Kamran choked back a sob. "So I let someone in. *Then* they realize I'm a worthless piece of shit. *Then* they leave? No, thank you, I'll stick to no-strings sex."

"Then I'll stick to spending all hours at the office, where I can't possibly meet anyone, and die alone," Lee said, arching an eyebrow. "When all I desperately want is to build a life with someone. And you know what – you *are* right I need to change. And I think I want to, for someone who gives my life meaning outside the office."

"Well, la-de-fucking-dah," Kamran groused, turning away so Lee couldn't see him crying. "I hope you find him."

Kamran hadn't cried in years. He literally couldn't remember the last time. It was like this awful mountain man had pried his shell off and was now poking his soft, vulnerable belly.

"Kamran," Lee said, sounding exasperated. "Oh…fuck it. Fuck it *all.*"

Kamran turned to see if Lee was going to finally leave him alone like any sensible person would. Except he turned straight into that granite-like chest. Then Lee's hands slid around the sides of his neck, into his hair.

And his gorgeous, full lips crashed right into Kamran's.

11

LEE

No, it wasn't ethical. Yes, Lee could be jeopardizing years' worth of work on the Bolt case. But in that moment, he really couldn't bring himself to give a shit.

He wanted Kamran so desperately it was like a knife in his heart. He just couldn't stand to see him crying, thinking he was nothing and nobody. And if he only stuck to hookups because he was afraid someone like Bolt would break his heart again, Lee had a feeling that he could do something to *fix* that, if only Kamran would give him a chance.

Kamran's lips were greedy and forceful as they kissed. Within seconds his hands were fisted around Lee's sweater, bunching the material as he pulled Lee to him. Lee splayed his hand over the small of Kamran's back, keeping him in place as his tongue plunged into Kamran's mouth. The other hand gripped the back of his neck as his fingers rubbed against the short hairs.

It was like fireworks on the Fourth of July. Lee couldn't remember ever feeling more explosive from a kiss before. Electricity surged through him, leaving his skin alight and his cock as hard as steel.

Kamran moaned, then pulled back, gasping as he stared at Lee. "What about ethics?" he rasped.

"Fuck it. You're worth breaking the rules for," Lee growled. "That's what I'm *trying* to tell you."

Kamran's eyes went wide, and he looked like he was going to argue, but Lee didn't give him the chance. He surged forward again, kissing Kamran deeply and pressing their bellies together. He ground his erection against Kamran's hip, feeling Kamran's matching length against his thigh.

Kamran whimpered and clawed at Lee's arms. "Want you," he uttered.

"Want you," Lee agreed. He pawed at Kamran's crotch, palming his dick through the denim. "Want to taste you. Please."

Kamran's breath was ragged as he nodded between frantic kisses. "Fuck, yes," he whispered.

Lee's knees hit the carpet with a thud that he was sure his family heard downstairs, but he didn't care. It felt like he'd been waiting months for this rather than twenty-four hours. He groaned as he kneaded Kamran's ass and pressed his face against Kamran's bulge. Kamran stood still for him, caressing his fingers through Lee's hair as Lee made short work of the button and zipper on Kamran's jeans.

He shoved them down to his thighs, utterly delighted to discover that Kamran hadn't been wearing any underwear this whole time. His cock was hard and leaking from the dark tip, and Lee wasted no time at all feasting on it. He wrapped his hand around the base, stroking it as he slipped the sticky head between his lips, lapping his tongue against the musky precum.

Kamran cried out as his knees buckled, but he managed to stay standing by grabbing Lee's shoulders and squeezing tight. Lee moaned as he sucked Kamran's length down, stretching his mouth around the width and rubbing the tip against his cheek. He gave Kamran's bare ass another squeeze, then moved his hands to cup his balls and massage them, stroking his taint. Everything was slippery with spit, making his fingers glide perfectly, and Kamran was already trembling.

"Lee," he cried, his breathing ragged. "Oh, god, Lee! I'm not going to last long!"

That was totally okay with Lee. He wanted to make Kamran unravel completely. He wanted to show him how amazing and beautiful Lee thought he was. Not something damaged to be fixed but something perfectly imperfect to be cherished.

He picked up the pace, sucking harder and bobbing his head like he could take all of Kamran's pain away through his cock. His length was red hot against Lee's tongue, and Kamran started thrusting with abandon, fucking Lee's mouth and hitting the back of his throat with the blunt head. Lee could feel himself dribbling down his chin, but he didn't care as he chased Kamran's release.

He didn't have to wait long. Suddenly, Kamran buckled again, scratching at Lee's shoulder and yanking his hair. *"Lee!"* he yelled in warning.

Lee kept swallowing, though, sucking down the bitter fluid that Kamran started shooting down his throat. He moaned as Kamran thrashed and cried out, shivering under Lee's hands as he saw his orgasm through to completion.

For a few seconds, he remained standing with the help of Lee's shoulders. Lee gently sucked and kissed his still hard member, then wiped his mouth and chin before looking up at his lover. "Was that okay?" he rasped. His voice was hoarse from the sudden throat fucking he'd received.

Kamran didn't answer. He just shoved Lee onto his back. Lee yelped, then laughed as Kamran landed on top of him, kissing his mouth fervently.

"Okay?" he repeated. *"Okay?* They should give you a promotion for *that.* I can't imagine any better witness protection, Agent Marshall. But now I'm going to need you to lie back and think of the Bureau, all right? Because if I don't return the favor right the fuck now, I'm going to explode. Again."

Lee grinned and caressed the side of Kamran's face, kissing his swollen lips. "I can assure you," he said, his voice low and full of sincerity, "I am *not* going to be thinking of work with my dick in your mouth. You're the *only* thing on my mind, Kamran."

Kamran bit his own lip before kissing Lee's mouth slowly. "Good," he whispered, then shimmied down Lee's body.

He hurriedly opened up Lee's jeans, then peeled them down his thighs, taking Lee's briefs with them. Lee's breath hitched as his sensitive cock sprang free, the air feeling cool against his dripping tip.

Kamran's eyes went wide when he saw it. Lee knew Kamran was far from a blushing virgin, but he also knew he was on the large side, like the rest of him. Kamran placed his hand on his chest and just stared at it for a few seconds, his mouth open.

"Well, that's a thing of beauty," he said, meeting Lee's gaze and giving him a wicked grin.

Then he dropped down, wrapping his lips around Lee's tip and squeezing the rest of the shaft.

Lee let out a guttural moan, arching forward and holding his head up. He didn't want to miss a second of watching Kamran's gorgeous mouth stretching to suck him down, his lips and tongue deliciously perfect as they explored Lee's throbbing cock for the first time.

Because there would be a second time. Lee was going to make sure of it.

That was about as coherent as his thoughts were going to

get for the time being. Kamran certainly knew his way around a cock. He jerked and twisted his hand as he bobbed his head, getting Lee's length to the back of his throat. Just as he was getting into a good rhythm, he pulled off, and Lee had to resist the urge to complain.

But his face must have conveyed something because Kamran laughed at him. "Don't pout, shnookums. I'm only just getting going."

"I thought I'd vetoed 'shnookums' as a pet name," Lee growled. "In fact, I distinctly remember—"

While he'd been ranting, Kamran had spat on his fingers. He shut Lee up pretty swiftly when he shoved his middle finger inside his hole, grinning like the devil he was as he started sucking the end of Lee's cock as he pushed his finger up to the joint, fluttering his eyelashes like the angel he wasn't.

"Oh...*fuck*. Oh fuck, fuck, fuck," Lee gasped as he squirmed on the floor, half on the blanket he'd slept under, half on the carpet.

He'd topped all the time with Billy, who'd been quite the pillow princess, so Lee couldn't remember the last time anyone had played with his hole other than himself.

Suddenly, he had the very real need to be topped by Kamran. Oh, *god*. He wanted to do *everything* with Kamran. But for now, he was a bit of a pillow princess himself, lying back and reveling as Kamran sucked him off and fingered his hole.

Lee had been on such a hair trigger since walking into Aquarium the night before he was amazed he didn't blow his load within the first thirty seconds. But he took several long, deep breaths, calming himself and sinking deeper and deeper into the bliss Kamran was giving him. He wanted this to last for as long as possible. He wanted to luxuriate, basking in a moment he'd convinced himself could never happen.

He'd fallen like a ton of bricks for Kamran. There was no going back now.

"Oh, baby, yes," he hissed as he carded his fingers through Kamran's thick hair.

Kamran stilled, looking up at Lee. He pulled off and wiped his mouth, then swallowed. "Uh – not 'baby' – if that's okay?"

Lee's heart dropped. "O-of course," he stammered. "I'm sorry. I didn't mean—"

But Kamran smiled and grabbed Lee's hand, bringing it to his mouth to kiss the backs of his fingers. "No, don't be upset. This is definitely a *me* thing. I just find it – uh – cringy. Sorry."

Lee nodded and moved his hand to caress the side of Kamran's face. "Don't be sorry. Thank you for telling me." He rubbed his thumb against Kamran's cheekbone, and for a second they locked eyes. Kamran's breaths were deep, and he looked pained.

Lee couldn't have that.

It was awkward with both of them having their jeans wrapped around their thighs, but Lee sat up and pulled Kamran to him to kiss his mouth. "It's really, *really* important to me that you're honest with me," Lee said, "and that includes setting boundaries. Don't ever be ashamed to ask for what you want. Definitely not with me."

Kamran looked like what he wanted was to wriggle away, but Lee held his neck and kept their gazes connected.

"Okay," Kamran mumbled eventually, smiling sheepishly. "But, uh, what I want right now is to guzzle your cum. Is that all right?"

He waggled his eyebrows, and Lee couldn't help but laugh, despite knowing precisely what Kamran was doing by deflecting the conversation. He didn't want to agree that he deserved to ask for what he wanted, but that was okay.

Lee could work on that.

"Okay, you minx," he said, trying out a different kind of nickname, and he was thrilled when Kamran preened. "Knock yourself out. You were doing a pretty spectacular job, so I guess I'd be okay with you finishing."

"Oh, I'm *honored*," Kamran said flirtatiously, pressing a quick kiss to the tip of Lee's nose. "If you'd be *okay* with it, then I suppose I'll continue."

"Good boy."

Lee wasn't sure where that slipped out from, and he immediately second-guessed himself. But Kamran fucking *blushed*, a beautiful crimson color that spread over his cheeks and neck, and he looked at Lee coyly through his beautiful lashes as he crawled back down to Lee's slightly deflated cock.

It wasn't deflated for long.

Kamran swallowed him down with gusto, making pornographic sounds as he sucked and licked and probed with his tongue. He used his spit again to lubricate his fingers, and this time he pushed two of them inside Lee's hole. Lee gritted his teeth and tried not to bellow too loudly just in case anyone was out in the hall. But fucking hell, Kamran was doing everything to drive him wild.

The deep breathing didn't work for long. He'd been close before Kamran had paused, and in no time, he was jutting his hips, chasing his release as Kamran worked him harder and faster.

It was almost like Lee had been holding his breath for months – *years* – until Kamran had come along and made him fucking chill *out*. His entire body was vibrating as he allowed himself to just let go and feel everything, to stop worrying and just fly.

All because of one man.

"Kamran—!"

But Kamran wasn't interested in his warning. He just sucked Lee harder, running his tongue along the top of his length and over the slit at the tip. He jerked him off furiously, the spit making his motions slick and perfect.

"Holy fuck, gonna come. Kamran, I—!"

His whole world shattered as he shot his brain out of his dick. He snarled and slammed his palm against the carpet, gnashing his teeth as he came and came and *came...*

A few moments later, he resurfaced, taking those deep breaths into his lungs that his brain was suddenly craving. He rubbed his forehead, his thoughts clearing in his post-orgasmic haze.

Oh no.

Had he just done something unforgivable?

Kamran was his responsibility – had he felt pressured into doing that? Lee had to make sure this case was airtight. If anyone found out he'd slept with a witness—

He was torn from his spiraling thoughts as Kamran flopped by his side and dragged one of Lee's blankets over them. "You know what I like about blow jobs?" he said casually, stroking Lee's damp hair back. "No mess."

Lee met his eyes to find them sparkling with mischief, and he couldn't stop himself from bursting out laughing. "No mess," he agreed.

He ran his hands along Kamran's bearded jaw, then pulled him in for a sweet, tender kiss.

"So…Mr. No Hookups," Kamran said. There was definitely a nervous edge to his words as he avoided Lee's eye contact. "How are you feeling?"

Lee couldn't help the low rumbling laugh that escaped his chest. "You thought that was a hookup? Oh, gorgeous…no."

Kamran raised his eyebrows. "No?"

Lee kissed him again, longer and harder this time. "No," he said firmly. "Not by a long shot. If that's okay with you?"

Kamran frowned slightly, looking at Lee as if he couldn't figure him out. But then he smiled. "That's okay with me," he said, pressing a kiss to Lee's jaw.

Lee touched his chin, tilting it so he could capture Kamran's mouth for a proper kiss. "Good."

He got the feeling they still had some way to go. Kamran was like a wild stallion, skittish and needing to learn that he could trust again. But Lee had a whole week off work. If there was any time to prove to both himself and someone else that he could be a good boyfriend, it was now. He didn't care if it was too fast. He wanted all in and to at least *try* with Kamran.

When the vacation ended, who knew what would happen. But for now, Lee was going to do everything he possibly could to make this work.

Which he hoped would include lots and *lots* of sex.

KAMRAN

KAMRAN COULD DO THIS FOR A WEEK. IT WASN'T REALLY ALL that different from what he'd signed up for in the first place by pretending to be Lee's boyfriend. It was actually much better now with all the orgasms.

And when the week was over, Kamran would accept that. He would. He'd walk away and not cry over Agent Lee Marshall. He certainly wasn't going to get his heart broken.

Nope. Nuh-uh.

Besides, it was difficult to dwell on those kinds of feelings when he was so busy all the time. Between touch football out on the front grounds, barbecues, and trips to see local sights, Lee kept dragging Kamran off to dark corners to make out like horny teenagers. And when they were alone…

Well, Kamran currently had his back pressed to the bathroom wall, hot water cascading down his tingling body as Lee kissed the fuck out of him and jerked them both off. It had been a long time since Kamran had fucked around with the same person more than once, let alone several times in a row. He'd remembered getting pretty bored with Chaz.

Along with avoiding a broken heart, it was one of the reasons he didn't do repeats these days.

He was not getting bored of Lee. Not for a second.

Lee had this way of fucking devouring him. Every time, it was as if he was a starving man and Kamran was a buffet.

Kamran thought he had a pretty good body. He worked out occasionally, but more often than not, he ate and drank what he wanted, then just fucked the calories away.

But he didn't think he was anything special, not really. It was more what he could do with his body (and his dick) that he was proud of. Not like Lee with his crazy bulging muscles. Except the way Lee looked at him and touched him, licking and nibbling and kissing every inch of him every chance he got, it was difficult not to feel like some kind of Adonis.

He was probably just sex starved, Kamran had decided. It had been a matter of days since Kamran's last good fuck, but Mr. Monogamy hadn't had anyone since his foolish ex had left him. Kamran knew that Lee was a workaholic, and he might be feeling different if he hadn't had Lee all to himself the past few days. But in his opinion, anyone who would voluntarily walk away from someone so amazing as Lee needed their head checked.

"Fuck, yes," he moaned into Lee's mouth as he began to peak for his *third* orgasm of the day.

He tried to grip the slippery tiled wall for support, but then Lee grabbed his side and dug his fingers in to steady him. Kamran was covered all over in the most delicious pattern of bruises and tiny scratches from the last couple of days, and he was unashamed to admit that he'd been staring at them all as he'd stood naked in front of the bathroom mirror that morning.

He couldn't keep Lee for long. He knew that. But for now, he felt liked he'd been claimed…almost in every way.

As he cried out and came all over his and Lee's stomachs,

he reminded himself that this was enough. That blow jobs and hand jobs and frotting were totally awesome ways of orgasming. But he couldn't help but be a little miffed that he'd begged Lee to fuck him senseless several times now, and yet they still hadn't gotten that far.

Kamran knew that Lee had stocked up on condoms and lube because he'd gone snooping yesterday and found them in Lee's nightstand. But whenever Kamran brought it up, Lee just told him 'soon.' Kamran wasn't sure what the hell he was waiting for, but he had to admit he was too chicken to push him on it in case Lee decided he'd gotten bored of Kamran already and went back to sleeping on the floor.

Rather than focus on what he didn't have, Kamran reminded himself of what was right in front of him. Namely, Lee's still hard cock. Kamran might have blown his load, but as he shuddered through the last ripples of his orgasm, he realized that Lee was stroking himself slowly, watching Kamran with a hunger in his eyes.

A hunger Kamran was more than happy to sate.

He dropped to his knees, moaning in pure joy as he took Lee into his mouth. Kamran felt like one of those snakes that dislocated their jaws to eat beasts bigger than themselves. He'd never been a size queen, not with cocks or boobs or anything. Pleasure came in all shapes and sizes, of that he could attest. But dear fucking *lord*, Lee was hung like a horse, and Kamran was thrilled with all the practice he was getting on how to fit the damn thing all the way down his throat.

If he could also get it in his ass, then he'd truly be happy.

Speaking of asses, he reached around to play with Lee's hole the way he liked. Kamran had been with big toppy guys before who lost their damn minds if he so much as brushed his hand in that direction. But the way Lee loved Kamran sticking two fingers up there while he blew him was a considerable turn-on. Lee wasn't some douche with a fragile ego. He knew what he liked, and Kamran loved giving it to him.

Maybe Kamran could convince Lee to let him fuck *his* ass first. Like a warmup to the main event before Kamran finally got the chance to impale himself on the giant cick he was currently sucking off like a champ.

"Kamran," Lee grunted, tugging his hair the way Kamran loved. He was a gentleman like that, always warning Kamran when he was going to come. But there wasn't a power on earth that would stop Kamran from swallowing the whole musky load as it hit. Again, it felt like a small triumph to him. That getting *something* of Lee's inside him was a victory.

Kamran cradled Lee's cock with his mouth, sucking and lapping at the tender flesh until he started to go soft. Lee groaned and tugged Kamran up to his feet again, wrapping his arms around Kamran's back and kissing his lips reverently.

"You're gorgeous," he murmured, nuzzling their noses together. "Thank you."

Kamran blinked at him, watching the hot water run down his strong clean jaw in rivulets. Kamran's beard was more like an extended goatee, but he was still making Lee's chin a little pink from the last couple of days of kissing and beard burn.

"Thank you for what?" he asked.

Lee smiled and stroked firm circles against Kamran's back. "I don't know. For being here with me, like this. For trusting me to care for you. For reminding me there are things worth living for outside of work."

Kamran hummed instead of answering directly. He hugged Lee and rested his temple against Lee's hard chest, swirling his fingers in the wet hair that trailed from between his pecs down past his belly button to the thick thatch around his groin. It was simpler to just be held by this big, strong man rather than dwell on his sweet words.

Kamran wasn't used to much of this pillow talk (or standing in the shower post-coital talk). Maybe it was the types of people he tended to fuck, but he expected a little snuggling with the women. However, the guys were usually 'tap-it-and-done.' Or if they let Kamran sleep over, it was because they wanted a round two, but he didn't do that very often. All these feelings with Lee were getting under his skin. Not because he didn't like it.

But because he did.

"Happy to be of service," Kamran said jovially as he stepped away from Lee.

They'd already washed their hair and bodies before the fun had begun, so Kamran moved out of the stream of water and ran his hands over his limbs, splashing off the excess water before grabbing a towel and stepping out of the tub.

"Hey," said Lee, catching up with him and touching Kamran's arm. He was gloriously naked and seemingly unbothered by it, but Kamran held the towel between them, like hiding his junk might make him less vulnerable. "Don't say that," Lee told him.

Kamran raised his eyebrows. "Say what?"

Lee bit his lip and studied Kamran for a second. "'Service,'" he repeated. "It makes this feel transactional. I don't want you doing *anything* if you feel you have to. Only because you want to."

Kamran softened. This big lug. Honestly, for such a scary-looking dude, he really was a teddy bear. "I promise," he said, discarding the towel over the edge of the bath and wrapping his arms around Lee's waist, "that I'm not doing a single thing that I don't want to or that I'm not enjoying."

He looked up into Lee's sparkling blue eyes. They were an

ocean that Kamran kept diving into, aware that the tide could probably drag him away to his doom any second now.

It was just a matter of time.

"Good," said Lee, sounding relieved. He carded his fingers through Kamran's wet hair. "You know, for Mr. I Don't Do Relationships, you're doing just great."

Kamran rolled his eyes. There Lee went again, being all schmoopy. "Four days doesn't count as a 'relationship,'" he said. "Besides, you're acting like it's a chore to keep getting each other off. Just to clarify, this is not a hardship, Agent Marshall."

Lee huffed, but at least he was smiling as he rocked Kamran back and forth. "I'm not just talking about sex. That's kind of the point, *Kamran.* You make a good boyfriend."

Kamran opened his mouth, but rather than argue, he just smiled and then moved to pick up his towel again, turning away from Lee. It was just an *act.* Kamran had promised Lee he'd be attentive and supportive in front of his family. The only change was that now behind closed doors, there was a little more authenticity to the charade. Kamran wasn't fit to be anyone's boyfriend.

No matter what Lee said.

He dried his hair off and then pulled on the sweatpants he'd been sleeping in when he and Lee hadn't been getting down and dirty. They were the same ones Lee had lent him on the first night, but Kamran was kind of possessive over them now. Even if they did hang precariously off his hips despite the triple knot Kamran had tied them with. They just made him feel good and no doubt helped him get into the boyfriend role by borrowing his man's things. That was more than likely what Lee meant. Kamran was simply doing a good job, which made him feel proud of himself.

Okay, Kamran admitted to himself as he slipped under

the covers and watched Lee wandering around in his towel for a few seconds. Maybe he *could* imagine what it would be like to be Lee's boyfriend, and it was pretty sweet. Lee talked a lot about how he didn't know how to be in a relationship without work ruining everything, but Kamran suspected that wasn't really true.

He just needed someone *worth* being in a relationship for to drag him away from the office. Hopefully, this week would remind him of that, and he wouldn't fall back into old habits when he returned to Seattle.

Without Kamran.

For heaven's sake, *of course* without Kamran. What was he even thinking, considering getting mopey over that? This was just a fling, and Kamran would be an ungrateful dick if he didn't appreciate how good he had it for the next few days.

He was safe, he was spoiled, and he was in no shortage of orgasms. If only…

He rubbed the mattress beside him, biting his lip and waiting for Lee to look at him. But Lee had just checked his phone and was frowning at the screen. That wasn't good. He wasn't supposed to be letting work creep in, and Kamran suspected it wasn't his Facebook that had made him pull that expression.

"Come here," he said, his voice sultry. He knew they'd both only just come, but Kamran could work wonders when he put his mind to it. He hadn't given up on his quest to get thoroughly fucked up the ass by his mountain man, and after some dedicated foreplay, he reckoned he could make some magic happen.

But then Lee blinked up at him, his face pinched with concern.

"Everything okay?" Kamran asked, genuinely anxious for his lover and his worries.

Lee sighed before placing the phone face down on his nightstand. "Sorry, hon," he said. "They think they might have a lead in the case, but that's for them to deal with this week, not me."

"My case?"

Lee nodded as he pulled on his own sweatpants, then slid between the sheets. He opened out his arms, and Kamran scooted over to cuddle up next to him, resting his head on his chest.

Because that was what a good boyfriend would do.

"You don't have anything to worry about, though," Lee said. "It's all happening in Seattle. They think they might…" He smiled down at Kamran. "Let's just say it'll hopefully be good news in the morning. Fingers crossed you won't have to worry about You-Know-Who any longer."

Kamran thought it was sweet and kind of cutely protective that Lee never said Chaz's name anymore. It was always You-Know-Who or Him. (Kamran could hear the capitalization in Lee's voice, which was also adorable.) But the truth was Kamran was rapidly becoming addicted to someone looking after him, even if it was in an official capacity.

Although it hardly felt official as Lee turned off the bedside lamp and snuggled down in the ridiculously comfy bed with Kamran wrapped up in his arms.

Kamran let his previous thoughts of another seduction attempt fade away as he simply enjoyed being held. He'd get Lee to fuck him before the week was through, he was certain. But for now, the moment didn't feel right to tease him about it. Lee had said he wanted to, so Kamran just needed to accept that and be patient.

Besides, Kamran was perfecting his boyfriend skills. And what felt much more natural now was to rub Lee's chest and kiss his shoulder. "You'll get him," he said, believing his words. "You're so close."

Lee sighed, but there was a smile to it that Kamran could feel in the dark. "Thanks, ba…hon." He kissed Kamran's hair, and Kamran appreciated him trying to brush over the fact that he'd tried to call him 'baby' again. Kamran wished he didn't feel like that word was a weapon, because Lee seemed to like using it. At least, Kamran felt he did, judging by the number of times he'd had to swallow it over the past couple of days.

But Kamran couldn't be that for Lee. They were from two different worlds. There was no sense in trying to fight it. Once this case was over and Chaz was locked up, Lee would go back to his fancy life with his fancy family, and Kamran would go back to his small, simple life.

But he'd always remember his time with Agent Lee Marshall with fondness, he was determined. So he closed his eyes and snuggled down to sleep, promising himself that he was going to keep enjoying the week and not overthink things. That wasn't his style, anyway. He was a go-with-the-flow sort of guy, and he needed to remember that. Lee was a gift for him to cherish for a short while.

And then Kamran would go back to his real life and let him go.

13

LEE

IT WAS NOT, IN FACT, GOOD NEWS IN THE MORNING. AT LEAST not the kind that Lee wanted to hear.

He scowled at his phone as he typed silently back to Duke.

LEE: I'm sorry, man – I told you, no. You don't need me there. I'm several hours away. You can video call me if you really need to.

He chewed his lip and watched Kamran sleeping. He looked so sweet and peaceful curled up to Lee's side. It was still early in the morning – not even seven yet – but sunshine was streaming around the curtains. The beams skimmed over Kamran, picking out the coppery strands in his dark hair. Lee stroked it with a featherlight touch so as not to disturb him.

For the first time in over a year, since Billy had left, Lee was putting his personal life first. He and Kamran only had a few precious days together, and Lee needed all that time to convince Kamran that what they had here was worth a real shot.

He knew it was fast. He knew that just because he and Kamran had spent a couple of (*seriously* hot) days in bed didn't mean they were on the path to a long-lasting relationship. All he knew was that everything within him was screaming not to let Kamran go. To give this thing between them a real try. Because as much as they were incompatible on paper, Lee was starting to suspect that maybe it was more of a case of opposites attract in real life.

He'd been so convinced that his family would never believe they were a couple because they were so different. But that was exactly *why* it felt like it was working so well. It was as if Kamran was waking up sides of Lee he'd long forgotten about. His fun, naughty sides. And Lee could see Kamran calming and steadying under Lee's reassuring presence.

Lee had no idea how long this might last, but at least for now, he wasn't feeling that gnawing pull to get back to the office. This week was no longer feeling like something he had to enjoy, but rather it had become something to cherish.

Because of Kamran.

Yet here Duke was, messaging him late into the night with their breakthroughs on the case, and now again at the crack of dawn. Except this time, he was summoning Lee back to Seattle.

DUKE: It's just for a couple of hours! No one knows the case like you do, and we've got to get this guy to roll.

Lee gritted his teeth. They'd been on a raid last night and had managed to bring one of Bolt's top goons in. Of course, the guy was refusing to say anything without a lawyer (Lee hated smart scumbags), and Duke wanted Lee to take a crack at him before they caved in to his demands.

Lee was partly flattered that Duke wanted Lee to try and get through to this guy over everyone else, but Lee was *on vacation.* Something he never ever did and had really hoped would be respected. Damn it. If he were a plane ride away, Duke wouldn't be able to try and pressure him like this.

It came down to what was more important – the possibility that Lee might be slightly better at rattling a suspect than his other perfectly capable colleagues ..

Or Kamran.

It was obvious to Lee that before – even when he'd been with Billy – the answer would have been proving himself at work. To show he was the best at everything that he could be. Because that was the only way to prove to his father that he'd made the right choice with his career. He didn't want to follow in the family footsteps just because that was what was expected. He wanted to forge his own path and make a difference to society.

But there was more to life than work, and he was beginning to see that with startling clarity.

Kamran stirred and made an adorable whimpering noise as he fumbled with his hand against the covers. Lee gently took it and kissed the backs of his fingers. "Go back to sleep, love," he murmured, feeling confident enough to call him that while he was asleep.

It upset Lee that Kamran didn't like being called 'baby.' The pet name felt so perfect for him. He was this tough, scrappy thing that had come out the other side of some real shitty situations, but he was still so fun and playful. Lee wanted to wrap him up and protect him from the world. He wanted him to be his baby. His good boy.

Kamran might have scoffed at the idea of Lee wanting a house husband – and to be fair, that was probably antiquated of him – but Lee didn't want his man to yearn for anything. That didn't mean sitting at home and not working. That meant the freedom to pursue whatever kind of life he wanted by Lee's side. To never struggle for money or worry about a landlord kicking him out or being alone for anything.

Lee wanted to give that to Kamran. He wanted to give him anything.

LEE: I'm sorry, sir, but you have plenty of people there who will do a fine job at interrogating the suspect. I am unable to come back to the office until I am scheduled to next Monday. You have access to all my notes, and if there are any queries, please call me. But I am on a long-overdue vacation.

He hit send before he could chicken out. Then he dropped the phone on the bedspread and cuddled up to Kamran again. He really was breathtakingly gorgeous. Lee felt like a criminal touching a priceless work of art. That wasn't going to stop him, though.

As Kamran murmured in his sleep and slung his leg over Lee's thigh, Lee bit his lip and considered Kamran's many requests to up their intimacy to the next level.

It wasn't that Lee *didn't* want to try anal together. Quite the opposite. If he were going to judge by what they'd already done together, it would be spectacular. But he was ashamed to admit that there was a part of him that still didn't quite trust that Kamran wouldn't slip away once he got what he wanted. It was unfair to judge him like that, but Lee couldn't help it. Kamran had been very clear that he used sex to protect himself, and his friends had told Lee before he'd even met the man that Kamran didn't do seconds.

Except here he was, still in Lee's bed, days after their first spectacular tryst. Was that just because he was sort of trapped here in Lee's family home? Or was it because this was where Kamran wanted to be?

Lee sighed. He wouldn't know unless he asked. But when he thought back to the pain and humiliation of Billy cheating on him and leaving him without (Lee felt) any warning, he couldn't blame himself for being wary. Kamran could just vanish into the ether, and Lee might never see him again.

His heart clenched at the thought. Kamran was so

different from the kinds of people Lee had grown up around in this family. Heck, even the guys he'd gone to school with. He was fresh and exciting but also raw and worldly. He made Lee laugh as much as he made him come. Even when he was being an infuriating little minx, Lee…

Lee loved him.

No. That was far too soon to think like that. This ache in his heart was just from the uncertainty of the situation. If they didn't have the time pressure of the vacation hanging over them, Lee wouldn't be feeling this desperate clawing in his chest, he was sure.

Because that was crazy. He hadn't even known the man a week. He couldn't love him already.

Could he?

His phone flashed, pulling him from his thoughts. Lee was strongly tempted to ignore it. He'd given Duke his answer. But duty and loyalty compelled him to at least read the response.

DUKE: Yeah, I've got other people here. They're all also after that promotion that really should be yours by now. But it's up to you. I'm sure we'll manage.

Lee's heart sank. *"Fuck,"* he growled quietly.

He respected Duke, professionally speaking. But the man dangled that damn promotion in front of Lee like bait on a hook, always jerking it away just when Lee thought he was going to get a bite. He'd worked his *ass* off for it. Was he really going to give it away for the sake of a few hours of his vacation?

He rubbed his forehead, feeling the tension in his skull. If it were just his family, Lee would probably already be in the car by now. Sure, his dad and brother would give him an unholy time for it, but he'd probably be back before the still life drawing class his mom had organized for the evening. He couldn't draw for shit, but the idea of drinking wine with

Kamran as they attempted to sketch a hot naked dude actually sounded like a hoot.

But would Kamran be okay until then? What if it took more than a few hours and Lee missed it all? What if Duke tried to convince him to cancel the rest of his vacation and come back to work on the case now that they had a key witness in their clutches?

Then Lee would say 'no.' Just like he would say 'no' if he tried to keep Lee there longer than a couple of hours. He wasn't going to throw his promotion down the drain, but he wasn't going to be whipped by this job unnecessarily anymore.

LEE: Fine. I'll be there in a couple of hours. But I have to be back here by five. I'm supposed to be protecting the witness, after all. You owe me.

DUKE: I'll owe you a promotion, I promise.

His boss added several winky faces, which made Lee roll his eyes and sigh. Duke knew he'd get Lee to come back if he implied it would be good for his promotion prospects. Lee hated how predictable he was.

But he'd made his decision now, so he needed to proceed with grace or not at all. He slipped out from the sheets and went to take a quick shower without waking Kamran. It tore Lee up to leave him, but he promised himself that he'd be back in a matter of hours and that he'd make it up to him when he did.

Maybe in the way Kamran wanted the most.

It was entirely possible that Lee had this all wrong. Maybe taking their intimacy up a notch wouldn't make Kamran leave because he'd gotten what he wanted. Perhaps it would show Kamran how all in Lee was for this thing between them and make him *stay*.

Lee huffed as the water cascaded down his body, and he hastily scrubbed the shower gel over his chest and limbs. Was he really thinking of asking such a playboy if he'd date Lee exclusively? This man had sex *all* the time – with men *and* women. Was monogamy even an option for him? Not to mention that Lee lived in Seattle and Kamran was based here in Pine Cove.

Was Lee totally deluding himself to think that he and Kamran could be boyfriends? Was that crazy talk?

All Lee knew was that he felt a sense of strange calm when Kamran was near, but it was the kind of calm that also made him feel like he was on fire and just about to jump out of a plane. And he knew that the sex was spectacular, even without going all the way yet. But would that be enough to keep Kamran satisfied in the long run?

Oh fuck, Lee wanted him so badly, and the idea of sharing him made his stomach tighten. He washed his junk and considered if he wanted to rub a quick one off to relieve his tension, but when things were so uncertain between him and Kamran, he decided to just leave it. That way, it would be even better when Lee returned that evening. At least he hoped.

He shut the water off and grabbed a towel to quickly dry off, but he needn't have worried. When he hurried back into his room, Kamran was still fast asleep. Lee couldn't help but admire him as he got dressed. His heart *ached* as he bit his lip, his thoughts swirling.

Was it right for Lee to want to keep such a man all to himself?

Kamran mumbled something sleepily and stretched. Lee didn't want to get caught staring at him like a weirdo, so he finished the knot on his tie, smoothed it down, then went to perch on the edge of the bed.

"Kamran?" he said gently, squeezing his shoulder. "Wake up, hon."

Kamran wrinkled his nose adorably before blinking his

eyes open. "Hey," he rasped, rubbing his face. "What time is it?"

"Early, you can go back to sleep in a sec," Lee promised him.

But Kamran wasn't stupid. He squinted at Lee. "Whyou dressed?" he slurred. "Suit?"

Lee leaned down and pressed a kiss to Kamran's forehead, feeling like a total piece of shit. "There's been a development. The office needs me, just for a couple of hours. I'll be back by this evening, I *promise*. Will you be okay here for a while?"

Kamran swallowed, his wide eyes more alert as he looked up at Lee. "I thought you weren't going to leave me alone?" he asked, his voice croaky with sleep.

Lee did his best to remain professional and not groan with guilt. "I know," he said, stroking the side of Kamran's face. "But they've got one of Bolt's men in custody. It's safer for you to stay here where nobody will think to look for you. I didn't want to go, but my boss needs me."

You liar, he accused himself silently. *Your* promotion *needs you.*

He cleared his throat and did his best to smile at his lover. "I promise I won't be long. But if you don't want to face my family, you can totally just hide out here and watch TV, and I'll text Gamma to bring you some food, and—"

"Hey, hey," Kamran said. He shook his head and sat up a little more, so they were closer to being at the same eye level. "I'm fine. You *promise* me it's only for a couple of hours?"

Lee shrugged helplessly. "The drive is also a couple of hours each way," he admitted. "But I swear I'll be back for the still life drawing class, okay?"

Kamran's gaze swept over him and he seemed to be thinking. "Okay," he said after a few moments.

Lee raised his eyebrows. "Okay?"

Kamran nodded. "If you promise you'll be back, I believe you. You're trying with that work-life balance, right? Well... this is a good test. If you really have to go in, then you'll do what you need to then come right back home, yeah?"

It was utterly ridiculous, but Lee's heart clenched at the way that Kamran said 'home,' like they lived together. That was jumping way ahead, but if it made Lee feel a little better about bailing for the day, he was going to run with it.

"I will, I promise," Lee told him sincerely.

Kamran smiled, but there was still some hesitation in his eyes that Lee could see.

"Okay, then," Kamran said with firm optimism. "You go get 'em, tiger, and I'll manage your family until then. Gamma and Mia will protect me."

"You mean they'll feed you," Lee said, raising an eyebrow.

Kamran grinned. "Same thing."

Lee exhaled. He really hoped that his dad and brother wouldn't be total dicks in his absence. "Right, well...the sooner I leave, the sooner I can come back," he said.

In that moment, he seriously considered blowing everything off. Kamran looked so *good* in his bed. But Kamran could be gone by next week, yet the promotion would last for his entire career.

He went to stand up, but Kamran snagged his hand before he could. "C'mere," he said, pulling Lee toward him.

His lips were so soft and warm as he kissed Lee thoroughly. His beard scratched against Lee's chin, making his toes curl deliciously as little shivers ran down his spine. Kamran held Lee's tie, not letting him go until he was apparently done kissing the crap out of him.

"There," he said with a final peck to the corner of Lee's tingling mouth. "Something to remember me by."

Lee took a steadying breath and looked down at Kamran, shaking his head. "Who could *ever* forget you," he murmured.

Kamran stared at him like he couldn't work out why Lee would say such a thing. He slowly licked his lips and frowned like he was going to argue.

Lee wasn't having that.

He pressed another firm kiss to Kamran's mouth, then rubbed his arm. "Go back to sleep, gorgeous. Breakfast won't be until nine. My folks have the caterers back in, so there will be more than enough. Then if you want to hang out or hide out, either is fine, just—"

Kamran laughed and pushed him. "Go," he said with a grin. "I'll be fine. You said it yourself. The sooner you go, the sooner you can come back to me."

In that split second, Lee made a decision. "And when I come back to you," he whispered, caressing the side of Kamran's stubbly jaw. "Will you be *ready* for me?"

He raised his eyebrows, making his request clear, he hoped. For a second, Kamran gave him a slight frown. Then his eyes went wide with delight.

"Oh *fuck*, yeah! I'll be ready for you, mountain man. I'll be on the bed face down, ass up if you want? Stretched and clean as a whistle!"

Lee chuckled and kissed his excitable lover sweetly. "Just be comfortable, however works for you. We can do the dirty drawing and drink wine and have dinner...then we'll come up here, and you can be all mine, understood?"

Kamran nodded frantically. "All yours, completely," he agreed.

"Good boy," Lee said, trying out that particular kind of praise again.

To his immense satisfaction, Kamran's breath hitched, and his pupils dilated. "Yes, Lee," he said hoarsely.

Lee picked up his hand and kissed the backs of his fingers. "Have a good day, Kamran," he said warmly as he stood.

"Hurry back to me," Kamran replied.

Lee's gaze lingered on him as he left the room. Then he was rushing down the hallway. In reality, their situation hadn't changed. But he could either worry about next week, or he could focus on today.

He had a man to hurry back to, and he intended to make sure that when he did, he would give Kamran every single thing he needed.

14

KAMRAN

MAYBE KAMRAN WASN'T INSANE.

Maybe someone like him actually *could* be with someone like Lee Marshall. Someone good and kind and loyal and decent. And *hot.*

Kamran had been with countless hot people, but attractiveness was all in the eye of the beholder. Some people didn't necessarily turn heads, but their personalities made them gorgeous and adorable. Some people could be on billboards and have personalities that belonged in the trash.

But Lee was stunning as well as lovely. Kamran had to question why anyone so morally upstanding, successful, and good looking would push so hard to be with *him*, but Kamran was also a selfish asshole. If Lee wanted to be with Kamran for longer than a fling, Kamran wasn't going to look that gift horse in the mouth.

Logically, Kamran knew that Lee just wanted to make the most of this week. What future could they have when Lee was living and working in Seattle and Kamran had finally built a life for himself here in Pine Cove? But the fact that Kamran was even *thinking* about a future together – or dating, or any of the long-term stuff – was quite remarkable.

He knew it was kind of ridiculous. And fast – had he mentioned fast? He'd spent more time choosing his last pair of sneakers than he had changing his mind about Lee Marshall. Sure, the guy was still kind of uptight and serious, but those didn't seem like negative qualities to Kamran anymore. They made him strong and dependable, thoughtful and sensitive.

All the things Kamran was pretty sure he'd craved in a partner but never allowed himself to accept that he could have.

Dependable meant commitment, and commitment was scary. Commitment made it much harder to pull the plug and run for the hills at a second's notice.

But Kamran was starting to think that he didn't *want* to run from Lee. He kind of liked Lee being around from morning to night and everything in between. He loved the way Lee fussed over him in ways that had nothing to do with protecting him from Chaz fucking Bolt. He always seemed worried that Kamran had enough to eat or that he was comfortable in the various social situations they'd been through this week. Hell, the man even insisted on grabbing a pillow to drop to the floor for Kamran's knees the last couple of times he'd given him a blow job. He was sweet and thoughtful and all Kamran's.

Kamran kind of liked the idea of keeping it that way. The thought of Lee going back to Seattle and dating some other lame guy who'd leave when the going got tough made his blood boil. Lee deserved *so* much better than that.

He probably deserved better than Kamran, but Kamran was a selfish asshole, after all. He wasn't going to give up such a good thing without a fight.

Oddly enough, Kamran wasn't bothered by the prospect

of fucking the same person for the foreseeable future. He'd have thought that alone would have made him want to run for the door by the time this protective custody thing was done. But he didn't feel any of those urges at present. As much as he didn't want to think about his time with Chaz, he did remember that he'd been perfectly happy to be monogamous when he'd thought he'd been in love, even if the sex had gotten boring when Chaz had only cared about getting himself off.

If anything, Lee cared *more* about Kamran's orgasms than his own, which Kamran could either feel guilty over or relish.

If it made them both happy, then he chose to relish.

The truth was Kamran just liked a lot of sex. Usually, that was with different people because that was emotionally less complicated. But he was pretty sure he could stay with the same person exclusively so long as there was still a *lot* of sex.

So far, Lee hadn't let him down in that respect either. The man was apparently insatiable when it came to Kamran's body. He'd been pretty hands on in the company of others, but that had been expected, what with them pretending to be boyfriends and all. But behind closed doors, it felt to Kamran like Lee was addicted to having his hands and lips all over Kamran's body. And his promise to Kamran right before he left…

Kamran shivered, then blinked as he forced himself back into the present moment. This was not the time to get a boner thinking about how Lee had promised to fuck him senseless later that night.

The family was gathered in the reception room with all the sofas where the welcome event had been held. They were playing some sort of family bingo game that Kamran had no chance of succeeding in as he barely remembered more than half a dozen of their names, let alone knew who had punched

Goofy on the nose at Disneyland that one time. But he was sitting with Joy and Mia, indulging in pink, fizzy cocktails while they played, and Sugar sat in his lap licking at a bowl of Jell-O. All in all, he was having a pretty good time.

Was this what family was supposed to be like? He knew that some of Lee's relatives were stuck up and prejudiced, but they were also loving toward each other. Some were loud, like Aunt Ginny who kept squawking at people for cheating, swigging on her third G&T of the game, or quiet like Cheryl, who was being the perfect hostess, making sure that everyone's drinks were kept full and that the plates of snacks weren't running low. As she made her way through the room, she touched people's backs and shoulders, smiling down with such warmth as she spoke a few whispered words to them that it made Kamran's heart ache.

Unfortunately, Lee's brother, Mikey, was the one running the game. He had an elaborate slide show to go along with the questions, but several times now the projector had frozen, or Mikey had gotten a slide upside down, making Kamran feel like maybe one of the younger generation should have been in charge of that particular element.

"Okay, there we go!" Mikey boomed into the microphone. He'd just put up a question with the answer right there on the slide with it, and he'd almost knocked the projector over in his haste to hide his mistake. "Next question! Who got bitten by mosquitoes so badly on their Bahamas cruise that they had to be hospitalized?"

"Oh, he's not even trying," Joy said, rolling her eyes and sipping her screwdriver cocktail. She stamped a name from the grid on the paper in front of her, then grabbed a handful of pretzels to start munching on.

Kamran looked at his own entry sheet, then picked a name at random like he'd been doing for the past hour or so.

"Why can't he pick *nice* trivia questions?" Mia

complained. "Like 'Who won their school talent contest with a rendition of Single Ladies on her flute?'" She looked up from where she'd been doodling on her paper to fix Kamran with a serious look. "It was me. I did that," she said, raising her eyebrows.

Kamran held up his hand for a high-five, which she gave him. "Wow, nice work, kid. I've got to hear that someday."

"Oh, good," said Joy, holding out a pretzel for Sugar to sniff. The tiny dog gave the huge salt crystals a tentative lick before chomping the whole thing into her mouth. Kamran chuckled at the crumbs that fell onto his lap.

"Good?" he asked, not quite sure what she meant.

She arched an eyebrow at him. "Saying 'someday' makes it sound like you plan on sticking around," she said as she wagged a pretzel at him. Sugar's big eyes followed every movement. "You're good for my Lee, I can tell. Don't let anyone here tell you any different."

Kamran bit his lip and looked around the room. He wasn't sure what any of these people really thought of him, but to be fair, he'd definitely kept his distance. For one thing, this was just for the week, so the fewer people he and Lee had to lie to, the better. But also…they were from a totally different world from Kamran. They oozed wealth and opportunity from every pore. Kamran had about seventeen dollars currently left in his bank account.

"I don't know," he said with a shrug.

Joy narrowed her eyes at him. "Is this moping thanks to him going back to the office today? Because I can assure you that I am going to whoop his ass when he gets back."

"Joy!" Kamran spluttered, glancing around as a couple of people on sofas near them cast them dirty looks. "I – he – it was an emergency."

Joy scoffed. "Really? They couldn't have coped without him for one day? There are about a dozen people on that team, I know it. He needs to stop trying to define himself by how many hours he works. That won't make him happy." She patted Kamran's knee. *"You* make him happy. I'm sure he realized that the second he got past the driveway."

Kamran bit his lower lip. That voice in the back of his head reared up again, asking why on Earth *he* would make Lee happy. But he reminded himself he was being selfish and holding on to a good thing for as long as he could.

Still, he couldn't find the words to agree with her. "Shouldn't you be playing the game?" he asked as Mikey droned out another question.

Joy chuckled and waved a hand at him. "I got bingo fifteen minutes ago. I always win these things. No one knows this family like I do, and for sure, no one knows Lee like me." She winked at him. "Trust me, he likes you, young man. And so do I."

Kamran opened his mouth to ask why Joy hadn't called 'bingo' if she'd won the game, but he realized he knew the answer. She didn't have anything to prove. She'd lived longer than anyone else here and was being gracious, letting someone else win for once.

There was probably a lot that Kamran could learn from her about being comfortable in his own skin. About being confident that he was good enough, just as he was. In fact, Lee could probably learn the same things.

He'd seemed cut up as he'd left this morning. Kamran hadn't known him long, but the time they'd spent together had been pretty intense, so he liked to think he was starting to get some insight into what made his mountain of a man tick.

He hadn't wanted to go to work today. He hadn't wanted to leave Kamran.

But he had because he was loyal and trust-worthy, both admirable qualities. But that didn't mean Kamran was missing him any less or couldn't wait to get him back to his bedroom. And not just for sex, surprisingly. He just enjoyed having someone who was all his, who cuddled him and talked quietly into the night until they fell asleep.

Someone who plugged a relative stranger's phone in to charge just because it was a nice thing to do.

Kamran had thought he'd been in love with Chaz. Chaz had always showered him with affection publicly, buying him flashy gifts and wrapping his arms around him when anyone else showed him interest. But he'd never once taken *care* of Kamran. He'd never come over when Kamran had been sick or calmed him when he was angry or bought a cheap, silly gift just because he thought it would make Kamran smile. Hell, even when he'd bought him clothes, he'd bragged about it so everyone would know.

He'd never sat in a changing room, dressing Kamran to the nines just because he wanted his man to have the best, to feel like a million bucks.

Had he been in love with Chaz at all? Or had it been just an illusion of security and months of familiarity? Because Kamran had only known Lee a few days, and their situation was totally up in the air, but he felt like he had an invisible string tied around his heart, and the pull was growing harder and harder the longer that Lee was away from him. He ached inside, worrying that Lee was okay and would be back soon. He felt like when Lee was by his side, he could be a better man. The *best* man.

Did he love Lee?

Was that the most ridiculous thought he'd ever had in his whole ridiculous life? Or could you really fall this hard and fast for someone if it was the *right* someone?

He realized people had begun stirring, the murmur of a dozen conversations starting up as people moved and stretched in their seats or got up altogether. The bingo must have ended, and Kamran had been too preoccupied by his thoughts to even notice.

"Well, that's an hour of my life I'll never get back," said Mia, rolling her eyes and folding her paper up with a huff. But then she smiled down at Sugar in Kamran's lap, and the little dog immediately began wagging her tail like mad. "Can I take Sugar for a W-A-L-K, Gee-Gee?" she asked Joy hopefully.

"Sure," Joy said with a big smile. "She's never had as many walkies as she's had this week. She's been thoroughly spoiled." She laughed and got her tablet out, no doubt to watch more Drag Race. "You take your time now. Gamma wants to see how these makeovers turn out. I think some of these gals don't like their families much if this is the way they dress their sisters."

She chuckled and jabbed at the tablet screen. Mia looked at Kamran. "Hey, you wanna come with? We could argue some more about Avengers versus the Power Puff Girls?"

She did a little jig in her seat, and Kamran had to say he was tempted. He kind of liked hanging out with the little chatterbox, and she almost managed to kick his ass in pop culture debates.

But he'd made Lee a promise.

"Ah, I'd love to, kid, but can we take a rain check? I got a couple of things I need to take care of. I'll be back down for the still life class, though."

"Mom won't let me join in," Mia said with a pout.

Joy scoffed, not taking her eyes off the screen. "I'll talk to her, sweetie. There's nothing wrong with the human body."

Mia raised her eyebrows. "Does that mean I can have some wine, too?"

"I'm not that distracted," Joy said with half a grin, looking at her screen. "Now, off with you. Walkies, Sugar!"

Sugar leaped from Kamran's lap and began barking. Mia

laughed and jumped up as well, running after her as they both headed to the gardens. Kamran smiled, watching them disappear.

"Now, off you go," Joy said with that same lingering half-a-smirk. "Don't do anything I wouldn't do."

Kamran didn't often blush, but he couldn't help but feel that Joy knew full well that he was going to run upstairs and finger himself while he jerked off. Oh…he was *definitely* sending Lee photos of *that.* If anything was going to make him hurry home, it was some naughty, tempting pics of what was waiting for him as soon as he got his ass back through the front door.

"Yes, ma'am," he said as he stood.

For once, Joy didn't correct him and tell him to call her 'Joy.' She just waved him off, then scowled at the screen. "Well, you're just trying to make yourself look better by making your sister look like crap! *Someone's* landing in the bottom two."

Kamran smiled to himself as he made his way over to the bar. He figured he'd get another drink, put some music on, have a little party for one, and send the evidence to his big hunk of a lover…

Yes, this was shaping up to be a very fun afternoon.

Or it had been.

"Mr. Amir," a voice drawled.

Kamran looked up from where one of the hired bartenders was mixing him another pink, fizzy cocktail. His stomach dropped as Mr. Marshall Sr. sidled up to him, looking him up and down as he clicked his fingers at the bartender. The guy stopped making Kamran's drink and immediately switched to pouring a glass of whiskey from a bottle that had been hidden under the table.

"Hiya, Donald," Kamran said cheerfully.

The bartender handed the whiskey over, then threw

Kamran an apologetic look. Kamran just smiled back at him, though. He understood that Donald here was the one signing the guy's paycheck and had power over him if he didn't do what he said.

Jerk.

"How are you doing? Did you nail the bingo?" Kamran asked playfully, but Donald just hummed and sipped his whiskey. Luckily, the guy behind the bar finished Kamran's drink so he could take it and have something to occupy himself with. "Wow, that's good," he said after taking a sip. "Thanks, man." He tipped the bartender a ten, which he felt was the polite thing to do after he'd made Kamran so many drinks now, but Donald looked at the transaction like the whole thing was baffling to him.

"Walk with me," he said, moving away from the drink station.

He didn't wait for Kamran. He just turned and left. Kamran had a good mind to tell Mr. Marshall to shove it, but he was still here to impress the family for Lee's sake. So he bit his tongue and followed like an obedient puppy.

"I notice it didn't take Leopold long to skedaddle back off to work," Donald said conversationally as they strolled through the reception room. People naturally parted for them like the red sea.

Kamran scowled. *"Lee* said it was an emergency," he said pointedly, but he wasn't even sure Donald heard him correct the name.

"There will always be an emergency, Mr. Amir. It's best you learn that now." He led Kamran out into the hallway, then turned to look at him. His gaze was piercing, making Kamran feel like he'd been skewered. "I'll cut to the chase, Mr. Amir."

Kamran hated the way he kept saying his name like that, but he felt powerless to challenge it. He was in Donald's house, his guest for the week and at his whim. Kamran didn't want to make things worse for Lee between him and his family, so he just nodded.

"Okay," he said tentatively, feeling like Donald was waiting for him to acknowledge the gauntlet he'd just thrown down.

"I had one of my people look into you. There is a surface-level presence of your career in NASCAR, but a simple scratch shows that you're not really employed by anyone there. You're just an Uber driver." He rolled his eyes and took another sip of whiskey. "So you are either deceiving my son or you both chose to try and deceive us. Me. I'm not sure which is worse."

Kamran felt a spark of rebellion ignite in him, fueled by the loving look Lee had left him as he'd parted that morning. "Maybe we agreed that you'd all judge me anyway, so why not tell a story to make me sound a little more impressive? Maybe it's *you* and your snobbery that pushed Lee to this."

Donald scoffed, shaking his head. "My son is terrible at relationships, so I'm sure this…whatever this is…will fizzle out soon enough. But just in case you manage to sink your claws into him for any longer than this week, I wanted to make something perfectly clear to you, Mr. Amir. This family and our legacy will not be made fools of. We do not suffer gold-diggers. So whatever scheme you have in mind, drop it."

"Wow," said Kamran loudly. He downed his drink and slammed his glass on a nearby table. "Did you ever think that I just *love* your son and want to be with him in *spite* of all this bullshit? Maybe if you didn't have such a low opinion of him, he wouldn't feel the need to throw himself into work and would know how to be better at relationships. It doesn't matter, though, because he has me now to show him how to be better. To show him that no matter how hard he tries, he'll *never* earn your approval, so why bother spending all hours at the office instead of at home? Either way, Lee's life is *none* of your business, so how about you just back *off?*"

A little squeak came from down the hall, and Kamran looked over to see Aunt Ginny. "Don't mind me," she said with a wave of her hand before scuttling off, gin and tonic clutched firmly in hand. Kamran sighed. Well, either way, this altercation was going to be spread all around the family. So much for Kamran being a polite boyfriend. He was going to be branded as a troublemaker.

But did he care? Quite frankly, *someone* needed to stand up to Donald for Lee. That way maybe Lee would start doing it himself.

Donald shook his head. "I've said all I have to on the matter," he told Kamran curtly. "I simply suggest you remember your place in all this and cause minimal damage in the long run."

Kamran laughed coldly. "You can bully him all you like. Lee isn't going to drop everything to come and work for you. He loves his job, and he's damned good at it. All you're doing is pushing your son away, and one day you might push him so far that he never comes back. Just think if you're *really* prepared to do that."

Shaking, he spun on his heels and stormed up the stairs. It was funny how fathers could manifest as total assholes in completely different ways. Donald wasn't screaming and throwing things. He wasn't calling Lee an abomination and kicking him out of the house. But he was still a complete tool.

Lee deserved so much better than that.

Kamran crashed all the way up to Lee's room, then slammed the door. He leaned back against it, trying to get his breathing under control and his hands to stop trembling. He had planned on a good time this afternoon, and that was what he was going to have. Donald Marshall be damned.

There was only one Marshall man who Kamran cared about, and he was going to be home soon.

And Kamran was going to be ready for him.

Luckily, Lee and Kamran had indulged in a little private partying the other night, so there was a bottle of tequila already up in the room with a couple of tumblers. It was really good stuff as well, not like the shots they served at Aquarium, so Kamran washed out one of the glasses and poured himself a healthy measure. Then he locked the door, put one of his favorite music playlists on his phone, then got the shower in the en suite running really hot.

That was better.

Kamran took his time as he sang along to the loud music. He undressed and sipped his drink, letting the small bathroom get nice and steamy. He rolled his shoulders and his neck as well until it cracked pleasantly. He was here for Lee. Lee was all that mattered.

Speaking of which…

He stopped just before getting into the shower. Instead, he turned around and flopped naked onto the bed, wriggling around on the covers feeling naughty. He reached for the lube in the nightstand, squeezing a healthy amount onto his palm before taking himself in hand.

"Oh, Lee," he moaned in the quietness of the room, stroking up and down his length. "You big, bad man. Come back here and fuck me already."

When he was good and hard, his cock glistening and leaking precum, he fumbled for his phone where he'd dropped it near him. He was no stranger to sending dick pics when requested, so it didn't take him long to get a decent shot of his hand wrapped around his throbbing member. He bit his lip as he opened up a conversation. They hadn't actually messaged each other before, as they'd been together pretty much since they'd met at Aquarium, so it gave Kamran a thrill that their first communication was going to be his raging erection.

"I'm waiting for you, gorgeous," he said out loud as he typed one-handed. "I'll be so ready, I promise."

He grinned as he pressed send, half hoping one of Lee's colleagues might accidentally see it. That would be one way to declare that Agent Marshall wasn't going to be such a slave to the office from now on.

Taking a couple of deep breaths, he squeezed the base of his shaft and tried to relax. He had some more fun yet to come, and he didn't want to spoil it for himself yet. He finally made his way into the en suite, feeling the steam creep all over his skin before he stepped under the sinfully hot water. He felt guilty for the environment that he'd let it run so long before he'd gotten under it, but not for Donald Marshall's water bill. Fuck that guy.

Or not. Definitely not, actually.

Luckily, it was very easy for Kamran to switch his train of thought back to Lee instead. He was so fuckable, after all. In fact, as desperate as Kamran was to bottom for Lee, he also *really* hoped that later down the line, Lee would let him top, too. Kamran had a feeling by the way Lee loved Kamran's fingers inside him that he'd be up for that, but bottoming was a mentality. He might not be into it.

But Kamran hoped he would.

He bit his lip and moaned loudly, thrilled, knowing no one could hear him. He was all alone as he fingered his hole, getting three digits inside him. He knew Lee wouldn't be home for a little while, but relaxing now would help speed up the process later. Plus, Kamran wanted to feel squeaky clean when he begged Lee to eat him out later. As much as he loved getting down and dirty with sex (there was *nothing* wrong with bodily fluids and functions), he just wanted as many ways as possible to show Lee how special this moment was to him.

Lee had alluded several times to Kamran's playboy ways. Not necessarily in a bad way, just trying to point out that they might not be compatible.

Kamran wanted to show him how wrong he was. He wanted to convince him that he, Kamran, king of hookups, was ready to make a commitment. There might be practicalities involved with where they lived, but Kamran hadn't wanted to at least *try* with someone this badly in years.

He could get fucked up by the ass by any number of people with dicks or straps-ons, that was all fun and fine. But Kamran knew this was going to mean so much *more*. This was Lee. The guy he'd wanted to climb and strangle at the same time the night they'd met. But now...

Now Kamran wanted Lee to hold him and make love to him. To claim him so utterly and completely.

He couldn't hold on any longer. With a guttural yell, he came all over his hand, cum exploding onto the tiles. He gasped and shook as euphoria flooded through him, leaning against the wall for support. His skin was extra sensitive as the hot water poured down him, and he hastily grappled with the dial to turn it down. The cool water was a shock but also kind of delicious. He trembled beneath it, floating down from his orgasm, taking his time.

Eventually, he began to feel bad about the environment again, so he rinsed his body, then stepped out of the shower, wrapping himself in one of the big fluffy towels to dry off. He wished he had a butt plug so he could stay stretched for Lee all evening, but what he'd done should help a little.

Next time, a seductive little voice whispered at the back of his mind. The fact that he was even fantasizing about a next time was so remarkable and pretty fucking sexy in and of itself. He bit his thumb hard, sending a thrilling zing through his body. Then he quickly finished drying himself off. He had a little while before the still life drawing class began, but hopefully, that meant Lee would be back soon.

Kamran was desperate to see if Lee had responded to his naughty message, but he made himself get dressed before looking. The longer he waited, the longer he gave Lee the chance to see it and respond. So when the music was interrupted by the ringtone just as Kamran was pulling on his chinos, he practically leaped across the room to answer it.

The number was unrecognized, but he figured that might just be because Lee was driving.

He was wrong.

"Did you like that?" he asked breathlessly as he jammed the phone to his ear, grinning as he anticipated Lee's sexy growl telling him what a naughty minx he was.

But the voice that responded sent a chill down his spine, killing any trace of good mood he'd had.

"Oh yes, baby, I liked it a *lot.*"

Kamran swayed before dropping onto the edge of the bed, grateful that it had happened to be nearer than the floor to him. "Ch-*Chaz?*"

He'd blocked Chaz's number, but he'd been an idiot to think he wouldn't be able to just contact him on another number. In fact, now he was thinking about it over the noise of the blood rushing to his head. It was kind of crazy that he'd waited this long to contact Kaman after the incident at his apartment on Friday night.

"I'd been waiting for you to use your phone and give me something useful," Chaz purred. Kamran shivered in fear, hugging himself. Of *course* Chaz would have had his number cloned or his phone hacked or whatever it was he'd done. "Gorgeous dick pic. I took that as a compliment."

"It wasn't for you," Kamran spat. "I don't owe you anything, Chaz. I told you to fuck off! Leave me alone!"

"Well," Chaz said with a scoff, "you should have thought of *that* before you started fraternizing with the enemy. Why, may I ask, are you sending erotic photos to Agent Lee Marshall?"

Panic threatened to flare through Kamran, but he kept it at bay. "He's an FBI agent? So what? Is there a law against sending dick pics to FBI agents if you happen to be fucking them?"

"There is if that agent happens to be the lead investigator in your boyfriend's case, then…yes. That's pretty illegal in my book, baby."

"Ex-boyfriend," Kamran snapped. "And I don't know what you're babbling about, but—"

"Cut the *shit*, Kamran!" Chaz screeched, making Kamran freeze in fear. "My guy, Jimmy, *saw* Marshall approach you in that dive bar you love so much. He *saw* you go out back. And when my guys came to escort you to me to have a little chat about that, you ran away from them straight into his arms!"

Fucking Jimmy. Kamran knew that bouncer was a creep. He just didn't think he'd go so low as to rat Kamran out to Chaz for money. What a weasel.

Kamran opened and closed his mouth, trying to rack his brains for any of his apps that would show his location. If Chaz had managed to get someone to hack his phone, then the point might be moot if they could just activate his GPS. But he wasn't giving up without a fight.

"Oh my fucking god, how desperate for my ass are you?" he asked scathingly. "I met a guy. I liked him. How the fuck was I supposed to know he was anything to do with you? We hooked up, and I wanted a round two, so I invited him over later. If you want to jerk off to my private dick pics, that is your sad little problem, Chaz!"

There was a pause. It lasted slightly too long for Kamran's liking.

"So you're at your place?"

Kamran licked his lips." Yeah," he said defiantly, despite the fact that his heart was pounding.

"The place my guys trashed?"

Kamran curled his free hand into a fist. "Yeah. thanks for that, by the way, you absolute fucker. I'll bill you for it when I've worked out the final clean-up."

"Huh," said Chaz. He didn't sound rattled at all. "It's funny because I don't think you *are* at home, baby."

"Don't call me that," Kamran snapped.

It was crazy, but even though him *not* saying it, 'baby' had somehow become Lee's word. Hearing it from Chaz's mouth was even more awful than before. Like it somehow now belonged to Lee and Chaz was polluting it.

"Okay, baby," he said with a mirthless laugh. "Why don't you look out the window?"

"Of my apartment?" Kamran said, his heartbeat kicking up another notch. He stood up regardless, though, stomping over to Lee's bedroom window. "Sure, but I'm telling you, you're wasting your…time…"

He almost dropped the phone from his ear. Because Chaz wasn't outside Kamran's apartment.

He was on the lawn of Lee's parents' estate.

15

LEE

"Are you fucking kidding me?"

Lee was so mad he was seeing stars. The edges of his vision were black as he stormed into Duke's office and slammed the door behind him. Duke looked up from his computer as Lee towered over his desk.

"Marshall? What's the—?"

"You already charged him," he snapped. "You got what you needed from Bolt's guy an *hour* ago, and you still let me drive all the way back here?"

Duke held up his hands and scowled. "Marshall, calm down," he said sternly. "There is still plenty to do around here. We need—"

"No," Lee interrupted, jabbing his finger at Duke. "You told me that you needed me to break him, to get him to confess. Apparently, he rolled over like a puppy within a couple of hours to save his own ass."

"And that's a bad thing because…?" Duke asked.

Lee balled up his hands. "Because you used my promotion to drag me away from my vacation, and then you didn't need me at all. Enough. I have more to my life than this job!"

Duke laced his fingers together. "You could have fooled me. Normally we can't drag you out of this place."

"Yeah, well, things change," Lee grumbled, rubbing his eyes. "This is bullshit, Duke, and I don't appreciate it. Either give me the promotion or give it to someone else. But stop using it to make me jump through every god-damned hoop you please."

Duke arched an eyebrow. "I'm sorry," he said coolly. "I was under the impression that you cared about this job."

"I do," Lee said in exasperation, throwing his hands out. "But it's not everything."

Duke shrugged. "I'm sorry you've got your panties in a twist, but while you're here, you might as well—"

"No," said Lee, fully aware that he was walking on thin ice by interrupting his boss a third time in so many minutes, but he couldn't bring himself to care. "I left Kamran alone because I didn't think it was safe to bring him here if you had one of Bolt's guys hanging around. He should be safe at my parents' place, but I swore I'd look after him until Bolt was in custody, so that's what I'm going to go do. I will see you on Monday morning."

"Don't you mean 'Amir'?" Duke asked, that annoying eyebrow of his raised again.

"What?"

"You said 'Kamran,'" Duke explained. "I assume you mean our witness, whose name is 'Amir,' if we're being professional."

"Oh, you spend a week glued to someone's side and not get friendly with them," Lee snapped. Then he sighed. He didn't really want to fight with his boss. "I apologize," he said contritely. "I just feel responsible for him. I don't want to let him down or fuck up this case."

"Sure," said Duke after a beat. "See you on Monday, Marshall."

187

Lee bit his lip and hesitated. His knee-jerk reaction was to try and make things better with Duke, to stay and do some work after all, seeing as he'd come all the way there.

But then he remembered Kamran's cheeky grin. His big, wide eyes as he made Lee promise to come back to him as soon as possible. The way he'd swallowed when Lee had promised him more in bed that night.

He was on vacation, and he was going back to his lover. *Now.*

So he nodded once and turned on his heels, yanking the door open and marching his way through the cubicles where his colleagues were hard at work. A few of them said hello, and one guy shouted out, "Hey! Get over here, you lazy bum!" But Lee just waved to them and kept on walking.

It wasn't that he suddenly didn't like his job. He was sure that come Monday morning, he really would want to get back to it. But he couldn't deny that he was pissed at losing the day with Kamran when he didn't know how long they really had together.

At least they still had the evening and night. In fact, Lee realized as he checked his watch, if he hurried, he could get back for the mid-afternoon bingo. His heart leaped. Not for the bingo – Mikey was in charge, so it was bound to be an uncomfortable affair. But because it meant that Kamran wouldn't be on his own.

So rather than continuing to be mad at Duke for ruining his day, Lee decided to focus on what he'd gained. He'd expected to be in with the suspect for at least an hour or two, so if he looked at it with a positive attitude, he'd just earned a couple of extra hours.

Until he hit traffic.

About halfway back to Pine Cove, Lee ground his Jeep to a halt behind the long snake of vehicles on the highway. Groaning, he checked his app and was soon informed of a three-car pile-up a mile or so down the road. No casualties, apparently. However, it was going to take a while to clear the debris.

He tried not to let his frustration get to him, but it was almost like the universe was telling him 'I told you so.' That work would always intrude and ruin his relationships. He felt like a total fool for allowing himself to be talked into coming back to the office. When was he going to learn? What was it going to take?

"I'm learning today," he said to himself out loud over the music that he had playing. "And Kamran is what it's going to take."

Complex Kamran, with all his bravado and flirting. Sweet, surprising Kamran, the secret figure skater. Tender Kamran, who clung to Lee with tears on his lashes when they were climaxing together. Lee wanted all the Kamrans, as many as he could find. He had no idea how the future might look for them, but he was willing to try.

So he made himself breathe deeply and not bitch at the universe for getting him stuck in traffic. An hour or so wasn't going to make a difference. Kamran would be waiting for him when he came back...and hopefully be eager and ready to try something new between them.

Lee adjusted himself in his seat as his cock let him know how much he was looking forward to that. It had only been hours since he'd been apart from Kamran, but it felt longer. It was like he was a drug, and Lee was addicted already. He breathed deeply, recalling the scent of Kamran's leather jacket and the new woodsy cologne Lee had bought for him.

Lee was tempted to message him to let him know what was going on, but until this traffic cleared, Lee couldn't give him an ETA, so he resisted. Instead, he turned up the music and sang along, letting his mind wander.

His family could be tough at times – Lee suspected that

he was never going to get along with his brother or dad the way he would have liked – but on the whole, he was having a fun vacation and was looking forward to the next few days they still had left.

Going back to the office had almost wound him back up again, but as the traffic got going finally, Lee relaxed, smiling as he thought of the fun evening ahead. He couldn't draw for shit, but there would be red wine and, more importantly, Kamran. They were making memories together all this week, and one day, Lee hoped he'd look back on this time fondly as the start of something really special.

He sighed with relief as he finally made it back to his parents' place. He parked his Jeep in the spot he'd moved it from that morning, then couldn't resist running his hand along the length of Kamran's Mustang as he walked past it. He loved how much Kamran loved that car, and hoped one day soon Kamran would take him for a drive in it.

It was funny how Lee had thought it was black when he'd first seen it in the dark, but now he knew it was midnight blue. Like Kamran, his car had deserved a closer look before Lee jumped to his conclusions.

That was why Lee was falling so hard for this guy. Kamran liked to pretend that he was superficial and flighty, only interested in sex and nothing more. But he was a complicated human being with a beating heart, full of so many passions. Lee wanted to hold him, to watch as he soared. He wanted to make sure nothing ever held Kamran back again if he could help it.

He'd always gotten his purpose from work. Billy hadn't needed him, not really. He'd had his own career that he'd been succeeding in. He'd been confident, and that was attractive, Lee couldn't lie. But Lee couldn't help but feel that maybe he was better suited to someone who craved that little extra TLC. Someone who needed to receive Lee's love and support just as much as Lee needed to give it.

Butterflies flittered in his belly as he jogged up the steps and through the front door. There were sounds of life coming from all directions in the house, and Lee wasn't too sure where Kamran might be. So he headed to the reception room, his anticipation building at the thought of being reunited with Kamran after only a short amount of time.

The bingo had obviously finished a while ago as there were only a dozen or so people lounging around on the collection of sofas. None of them were Kamran, but one of them *was* Gamma, so Lee made his way over, smiling as he approached.

"Tell me you won," he said by way of announcing his arrival.

Gamma looked up from her screen, her face breaking into a big smile as she saw it was Lee in front of her. "You're back," she said, sounding delighted. She paused the show, then leaned over to whack Lee on the arm with the tablet. "You never should have left."

Lee blinked at her as she raised her eyebrows at him. Sheepishly, he lowered himself into the armchair beside her. "I know," he said, offering her a small smile. "It was a complete waste of time...but I shouldn't have left either way."

Gamma tilted her head. "Go on..."

Lee sighed. "I think...I think I needed to go, though, Gamma. I needed to realize that work isn't everything to me, not anymore. I don't think, at least. I know it's been fast with Kamran—"

"Not that fast," she interrupted. "You've been dating a few months now."

Guilt threatened to rise up in Lee, but the white lie wasn't really the issue. A few months, a few days – it felt like it didn't actually matter. He knew how his heart felt about Kamran, and that was all that counted.

"But that was in Seattle when we were both working," he said, improvising. "Being here, living together, having a vacation – it's all made me realize that I've been finding my worth from my job, and that's not the same as people."

"Or just that one special someone," Gamma agreed with a twinkle in her eye as she grinned. She reached out to squeeze his knee. "Good boy, that's what I was hoping to hear. I mean, you should have realized it before you left, but no one's perfect." She winked, but Lee considered her words carefully.

"I've been working toward this promotion so hard... because I think I didn't believe I'd meet anyone special. That I wouldn't want to trust my heart to someone again after Billy broke it so badly. I guess I thought I needed a promotion to fulfill me."

"And now?"

Lee licked his lips and met his grandmother's gaze. "What if I let this work opportunity go and things don't work out with Kamran?"

"Then you'll find another nice man," said Gamma matter-of-factly. "But don't be so quick to dismiss *this* young man. He's special." She patted his arm. "You're more than your job, Lee. You don't need to prove it to your father, and you certainly don't need to prove it to me or anyone else. So long as you know it, that's enough. You *deserve* happiness, sweetheart."

He nodded. "I think maybe you're right."

Gamma scoffed. "I'm always right," she said smugly, going back to her tablet and whatever episode of Drag Race she was up to. "Now off you go. Kamran went upstairs about half an hour ago, maybe forty-five minutes." She winked at him, looking less like a sweet old lady and more like a devil. "I think he's *waiting* for you."

A fierce blush tried to creep up Lee's neck onto his face, but he loosened his tie and shook himself, refusing to let his grandmother embarrass him like a naughty schoolboy. "Okay, thank you. I'll, um, go find him, then."

"You do that, hon," Gamma said with a chuckle, starting her show back up again.

Lee nodded and said hello to several of his relatives as he crossed the room. The drawing class would be starting in a little while, so people were starting to drift back in. But Lee wasn't going to be distracted.

He had a mission.

He did a quick sweep of the kitchen and patio just to be sure, but Kamran wasn't there. So he made his way to the stairs, jogging up to his bedroom. Anticipation bubbled through him like freshly poured Champagne. Maybe he was right, and this little break from Kamran today was enough to show him exactly how much he valued their relationship – how much he wanted to fight for it.

If Kamran wanted that too.

Lee took a deep breath as he neared the door. At some point, he needed to stop tiptoeing around the situation and make his feelings and intentions clear. He couldn't make Kamran leave behind his playboy ways or want to commit to a relationship, but he'd never take a chance if Lee didn't make it crystal clear that was what he wanted.

He knocked twice, his heart leaping into his chest. "It's me. Can I come in?"

He waited, but there was no answer. It seemed completely quiet beyond the door. Was Kamran in the shower? Maybe he'd fallen asleep?

Lee knocked again, but still nothing. Realizing it was entirely possible that Kamran wasn't in there and was, in fact, somewhere else in the house or on the grounds, he turned the handle and let himself inside.

Nothing.

The bathroom door was open, but the shower wasn't running. A wet bath towel had been left on the end of the bed, though, which wasn't like Kamran from what Lee had seen that week. He'd been overly respectful of Lee's space and all the clothes and such that Lee had bought for him. He was always careful to fold things away and hang stuff up.

Maybe he'd been in a hurry, Lee thought as he picked the towel up and returned it to its home on the heated radiator. It was no big deal. The bed wasn't soaked or anything. Still...

Lee looked around but couldn't see any of Kamran's things that suggested he'd be back soon – like his phone or wallet. He was probably downstairs enjoying himself, but Lee didn't want to waste time hunting for him anymore. He decided to call him.

He hadn't checked his phone in a little while, so he was surprised when he unlocked it to see a message flash up from Kamran himself. A thrill rushed through him, and he wasn't disappointed.

It wasn't like Lee had never gotten a dick pic before, but he still gasped in the otherwise empty bedroom as Kamran's hard, glistening cock popped up on his screen.

KAMRAN: I'm waiting for you, gorgeous. I'll be so ready, I promise.

Lee gulped. Well, now he was really dismayed that Kamran wasn't in the room waiting for him like he'd promised. Lee had the sudden urge to make them late for the still life class. He took a second to admire the photo before realizing that the real deal was somewhere very close by, and he could *summon* its owner back to the bedroom.

Grinning like a horny teenager on his first booty call, he pressed the phone to his ear, waiting for the ringtone. But to his disappointment, the call went through to voicemail after several rings. He probably had it on silent. Lee sighed. They had plenty of time tonight for some intimate fun, and Lee didn't want to rush that anyway. It would be better if he went and found Kamran now, and then they could be sociable for the evening as planned.

So Lee trotted downstairs, intending to do a sweep of the place. He knew the house was big, but hopefully, Kamran couldn't have gotten that far. Lee guessed he'd sent the picture then showered, so he'd probably only missed him leaving the bedroom by ten or fifteen minutes.

More people had gathered in the reception room, and his mom was setting everyone up with paper and various different art supplies. A very handsome guy was standing on a plinth in the middle of the room with a towel wrapped around his otherwise naked body. Aunt Ginny was talking to him, twirling her red hair around her finger like a lusty schoolgirl, apparently oblivious to the big engagement ring on the same hand. It showed how smitten Lee was that he barely gave the model a second glance. He was only interested in Kamran.

Sadly, there was still no sign of him among the congregation. "Hey, Florence," Lee asked as he spotted his sister nearby. "You haven't seen Kamran recently, have you?"

"Oh hey, you're back," she said happily as he walked over to where she was standing. "I'm impressed. I thought we'd lost you for the whole day." She grinned and punched his arm lightly.

He shook his head and chuckled. "Shut up."

"It's only because I love you," she told him with a wink before sipping her white wine. "I think this is gonna be fun, don't you? Paul has the rest of the kids and told me to enjoy myself." She jerked her thumb over her shoulder at the model, then waggled her eyebrows. "He's not bad, is he? I mean, he's not *Kamran*, but I'm sure you can still appreciate objectively."

Lee laughed along with her. "Yeah, he's okay. But it's Kamran I'm interested in right now."

"Oh, yeah," said Florence with a frown as she looked around the busy room. "He did the bingo with Gamma and Mia – I think she's kinda taken with him, so cute," she added. "But uhh...not since then, actually."

Lee nibbled his lip. "He's probably outside or something."

"Who?"

Speaking of Mia, she appeared at Florence's side with Sugar in her arms. The little dog looked up at them sleepily before tucking her head under Mia's arm.

"Kamran," said Lee, looking around the room again as if that might somehow summon his lover to him. "I've called him a couple of times, but it's going to voicemail."

"Oh, he left," said Mia with a frown. "I assumed he was going to meet you or something."

Lee's heart skipped a beat. "No, I haven't seen him since this morning. What do you mean he left? When?"

Mia looked between him and her mom. "Uh...about fifteen minutes ago, maybe? I was outside and said hi, but I don't think he heard me. He seemed like he was in kind of a rush."

Fear lanced through Lee. Where would Kamran have gone? Had he left the house? Why would he risk doing that?

Unless Bolt had gotten to him.

Or he'd been working for Bolt this whole time and had used Lee's absence as a chance to slip away.

No. Bolt's people had threatened Kamran. Kamran had come to Lee voluntarily. He'd been really rattled.

Unless he was a really good actor and had been playing Lee this whole time?

No! Lee's gut told him he could trust Kamran. It was crazy to jump to conclusions like that. But why would Kamran leave the safety of the estate otherwise?

"Are you sure he left?" Lee asked Mia.

She frowned, looking down at Sugar as she seemed to think. "Well, he walked toward the parking lot. Then a minute later a sporty red car zoomed out. I kind of assumed that was Kamran's car, seeing as he's a racer and all?"

Lee shook his head, unlocking his phone and redialing Kamran's number. "His is the dark blue Mustang." Once again, it rang until the voicemail activated. Lee disconnected the call before Kamran's flirty 'leave a message!' recording could torment him again. "Damn it!" he cried.

Real fear was rising in him now. Surely, Kamran wouldn't be so foolish as to leave the house when he knew that Bolt was looking for him. But whose car had that been? And why would Kamran just walk out when he was safe within these walls?

"Trouble in paradise?"

Lee gritted his teeth and turned to face his father. "I—"

He realized he couldn't explain why he was so worried without divulging that Kamran was actually an FBI witness. But as stupid as it was, he didn't want his old man to think that his and Kamran's relationship was on the rocks, either.

"Uh, no," he said, squashing down his panic.

"But your new boyfriend has run off, yes?" said his dad.

Was it Lee's imagination, or did his dad's lip twitch a fraction? Lee knew that look. It was when his dad knew he'd already won and was trying to hide his triumph poorly.

Lee frowned and turned to face him fully. "Did you *say* something to him?" he demanded.

His dad shrugged, sipping his whiskey. "I merely let him know that I was perfectly well aware that his so-called career was a complete fabrication and asked if you knew as well or if he was attempting to dupe all of us."

197

Mia blinked at looked at Lee. "Kamran's not really a racing car driver?"

Lee could have screamed. "Yes, he is," he said, glaring at his dad. "Just not for NASCAR. He's a stunt driver, and he works here, in Pine Cove."

"He's an *Uber* driver," Lee's dad scoffed.

"He's a good man," Lee shot back. "But I knew you'd never see that, so I came up with a stupid story. It was all my idea, okay, so whatever you said to Kamran, you'll take it back."

"Will I now?" his dad said coolly.

Lee threw out his hands. "Why is *everything* a fight with you? Why did you have to go around sticking your nose into things? None of this matters. I need to find out where Kamran has gone and why he isn't answering his phone."

"Why would you say he's from Seattle if he's really from Pine Cove?" Florence asked, looking at Lee with confusion. *Damn it.* He'd just made things even worse. He knew his sister wasn't ganging up on him. She was just worried, but he didn't know how to dig himself out of this.

Luckily – or *unluckily* – he didn't have to.

"Because this whole thing is a sham," said Mikey, sauntering over. By now, most of the room had turned to look at Lee and the people around him, including the model who was still in a towel, looking thoroughly confused by what was going on.

Lee's stomach dropped. "What?" he demanded. He really wasn't in the mood for his jackass brother right now. But it seemed like Mikey didn't care what Lee wanted, as usual.

Mikey gave him a pitying look that made Lee want to punch his brother's smug, pudgy face. "I heard you the other day, on the landing after Kamran was so rude to me in the kitchen. I followed you, hoping he might want to apologize. But I heard the truth! That man isn't your *boyfriend.* He's your *witness.* You literally brought your work here to Mom and Dad's house."

Cold terror crawled up Lee's throat. Mikey had followed them, and naturally he'd sat on this information until he could use it to do the most damage. *Damn him!*

Of course that was the moment that his mom appeared by his dad's side, looking tearful. "Sweetheart? What's Mikey talking about?"

"I—" Lee didn't know where to begin. Humiliation was seeping through him like an oil slick. "It's not like that." *Not anymore!*

"Then what is it like?" his dad asked. He looked thoroughly unimpressed, and shame washed through Lee along with all his other emotions. "Because what it's sounding like is that you and this person have delighted in mocking your whole family for the past few days."

"No," said Lee firmly, locking eyes with his dad's. "That's not it. How Kamran and I came to be together…okay, yes, it's a bit complicated, but I…he…"

"Oh, for heaven's sake!" Lee turned his head to see Gamma waddling over to them, wagging her finger with a furious expression on her face. "What's all this nonsense?"

"Lee's boyfriend is really a witness he's protecting," Mikey cried. He always had relished tattling on Lee every chance he got.

"Bullshit," Gamma declared as she came to a halt in front of them all, her hands on her hips. She only came up to most of the adults' shoulder height, but she still glared up at Lee's dad and Mikey all the same. "You boys are always picking on my Lee. He works hard, but he'd never trick his family or put them in danger like that."

Guilt overwhelmed all Lee's other emotions, and he shook his head, his throat dry. "Actually, Gamma—"

But she silenced him with a crooked finger pointed at his

nose. "Maybe how you met is a little more complicated. Maybe you met on one of those kinky apps and are embarrassed."

"Gamma!" Mikey blurted out, scandalized.

"Can it, you," Gamma said, narrowing her eyes. "Don't think I haven't noticed that *your* wife isn't actually *here*. She's finally divorcing you, and I can't say I blame her. So how about you worry about your own damn self and quit bullying my Lee here."

Mikey's mouth opened and closed like a goldfish. Lee might have felt a great deal of satisfaction at this turn of events if he wasn't preoccupied by significantly more pressing matters.

"I didn't mean to lie to anyone..." he began.

Gamma waved her hand and looped arms with Mia, petting Sugar's head. "Who cares. We talked about this earlier. All that matters is that you're here now and you tell that boy how you really feel about him. Where is he, anyhow?"

Lee's heart was hammering in his chest. He'd been caught out. His mom looked devastated and his dad furious. But Gamma was steaming ahead like none of that mattered.

Did it?

He rolled his shoulders. He was done hiding. He was done trying to get his dad and brother to respect him when anything other than working for the family company was always going to be not good enough for them. This was his truth, and he needed to own it.

"Yes," he said, looking between his parents. "I can't explain the circumstances, but I met Kamran because he's involved with my case. I brought him here to protect him so I wouldn't have to miss the reunion. It was his idea to pose as my boyfriend to avoid any awkward questions. But all that's changed now, and we're together. I think…I think I might even…"

"Love him," said Gamma and Mia in unison. "Duh," Mia added with a wink.

"This is completely ridiculous," Mikey scoffed, clearly keen to switch the focus away from his divorce and back to Lee. "I have no idea what's true or not, but you're ruining Mom and Dad's evening—"

"Lee?" his mom interrupted. "Do you?"

Lee rubbed the back of his neck. "What?" he asked gently. He *hated* the idea that he'd let her down or embarrassed her in any way.

But she gave him a small smile. "Do you *love* him?"

Lee licked his lips and looked around at his family. "I think so, yes."

Gamma beamed at him.

Mikey threw out his hands. "Well, tough. Because he's run off. Now can we please get on with—"

"What do you mean he's run off?" Lee's mom asked.

"I saw him leaving," said Mia, sounding apologetic. "I bet there's a logical explanation, though!" she added hastily.

"Or a sinister one," Lee growled. "Kamran was in witness protection for a reason. So now the cat's out of the bag—"

"GO!" Mia shouted.

"What are you hanging around here for?" Florence asked, aghast.

Gamma slapped his arm. "You think he might be in danger, and you're standing around here arguing with these nitwits? I taught you better than that, Lee Marshall! Go find that man and tell him you love him, before you give me a heart attack."

Lee looked between them all. His father hadn't spoken in a while, but what did Lee expect? For him to suddenly support Lee unconditionally when he'd been looking down on him his whole life?

Screw it.

"Okay, I'm going to look for him," he said to his grandmother. "And when I bring him back, it'll be as my real boyfriend."

"Attaboy," she said.

"Good luck!" Mia cried.

But Lee was already running for the door.

He had to find his man.

16

KAMRAN

"There we go," Chaz gloated over the phone as Kamran looked down at him. "Don't you feel better for telling the truth?"

Technically, Kamran hadn't told the truth. Chaz had just caught him out in his lie.

Kamran swallowed, fighting the fear that was washing through him. "Leave me *alone*, Chaz. It's over."

Chaz laughed darkly, a horrible sound that made Kamran shiver. "I wouldn't take you back if you begged – which I'm sure you will," he added with a growl that Kamran wasn't ashamed to say made his stomach flip with fear. "But with regards to the little matter of you *ratting me out to the FBI*, I have to say, yes, I'd like to chat."

"I haven't told him anything, I swear," Kamran said, trying not to let his voice shake. "Look, you scared me when those guys busted into my place. I told Marshall I wanted to stay at his place for a while. That's it."

Chaz was hovering by the tree line, so Kamran wondered if anyone else had seen him lurking around like the total creep he was. Even though he was far away, Kamran could still make out his body language and imagine the facial expressions that went along with them. He was currently staring up at Kamran through Lee's bedroom window, his hand in his jacket pocket, looking totally at ease.

That was when he was at his most dangerous.

"Oh, baby," he said with a pouty voice. "The thing is, I *just* don't believe you. So how about you come down here, and I'll take us for a nice drive. You used to love that. I've got my *Jag*," he added in a sing-song voice, like that would possibly tempt Kamran these days.

"Why the hell would I come out there?" Kamran spat. "I think I'll stay up here, thank you very much. Lee's family are all over this house…*and* they have a security detail."

He knew the Marshalls had plenty of cameras, but there wasn't any actual security personnel, much to his dismay. Chaz didn't know that, though.

Except Chaz was always one step ahead of Kamran, the fucker.

"Yes, you're right," he agreed with a mocking cheeriness. "This guy has a ridiculous amount of family – the complete opposite of you," he added with a nasty laugh. "Like this girl I can see walking some kind of rat around. Do you think I should have a chat with her instead of you?"

Mia.

All the blood drained from Kamran's body. "You stay *away* from her!" he snarled. "This is between you and me, Chaz!"

But Chaz just laughed. "Oh, baby. If you won't come meet me, I'll have to think of something else, won't I? It's not *my* fault you're being stubborn. I bet no one would miss this kid. She's so skinny, and that *thing* she's chasing after…"

"No, I—" Kamran cried, but he didn't know what to do. He didn't want to go with Chaz, but would he really stoop so low as to threaten a teenage girl?

Kamran was pretty sure he knew the answer to that.

Fuck! Of all the times for Lee to leave him...wait. Wait a minute. Had Chaz been watching him, poised for the perfect moment to strike?

Had he gotten one of his guys caught on purpose so that Lee would leave?

Before Kamran could work out what to say, Chaz continued speaking, apparently not done with his threats yet.

"Perhaps you don't give two shits about the kid," he said with a shrug. "I get it. She's a bit too young for even you to fuck. Maybe I could take a visit to some of your other friends?"

He took the phone away from his ear as revulsion rolled through Kamran. He wanted to scream at Chaz for talking about Mia like that, but he was too afraid of making things worse. As Kamran breathed through his nose, trying to get a hold of himself, Chaz finished what he was doing and smiled up at the window as he put the phone to his ear again.

"There you go," Chaz purred. "I just sent you a few little treats. Let me know what you think."

Kamran licked his lips, but he felt he had no choice but to do what he said. He went to the messages that had come through from the unknown number that Chaz was using.

Kamran thought he was going to throw up.

There were several photos, all of his friends. The first few were of Robin, Dair, Jay, Angel, Taylan, and Hudson. They were walking their many dogs together at the park near the lake. There were a few different angles of that. Then there were photos of Swift and Micha putting little Imogen on the school bus at the stop by their house. Elias picking Ben up from the bakery where he worked, leaning over the counter to give him a kiss. And finally, Emery and Scout at Scout's boxing gym, hugging and laughing.

His hand shaking, Kamran put the phone back up to his

head. "Chaz…" he began, his voice catching. But Chaz was the one in charge here.

"I mean, who needs *that* many dogs," he said with a cruel laugh. "They wouldn't miss one or two, surely? And kids, *yuk.* So expensive. And annoying. Or what about those businesses, built from the ground up? So much work. They'd probably be relieved to get the insurance if they burned down. And if someone just *happened* to be inside, well…"

"STOP!" Kamran cried, his chest heaving. He couldn't see straight, but there was no way in hell he was going to let anything happen to his friends or Lee's family. His life wasn't worth that. They were all ten times more worthy than him. He was scared, but he wasn't an idiot.

He was expendable.

Even though…

Even though he just felt like he had something worth living for. Like he'd just seen the light after years in the dark. He didn't want to lose Lee or let him down, but there was no way Kamran would let anyone else get hurt instead of him.

"I'll…I'll come down," he croaked, wiping the tear that escaped from his eye. He turned away, hoping that Chaz hadn't seen. But what did it matter, really?

Chaz had won. Kamran had lost.

"Good boy," Chaz said.

Revulsion surged through Kamran. When Lee said that, Kamran wanted to drop to his knees and beg to be good for him. But from Chaz's lips, it was disgusting. A shiver flurried over his skin, and he swallowed his nausea.

"I'm coming down," he managed to croak out, turning away from the window.

"Excellent," Chaz replied. "Stay on the line now, so I know you can't call Marshall before you get here. And don't even *think* about trying to warn anyone what's happening on your way down. I'm still perfectly capable of ruining someone's day. In fact, I think I'd quite enjoy it."

Kamran screwed his eyes shut, dread welling up inside him. He was completely at Chaz's mercy. He'd been such a fool to think he could flip on him. Chaz might have respected his wish not to get involved in whatever heist he was planning, but Kamran had always known talking to the FBI was a one-way ticket.

He didn't want Chaz to hurt him – or worse – and he definitely didn't want anyone else to get hurt. But alongside the fear of what was about to happen to him, rage was coursing through Kamran. Chaz was going to get away with everything. All that money he'd stolen, the lives he'd ruined. All because Kamran had…

No, actually. Kamran hadn't done anything wrong. In fact, he'd tried to do what was right and noble for once in his life. He'd tried to not be selfish and put the greater good first. Where had that gotten him?

Truly fucked, and not in the good way.

"Are you still there, baby?" Chaz asked in a teasing voice as Kamran hurried down the second flight of stairs.

"Fuck you," he snarled.

Chaz just laughed in response, apparently completely unbothered by Kamran's resistance. Chaz knew he held all the cards, so why would he care?

Kamran kept his head down as he hurried through the house, not making eye contact with anyone, trying to be as invisible as possible. The last thing he wanted to do was to give Chaz the excuse to be cruel to anyone. He grabbed his leather jacket from the cloakroom by the front door, quickly shrugging it on before pressing the phone back up to his ear.

"You're by the car?" he asked, scanning the front lawn and not seeing any sign of Chaz where he'd been previously standing.

"Ready and waiting," Chaz confirmed cheerfully. "I wanted to park it next to your Mustang, but there are so many damn vehicles here. Who are these people? I could make a killing from just a handful of these cars."

Kamran almost spat out that Chaz should stay away from both his and Lee's family's cars, but he didn't want to escalate the situation any more than it already was. So he just marched around the house, heading toward the parking lot. He was pretty sure he heard someone call his name, but he kept his head down and ignored it.

He was probably never going to see these people again, so what did it matter if they thought he was rude?

Oh, fuck. Another wave of terror washed through him. What was he walking into? What was Chaz going to do to him?

His numb feet were on autopilot as they walked him around into the lot. He couldn't let himself dwell on anything because he didn't have a choice. He just had to move forward and protect his friends. They were what mattered. Their lives, their happiness.

He wished his happiness mattered, but that just wasn't the world he lived in.

As his shoes crunched over the gravel and Chaz's red Jaguar came into view, Kamran saw Chaz leaning against it with a shit-eating grin on his face. He waved at Kamran, then hung up the call, meaning Kamran could finally hang up too and slip his phone back into his pocket.

He didn't know what to do. He just needed more time to *think.* But he was still walking toward Chaz like a man walking to the gallows.

"Take your fucking time, sweetheart," Chaz said, shaking his head. "I've got places to be, people to see. Get your ass in the car."

He pushed himself away from the door so he could open

it and slide inside the driver's seat of the cherry-red Jag. This car was one of the reasons Kamran had been drawn to Chaz in the first place. What an idiot he'd been.

Kaman had to cross behind the trunk to get to the passenger side, and he glanced down at the tires, begging the universe for a slow puncture. If he could get Chaz off the road, maybe he could make a run for it…

Wait a minute…

A flash of inspiration struck him like a bolt of lightning, but he had to act fast. Otherwise, Chaz would notice.

Out of habit, he'd still been carrying his keys in his pocket all this week. Without hesitating, he grabbed the bundle from his jeans, then swooped down to wedge the biggest, sturdiest key against the back tire.

The decades' old key to his beloved Mustang.

He glanced one last time at the engraved stallion running free on the head of the key, then stood and continued to walk, hoping Chaz hadn't noticed anything. The key might just fall over. Or it might jam into the rubber and buy Kamran the time he so desperately needed. Either way, he felt like by sacrificing the key, he was losing his car forever.

But would he even get to drive it again if he didn't get away from Chaz? He had no choice. There were more important things at stake.

His heart was racing so fast in his ribcage that he was amazed it didn't burst out of his chest. But Kamran managed to hurry around the car and yank open the door before Chaz looked up, wondering where he was. Probably because Chaz was scowling down at his phone. Kamran didn't ask why. He just counted his lucky stars as he dropped into the leather seat and tugged the seat belt across his body.

"Right," Chaz said loudly as he shoved his phone into the inside pocket of his jacket. He flashed a smile at Kamran that caused his guts to writhe, then turned the key, making the ignition roar to life. "Let's get this show on the road."

He squeezed Kamran's thigh, but Kamran flinched away from him as much as he could in the compact space of the car. Chaz just laughed, reversing out of the parking spot, flinging the Jag around in a quick turn, then speeding out of the Marshall's estate.

Kamran closed his eyes. He wasn't a religious person, but in that moment, he prayed to whoever might be listening that Chaz had rolled over the keys and lodged the Mustang one in the tire.

He wasn't sure what his little stunt might accomplish. If he ran for it, Chaz could still threaten his friends and Lee's family. All he knew was that he just needed a chance to think, to try and find a way out of this before things got messy.

"So," Chaz said, throwing Kamran a smile that didn't reach his eyes. "How are things, baby cakes? Tell me *allll* about your new man and what you've been chatting about."

"I haven't told him anything," Kamran muttered, staring mulishly out the window. "I already explained. We met at the bar and—"

"Yeah, sorry, I don't believe that," said Chaz. His eyes were fixed on the road, but his tone was laced with malice. "Try again, baby."

Kamran swallowed and clenched his fists. "Okay, all right," he snapped, giving up the pretense. "I went to him for help after your guys broke into my place and *trashed* it. I was scared. But I really haven't told him much, just that we used to date and…"

"And?"

The words stuck in his mouth. How could he not incriminate himself? If Chaz knew that Lee knew all about the job Kamran had driven for Chaz…

Well. Why would he let him live?

"God damn it, Amir!" Chaz yelled before Kamran could finish what he'd been saying. "You told him about the First National job! You fucking idiot. Why do you always do this to me? You had no right to do that! *Urgh!*" He slammed his palm against the steering wheel and bared his teeth. "Okay, you know what's gonna happen now? You're going to come back to Seattle with me and pull the job. You *owe* me that. No one can drive like you."

Kamran's breath was ragged. "O-okay," he said. "I'll do it, no problem."

Doing the job gave him more time, just like he wanted. It wasn't game over yet. If he could find a way to talk to Lee, then maybe they could work some way out of this that kept everyone safe and put Chaz behind bars. So long as he had time, he still had a chance.

"I wasn't asking. I was telling," Chaz spat. "What the fuck is wrong with this thing?"

He tugged at the steering wheel, and Kamran's heart leaped. "What's the matter?" he asked, mentally crossing his fingers.

"I don't know. Something feels off. For fuck's sake! I don't have time for this! I'm going to check the damn tires."

Chaz snarled and pulled the car over to the shoulder. It was a relatively quiet road, so Kamran wasn't confident about flagging down another car, but he wasn't sure he wanted to anyway. That could put an innocent passerby in serious danger. But for now, his abduction was being paused, and he just had to play it by ear and be alert for any possible chance he had to escape.

"Of all the…are you fucking kidding me…" Chaz grumbled as he killed the ignition. "Don't fucking *move*," he snarled at Kamran.

Kamran threw his hands up. "Where would I go?" he asked, looking around at all the nowhere they were surrounded by. It was woods or fields, and dusk was starting to fall. He didn't like the odds of running from Chaz on foot, especially when…

Yup. As Chaz got out of the car, he purposefully flashed the handgun he had strapped to his side under his jacket. "Be a good puppy dog and *stay*," he said.

Kamran bit back the snarky retort he was tempted to throw. It wouldn't do him any good to make Chaz any madder. But he suddenly realized that he still had his phone on him, and he reached slowly toward his pocket…

Just as Chaz stuck his head back in the car.

"Yes, it's a fucking flat," he groused. "I can't see from what. The tire must have swallowed that."

Kamran's heart skipped a beat. He hadn't even thought of that. If the distinctive key with the horse on it had been sticking out, Chaz could have easily suspected him. But it seemed like the universe was on his side, after all.

Chaz clicked his fingers at Kamran. "Get out here and help me change the damn tire. Since driving and cars and shit is all you're good for, you can earn your damn keep. I can't *believe* you made me come all the way out here!"

Kamran only hesitated a second, but he wasn't going to argue with that gun. So he gritted his teeth and unclicked his seat belt.

It probably took them around half an hour to swap the tire over to the spare as the daylight faded around them. Chaz continuously barked at Kamran to hurry up without actually helping him and making the job last longer, all the while Kamran's phone was burning in his pocket. Had Lee seen Kamran's flirty message? Had he tried to call him or just messaged back? Was he still miles away in Seattle?

While Chaz was watching him like a hawk, he had no way of knowing.

"Fucking finally," Chaz said, wiping his hands on a cloth,

then throwing it back into the trunk. "You're a pain in my ass, Amir. If you'd just come with my guys the other night, we wouldn't have to be fucking around like this now. Get back in."

Kamran swallowed. His distraction had come and gone, and he was still no better off than he had been. What the hell was he going to do?

Once they were both back in the car and belted up, he looked to Chaz, expecting him to fire up the ignition again. But he just sat there, his hands wrapped around the steering wheel. Kamran opened his mouth to ask what the holdup was, but then he remembered that he actually didn't want to get moving, so he sat patiently waiting for Chaz to move or speak, trying not to let his nerves eat him alive.

"You know what," Chaz eventually said slowly. "I don't like loose ends. I think I'd like to have a little chat with Agent Marshall."

Ice flooded through Kamran. "Chaz..." he said. Begging would only make things worse, he knew, but he wanted to keep Lee *out* of this. He was so ashamed he couldn't bear for Lee to be anywhere near this part of his sordid past. Besides, even though Lee was built like a tank and no doubt was very capable at his job, Chaz was a vicious fucker who didn't play fair.

He turned and cast a shark-like grin at Kamran. "Yes, I think I'd like to see Agent Marshall in the flesh. We're still close enough to this podunk town you've been wasting away in. Call him up. Tell him to come meet you."

Kamran blinked at him. "What...here? By the side of the road?"

Chaz let out an exasperated noise from the back of his throat. "Do I have to think of everything? No, not *here.* Surely, you must know somewhere around here that he can find. Somewhere *quiet.*"

Kamran's blood was rushing through his veins, his pulse thrumming in his ears. "C-Call Lee? But he might still be in Seattle."

Chaz raised his eyebrows, looking dangerous. "Do I need to repeat myself?"

"Somewhere quiet," Kamran repeated, nodding even though inside he was screaming. Chaz was asking Kamran to lure Lee into a trap. That much was obvious. He probably didn't want to even talk to Lee. He was probably just planning on blowing his head off.

So Kamran needed to think of a place that Lee knew inside and out. Somewhere quiet...

"There's an ice rink that's closed this week for renovations," he said, managing not to stutter. "He'll know it. The parking lot is big."

Chaz laughed, an awful, chilling sound. "Look how quickly you gave him up to save your own skin. I almost feel sorry for the sap. Fine, call him. Tell him you got a cab, and you have a surprise for him, but he has to hurry up and meet you there."

His hands shaking, Kamran finally retrieved his phone from his jacket pocket. Sure enough, he had several missed calls and text messages, but he ignored them, just going straight to calling Lee, his heart in his throat.

He hoped he'd live to see Lee forgive him.

LEE

As HE'D BEEN INTO THE OFFICE, LEE ALREADY HAD HIS BADGE and gun on him, so he was ready to go. But somewhere between running out of the front door and reaching his Jeep he realized he had absolutely no idea where to start looking for Kamran, and time was of the essence.

He could try his home, but Lee was pretty sure Kamran would know not to go there in case Bolt had someone watching it. The same with Aquarium. So what else could he try? His car was still sitting next to Lee's, so it sounded like Mia had been right about the red Jag. Was that one of Chaz's cars? Lee had looked over the case files so many times over the years, it all blended together. He honestly couldn't remember.

Just before he got to his car, he paused to look at something glinting in the evening sunlight, nestled between the stones covering the drive and parking lot. It looked like a couple of house keys and the twisted ring that presumably had held them together before. He frowned, wondering where they had come from and if they were relevant. But he didn't have the time to ponder. So he just stored the information away for later in case it became pertinent.

He unlocked his car and dropped into the driver's seat, chewing his lower lip. He couldn't let fear cloud his judgment, but unlike any other case he'd ever worked on, this was deeply personal. What if Kamran was in trouble, counting on Lee to save him, and he didn't get there in time?

No. He couldn't think like that. It was counter intuitive. What other options did he have?

The obvious starting place was to try calling him again, but when it went to voicemail, Lee began research 101 and started checking his social media. Kamran didn't have a Twitter, and his Instagram was pretty sparse, until Lee realized that was probably an account set up by *his* tech guy to support the NASCAR lie.

Guilt threatened to creep in again, but Lee shoved it away. Gamma had said none of the lying mattered, only Kamran's safety, and she was right. So Lee shook the feeling off and tried Kamran's Facebook next. As expected, almost none of it was public. The two of them hadn't connected on the site yet because they hadn't had any reason to, so Lee couldn't see any posts that might be helpful.

He was about to close that app and call his tech people again to see if they could do a deeper search into Kamran's online presence when he spotted the 'friends you have in common' section. He blinked, not sure he was seeing things right. He'd have assumed that he and Kamran couldn't possibly have anyone they knew in common, but there it was, clear as day.

Swift Coal.

Kamran was friends with Lee's old football buddy? How could that possibly be? Was it a casual acquaintance, or were they actually friends?

There was only one way to find out.

Hoping that his number hadn't changed after all this time, Lee quickly found the right contact details and hit the call button. It started to ring, so that was a good sign. He gripped the steering wheel with his free hand and held his breath.

The dial tone stopped, and there was a pause before anyone spoke. "Lee Marshall?"

Lee exhaled and gripped the wheel harder. "Swift Coal? That you?"

"Yeah," said Swift, sounding completely baffled. Lee couldn't say he blamed him. It had to have been fifteen years or so since they'd actually seen each other. "Damn, it's been a while. How's it been? Is everything okay?"

"I'm actually calling on official FBI business," Lee admitted. "And there might not be much time to explain. But do you know Kamran Amir?"

"Kamran?" Swift repeated. It sounded like there were people talking in the background, but then maybe Swift moved because it seemed to get quieter. "Yeah, I know Kamran. What's going on. Is he okay?"

Right. It wasn't actually a lead, but the fact that Swift *did* know Kamran wasn't a dead end either. Lee rubbed his eyes and tried to keep his heart rate steady. "I can't go into too many details, but I was wondering if you'd heard from him. I need to find him, and he's not picking up his phone."

Swift paused. "I haven't, no. But he's much better friends with some of the other guys. He would have been more likely to message Scout or Emery. Lee, what's going on. How the hell do you know Kamran?"

"I'll explain everything, I promise," said Lee clinging on to hope. "But for now, could you give me their numbers?"

Another pause. "I know you said it's urgent, but they're actually on their way over here now. The whole gang is. You could try calling them, but they might be driving. Or you could wait until everyone arrives, and I can put you on speaker. That way you can see if anyone else has heard from him. I know they'd want to help."

It was stupid – there were so many more pressing issues and uncertainties in that moment – but Lee's eyes pricked with tears. Honestly, the way Kamran had told it, he didn't have any friends or anyone who cared about him. Yet Swift was saying there was a whole group of people who would be worried for Kamran's well-being?

Why wasn't he surprised? Kamran probably didn't even realize that.

Lee cleared his throat. "Hang on. Does that mean you live in Pine Cove?"

"Well, actually, we're meeting at my parents' house," Swift explained. "But yeah, we're in Pine Cove."

"So am I," Lee said, starting the ignition. "Send me the address. I'll be there ASAP and ask my questions in person. If that's okay?"

Swift scoffed. "Of course it is. I'll send it right now. See you soon."

He hung up without ceremony, and before Lee had reversed his Jeep out of the parking slot, his phone pinged with a message. Within seconds, he had the address programmed in, and his ETA was showing as less than fifteen minutes.

He floored it.

<hr />

LEE WAS sure he'd visited Swift's place when they'd been at high school, but it was so long ago he couldn't say the Coal family home seemed familiar as he pulled up to a halt at the end of the driveway. It was a three-story home in a log cabin style surrounded by pine trees with several cars parked up in front. They were having quite a gathering for a Wednesday night, but Lee wasn't going to question it if there was any chance that someone might have an inkling as to where Kamran had gone.

He knocked on the door and stood back on the front porch, waiting for someone to greet him. The sound of music and voices drifted faintly through the air, and he wondered if people were gathered around the back. The house was open around the sides, so he was just considering going around the back to find Swift when the front door swung inward.

A small girl of about six or seven looked up at him. She frowned as she pushed a pair of sparkly glasses up her nose. "Who are you?" she asked confidently.

"Imogen, that's not polite," a voice cried. A second later, a slight man with light brown skin, dark curly hair, and tattoos decorating his forearms appeared, wrapping his arm protectively around the girl's body. "Hi, sorry. You must be Lee?" the guy said, offering out his hand. "I'm Micha. Swift said you were coming to talk about Kamran or something?"

"That's right," said Lee, shaking Micha's hand. "FBI Agent Lee Marshall. I'd appreciate any help in locating Kamran that you can offer." *As fast as possible before my heart breaks,* he added mentally.

"Kamran?" Imogen said with a frown. "Are you arresting him?"

"No, sweetie," said Micha quickly, but then he glanced at Lee. "You're not, are you?"

"Absolutely not," said Lee emphatically. He smiled at the little girl. He kind of loved how protective she was over Lee's man. "I want to keep him safe, in fact. And your daddy's friend, Swift, said he might be able to help me."

Imogen laughed and pointed at the guy hugging her. "Silly. Swift *is* my daddy. Micha is my papa."

Lee blinked as he took a second to realize what that meant. "Oh," he finally said in surprise. "Right! Excellent."

He beamed at Micha. Lee really hadn't been paying attention to social media if Swift Coal had gone and gotten a male partner and a daughter right under his nose. That was kind of crazy but in a good way.

He remembered his urgency and got back to business. "May I come in?"

"Sure, sure," said Micha, gently pulling Imogen back with him and waving Lee in. "Everyone's out back. Our two friends are now officially a couple after a really long time of being idiots, so we're having this impromptu party," he explained, shutting the front door. "It's basically an excuse to tease them. I'd offer you a drink or something, but I guess you need to get going?"

"I need to find Kamran," Lee agreed as he followed Micha and Imogen through the house. "But thank you. That's kind of you."

"Imogen, hon, why don't you go play with your toys in the front room while the grownups talk, okay?"

She looked like she was going to put up a fight, but then she shoved her glasses up her nose and nodded once. "Okay. But will you come get me if something important happens?"

Micha smiled fondly at her. "I promise."

She narrowed her eyes for a second, then scampered off. "It was nice to meet you, Mr. Agent Lee!"

Lee smiled at her retreating form, then followed Micha through the kitchen, which was littered with the evidence of a lot of side dishes being made.

As he stepped outside, a brief but strong image flashed through his mind, picturing what it would be like if he were here with Kamran as his boyfriend to have fun for the evening. There were over a dozen people around a barbecue, all holding drinks, chatting, and eating snacks. There were bunting and fairy lights hanging from the nearby trees, and pop music was playing from a Bluetooth speaker. It all felt ridiculously cozy and welcoming, very different from the reception party at Lee's parents' house on Friday night.

"Lee!" a voice cried, pulling his attention. A muscular blond guy jogged over to him, and Lee realized a second later it was Swift.

"Jesus, man," he said as they embraced, clapping each other on the back. "You grew up!"

"So did you," said Swift as they pulled apart. "Wow. And the FBI? When did that happen?"

"A while ago," he admitted as he scanned the crowd. "So, Kamran isn't here, is he?" It was a faint hope, but Lee had clung to it. However, Swift shook his head. Micha would have said something at the front door anyway, but Lee had needed to check.

"We haven't heard from him in days," said a redheaded guy.

"Is everything okay?" asked a dark-haired guy who looked strikingly similar to the redhead. Wait – they had to be Robin and Jay, Swift's younger twin brothers. Lee remembered them being in middle school. Damn.

"Whoa – it's *you!*" another voice cried. Lee turned around to see a slim Asian guy in a crop top with 'Sounds gay, I'm in' written in shimmery rainbow-colored letters on it. He was dragging a much bigger guy behind him...wait...

"You're from the bar," Lee said, his heart leaping. It was Glitter and Beefcake. "I'm Agent Lee Marshall. I'm looking for your friend Kamran Amir. You pointed him out to me in Aquarium on Friday night."

"Emery," said Glitter, pointing to himself, "and Scout. I know we did." He turned to the rest of the group. "You know how I said that Kamran *might* have met a guy? Well...what I meant was that he definitely did. This guy."

He waved his hand up and down Lee like he was a prize in a game show.

A woman with black curly hair frowned at him. She was holding hands with another woman with a pixie-cut. It kind of seemed to Lee like everyone was coupled up and either standing close to or holding hands with someone.

Had Kamran felt left out? Was that why he hadn't talked about these people at all?

"I'm confused," said the black-haired woman. "Are you an FBI agent or Kamran's hookup?"

"Uh…both, kinda," he admitted, deciding not to beat around the bush. "He's in trouble I was protecting him. Things happened between us—"

"Aww, yeah," said Emery doing a little dance, but Lee pressed on.

"However, he left my parents' home just now and I don't know why he would have done that or where he could have gone. I'm worried somebody might be trying to coerce him."

"What, Kamran?" the blond guy standing beside Jay asked, sounding confused. "Are you talking about the protestors from the movie set? Because I thought that business was all taken care of?"

Lee shook his head. "I can't discuss my case, but it's nothing to do with a movie set. I am concerned that it's serious. Urgent. Have any of you heard from him?"

The group collectively shook their heads.

"Shall we post in the group chat?" the short-haired woman asked.

"I can call him," Emery offered.

"I could try Facebook Messenger," the guy who'd asked about the movie set asked.

Lee nodded at them all. "I've tried calling, but there's a chance he might respond to someone else if…" *If this is personal and Kamran is hiding from* me.

No. Stop it. That might make sense if Kamran had left in his own car, but that didn't explain the red Jaguar. Had a different friend picked him up, maybe? Why else would he leave voluntarily with someone else?

He was getting nowhere going around in circles. He needed a lead.

He cleared his throat. "I'd appreciate trying from all angles," he said instead. "Do you know of anywhere he might go to think that I could try looking? Anywhere that's special to him?"

"His car," said one of the other guests with short, dark hair. A Pomeranian dog was sitting by his feet, perfectly well behaved while they were all talking.

Lee shook his head. "It's still at my parents' house."

"Aquarium or his house?" suggested Robin.

"No, I don't think so," said Lee without explaining.

"My bakery's shut for the day," another smaller guy told Lee. "He sometimes swings by to see what we have left at a discount, but I didn't see him before I closed earlier."

"Do you think he's really in danger?" Micha asked, the concern clear in his voice.

Lee nodded and held up his hand. "I'm sure everything's fine," he said in his practiced Dealing-With-The-Public voice. "But the sooner I find him, the sooner I can put everyone's minds at ease."

The black-haired woman narrowed her eyes at him. She seemed kind of intense. Was she Swift's scary goth sister, Ava, perhaps? "You just said you were worried and that it was urgent. Which is it?"

"Uhh…"

Lee was saved from answering by his phone ringing. He snatched it from his pocket at lightning speed, relief crashing over him like a tidal wave as he saw the caller ID.

"It's Kamran," he said, unable to stop the catch in his voice or the grin that split his face. The group around him reacted with smiles and happy gasps as he hit the answer button and turned away, walking a little apart from them as he answered. "Kamran! Are you okay? I was worried."

"Hey, baby. I'm fine. I'm so sorry I scared you."

Lee opened his mouth to say it was fine when his brain caught up with what Kamran had just said.

Baby?

Red flags sprang up all over Lee's mind. Kamran had made his feelings very clear on that word. He sounded cheerful, but was something seriously wrong? Was he trying to tell Lee something?

He needed to test it.

"That's okay, baby," he said, doing his best to still sound relieved. "I was just worried. I came back, and you weren't there."

"I know, baby," Kamran said without pausing in the slightest. Right. Something was definitely wrong. "I got carried away and lost track of time. I'm so sorry. I have a little surprise for you, though. Can you come meet me?"

Lee licked his lips. If Kamran was calling him 'baby' and using his flirty voice, then someone might be listening in. Someone who might need convincing that Lee didn't suspect a thing was up.

"A *sexy* surprise, baby?" he asked with a little growl in his voice.

Kamran hummed. "You'll just have to find out, won't you? Can you come to The Lodge? I got a cab here, so you won't see my car. But I'll be waiting outside. I'm all ready for you."

Goddamn it. Despite the seriousness of the situation, Kamran's sultry voice saying those things still made Lee's cock perk up. *Not now,* he told it.

"I'll get there right away," he promised, hoping Kamran knew exactly what he meant. "See you soon, baby."

"Can't wait," Kamran promised.

Then the call went dead.

"Where was he?" Emery demanded as Lee turned back to the group of friends, who had apparently all been watching him.

"What's going on?" Film Set Guy asked.

"Is he okay?" added Pixie Hair.

Lee shook his head. "I think he's in trouble. He's asked me to meet him at The Lodge, but I suspect it might be a trap."

"The ice rink?" said Ava. "But it's closed while they swap over for the season."

"I know," Lee agreed, checking his watch. "Okay, I'm going to go—"

"Even though you know it's a trap?" clarified the guy beside Robin. A quick glance at his ink suggested Marine to Lee.

Lee nodded. "I'll get a look at the situation, and then if I think it's safe, I'll call local law enforcement. But I don't want to involve them without knowing what they're walking into first. I don't want to risk any casualties."

"You think it's that serious?" asked Scout.

Lee shook his head. "I won't know until I get there. If you don't hear from me in half an hour, call 911. I might need backup. But hopefully it won't come to that." He checked the time on his phone. It had already been a couple of minutes since Kamran had called. "I have to go. Thank you, everyone, for your help."

"Bring Kamran back safe to us," Emery called out, but Lee was already running around the side of the house back to his Jeep.

The drive seemed to take forever. Every time he glanced at the dashboard clock, it was as if each minute was lasting five. But he drove slightly faster than the speed limit allowed, hoping no unsuspecting local cop pulled him over. He would have put his emergency light on, but he didn't want to alert Bolt that he knew anything was wrong.

He assumed it was Bolt, or more of his men, perhaps. Was the rest of the crew back in Seattle, or was there a Pine Cove contingent still hanging around, waiting to pounce on Kamran? God *damn* it. *Why* had Kamran ever left the safety of the house?

There was no point dwelling on that now. Lee had to focus. The Lodge would be relatively busy during the day with staff changing over some of the décor and a few of the seasonal stalls, but in the evenings, he was pretty sure the location would be dead. Did Kamran know that? Had he picked to meet there for that reason? Or did he even remember that the place was shut down for the week?

As Lee pulled into the empty parking lot, he only had questions, no answers. Darkness had fallen, and the gray concrete was illuminated by the streetlamps evenly placed throughout the parking spaces. On the front steps stood a lone figure, silhouetted against the streetlamps. They waved when Lee came to a halt about twenty feet away.

Was it Kamran? Where was Bolt? It didn't seem like there were a couple of dozen mobsters ready to pounce, so Lee reached for his phone, making the decision to call the local detective who Duke had given him the number for.

There was a knock at his window.

Lee looked up to see the gun pointed at his face. Holding that gun was Charles Bolt. Bolt wagged his finger. *Uh-uh.* Then he pointed to Lee's phone. Lee weighed up his options before placing the phone on the passenger seat. Bolt pointed at Lee's chest.

Fuck it.

Lee didn't know if there was someone with a gun also pointed at Kamran's head, so he didn't risk any funny business. He carefully unholstered his gun, then laid it beside his phone.

A quick glance at the time told him that he still had a little over ten minutes before Kamran's friends would consider calling the police, and that didn't factor in how long it would take for any units to respond.

He was almost certainly screwed, but that wasn't actually the thought that broke his heart as he slowly reached for the car door.

It was entirely possible that he'd just let Kamran down in the worst possible way, and if that were the case, he'd never forgive himself for as long as he lived.

However long – or short – that time might be.

18

KAMRAN

"Get out of the car," Kamran urged, his pulse going through the roof. "C'mon, Lee. Chaz is *right there!* What are you waiting for?"

But he was obviously waiting for something. Kamran couldn't see exactly what he was doing from this distance, but the headlights were still on, and the engine was idling. Kamran had already waved. He didn't know what else he was allowed to do.

He knew what he *wanted* to do. He wanted to break into a sprint, run to the Jeep, throw himself inside, kiss Lee senseless, then drive far, far away from Chaz and his bullshit. Well, maybe drive, then kiss. Because of all the guns. He definitely knew there would be kissing involved in any case.

Except he couldn't do any of that. Because apparently Kamran had been smart to run from his apartment and never go back. The three goons who had fucked up his place, and would have no doubt fucked him up too, hadn't left town. How did he know?

Because two of them currently had their guns trained on Kamran, and Cigarette Breath was somewhere pointing his piece at Lee. Not that Lee really needed the extra coverage, not when Chaz now had his gun pointed right at Lee's head.

A whimper escaped Kamran's throat as he watched Lee get out of the now dark and silent Jeep with his hands up. His legs felt like Jell-O as he watched on helplessly. He'd thought he'd been so clever calling Lee 'baby' in their call, and when Lee had called him it back...well, not only had Kamran really thought that Lee had understood the code, but god damn it, Kamran had been so comforted. From Lee's mouth, that word had felt like a warm, heavy blanket. For a minute, he'd actually hoped that Lee was going to come to his rescue.

But this was a trap after all, and they were outnumbered, no matter what. It wasn't like Lee's FBI buddies were going to click their heels three times and magically appear from Seattle.

No. They were outgunned and on their own.

But...at least they were together.

Fuck! No, that was so selfish. What the fuck was wrong with him? He didn't want Lee here, where he was undoubtedly going to get hurt! But Kamran was a selfish creature, and now that they'd fallen mercy to Chaz's devious scheme, he couldn't help but yearn for Lee to hold him one last time, to kiss him and...

And to tell him he loved him.

That was fucking nuts, but as he watched Chaz frisking Lee before starting to march him over the parking lot, Kamran couldn't help himself.

He was pretty sure he was in love with Lee. His heart ached like a wounded animal. It throbbed with pain at the thought of them being torn apart. It was as if Lee was the first person to really see Kamran for who he was and to not only accept that but also to cherish him for it.

And now Kamran was going to lose it all.

There were no words for how much he hated Chaz Bolt in that moment. How many ways could one person ruin another person's life?

But without Chaz, Lee would have never walked into Aquarium that night…

Urgh. Kamran was just angry at the whole universe and all the fuckery that had led to him standing on these steps, watching as Lee and Chaz approached.

"Look who I found," Chaz announced triumphantly, shoving Lee toward where Kamran was standing. Lee had his hands up with a mulish expression on his face. Chaz smirked. "Well done, Kamran. Your little charade worked like a charm in getting him here."

"No, I—!" Kamran spluttered desperately, but Lee shook his head.

"I knew you tried to warn me," he said gently, looking Kamran in the eye. "I was just stupid thinking I could handle the situation by myself."

Kamran's heart threatened to break. Lee had known it was a trap, and he'd come anyway?

For Kamran?

Also for the case he'd been working on for years. But as Kamran looked back into his lover's eyes, he couldn't help but feel like that wasn't it.

Lee had come for *him.*

At least if this really was the end, Kamran would know that there was someone on this godforsaken planet who gave a damn about him.

"I'm sorry?" said Chaz, his cheerful tone dangerous. "Tried to warn him how? Are you fucking with me, Kamran? Did you forget who's in charge here?"

Kamran glared at him. "Well, it didn't work, did it? And you're the one with the gun, so no, I didn't forget."

"No, it didn't work," Chaz agreed with a smirk, shoving

the gun into Lee's back to make him stand beside Kamran on the steps of The Lodge. To think – the last time they'd been here had been such a joyous day. "Although Kamran is a champion dick-sucker. I'd probably be thinking with my downstairs brain if I didn't now know what a fucking slut he is—"

He barely got the last word out before Lee's fist cracked against his jaw, the noise ringing through the night. Kamran gasped and jolted backward, but Lee was already stepping away with his hands raised. Probably because the three goons had materialized out of the darkness and all had their guns aimed at Lee and Kamran.

"Motherfucker," Chaz growled, spitting out a glob of blood onto the asphalt. Then he shook his head and waved his own gun. "It's cool," he told his men. "I'll give him one for free. For now." He rubbed his thumb against his bleeding lip. "But don't think I won't remember that later. Now talk, Marshall."

Lee glanced at Kamran, then back to Chaz. "What do you want to know?"

Kamran bit his lip, wishing he could telepathically communicate with him. But they were probably in trouble, no matter what. Lee was an agent on Chaz's case, and here Chaz was threatening him with a gun. There was no going back from that.

"Oh, *don't* fuck around with me, okay?" Chaz snapped, waving the gun haphazardly, making Kamran's insides turn to liquid. "It's *his* pants you're trying to get into, not mine. What's been the pillow talk, hmm? I want to hear from your lips what you *think* you know about me and anything…illegal or whatever."

"You mean like holding people at gunpoint?" Lee asked with a raised eyebrow.

"I hate to break it to you, Chaz," Kamran added hotly,

emboldened by Lee's presence, "but we had more important things to do in bed than talk about *you.*"

"Fine," said Chaz coldly. He leveled his gun right at Kamran's face. Kamran stopped breathing. "Tell me what you know, or I start using this ho as target practice."

"If you harm *one* hair on him—" Lee snarled, sounding like a savage beast.

"You'll what?" Chaz demanded with his cruel laugh. "Tell me off? I'm the one with the firepower here, so you'd better just—"

The police siren cut through the night. Kamran flinched, swinging his head around to see three sets of flashing lights hurtling toward them across the parking lot.

Lee was trained for this, though. As Kamran was still gasping, adrenaline flushing through his system, Lee used the split second of distraction to somehow snatch Chaz's gun from him. His free hand grabbed Kamran's T-shirt and hauled him behind Lee, the gun now firmly pointed at Chaz's face.

"Hold fire!" Chaz yelled at his goons. His hands were up and his eyes wide. A vicious wave of triumph crashed through Kamran, but it didn't last.

"Police! Nobody move!" someone bellowed over the wailing sirens.

A shot exploded through the night. Kamran couldn't tell from whose gun. All he knew was his ears were suddenly ringing as more shots fired and Chaz dove behind the other side of the steps for cover. Lee was yanking Kamran back toward the front door of The Lodge, shouting something that Kamran couldn't make out.

There were more sirens, more gunshots, and the sound of breaking glass that brought with it the wail of an alarm system. Kamran's breathing and heartbeat seemed loudest of all, though, drowning out everything else. He stumbled as

Lee pulled him inside the darkened building through the broken, open door. Everything looked eerie from being bathed in emergency red lighting.

"Come on," Lee urged as voices followed them. Kamran ran by Lee's side as they sprinted past several of the closed food and craft stalls, footsteps following them not far behind.

Lee suddenly pulled them down into the seated area where Joy had been watching them all skate the other day. The partition gave them some cover, and sure enough, Kamran heard a couple of pairs of feet racing past. Mercifully, the alarm stopped. His ears appreciated it, but Kamran didn't know if it being silenced was a good thing or bad.

"Are you hurt?" Lee asked in an urgent whisper. He began patting Kamran down with his free hand, but Kamran grabbed it with both his hands, clutching it to his chest as tears sprung into his eyes.

"I'm fine," he croaked, shaking his head. "I can't believe you came for me."

Lee's gaze suddenly softened in the dim light. He pulled his hand from between Kamran's and cupped the side of his cheek with it. "Of *course* I came for you. I was so scared when I realized you'd left the house. But, sweetheart, why would you leave when you knew Chaz was looking for you?"

A sob threatened to bubble up through Kamran's chest. "I'm sorry," he hissed, blinking back tears and placing his hand over Lee's. "I'm so sorry, I didn't want to leave, but I just didn't know what to do! He threatened my friends – he had photos of them – he threatened *Mia!* He said I had to come out. I didn't want to, but—"

The rest of his words were lost as Lee yanked him into a bone- crushing hug, rubbing his back fiercely. 'It's okay," he said urgently. "I knew there had to be a reason. You didn't do anything wrong. Of course you wanted to protect your friends and…and thank you for protecting my family, too. You must have been so scared, sweetheart. I just wish I'd never left you alone."

Kamran choked back a sob. He had been scared out of his mind. Relief that Lee didn't blame him washed over him. More than that, though, he cared that Kamran had been afraid. Kamran would have hoped he would, but having it confirmed threatened to break something in him. He swallowed it down. They weren't out of the woods yet.

"You're here now," Kamran said, meaning it. And before anything else could transpire, he grabbed either side of Lee's face and crashed their mouths together in a searing hot kiss. There. Now if anything dire happened, Kamran had gotten his wish. Lee had held him and kissed him one last time.

Except it wasn't *enough,* god damn it! Kamran was just as selfish as ever, and he wanted everything from Lee!

That meant staying alive.

Reluctantly, he broke the kiss. "We need to get out of here," he whispered, staring into Lee's ocean-like eyes.

Lee nodded, pressing one more quick kiss to Kamran's lips. "Stay down," he rasped.

But Kamran shook his head. "Don't leave me," he begged. *Not again. Not ever.*

Lee gave him a smoldering gaze. "Never," he growled, giving him another kiss. "But I need to help the local PD and get you to safety. Stay here, and I'll come back, I swear."

Was it crazy that Kamran trusted Lee with his life already? Maybe. But he did.

"Okay," he said, nodding and pushing Lee slightly to encourage him to go. "Be safe."

"I will," Lee promised.

"Wait!" Kamran squeaked before he could leave like Kamran had just told him to. They were going to get out of here – *alive* – but just in case something happened, Lee needed to know how Kamran felt.

How he'd never felt about anyone before.

"I – I love you," he croaked.

Lee's entire body sagged as he beamed at Kamran. "I love you, too, sweetheart," he said, making Kamran's heart leap, despite already thumping so hard in his chest from fear. "I really do love you."

He leaned in and kissed Kamran. It only lasted a matter of moments, but the heat of it promised *much* longer than that.

"Don't move. Stay safe," Lee murmured, rubbing his thumb against Kamran's jaw, their gazes locked. "I'll be back for you soon."

Kamran nodded, trusting Lee completely.

A few seconds after Lee vanished from the seating area, Kamran became painfully aware of all the sounds around him, or rather, the lack of. There were muffled noises that he guessed were from outside, but he couldn't really tell what they were. It felt like all the shouting and gunfire had ceased for now.

What did that mean? Had the local PD caught Chaz and his guys? Or had Chaz and the others shot their way out like Butch Cassidy and the Sundance Kid? Kamran squeezed his eyes shut and bit his knuckle, praying that no one good had gotten hurt. He didn't give a shit about Chaz or his goons, but if the cops got shot, it would be Kamran's fault.

And if *Lee* got hurt...

No, that didn't bear thinking about.

In the moments of relative calmness that followed, Kamran realized he wasn't sure how the police had known to show up, but he was just glad they had. Now Chaz was the one who was outnumbered and outgunned, and Kamran prayed to whoever might be listening that they would all make it out unscathed.

"There you are."

Kamran snapped his head as Chaz rounded the corner into the seating area, his gun pointed at Kamran's chest once again.

"Fuck!" Kamran screamed. He grabbed the nearest chair, hurtling it toward Chaz as a shot exploded through the quietness of the lodge. He had no idea where it hit, other than not his body. He offered a quick moment of thanks to the universe as he ran in a crouch, upturning tables and chairs behind him as he went, but Chaz tried to shoot him *again.* He needed a wall between them.

He didn't think. He just vaulted over the partition.

Onto the ice.

"Shit!" he hissed. He might have had a wall between him and Chaz for a second, but as soon as Chaz aimed his gun over the wall, Kamran was a sitting duck, completely exposed on the rink.

He pushed himself to his feet, wishing he had his skates on, but he'd have to make do. He burst into a run, heading for the enclosed foliage in the middle. Thank fuck it wasn't all ice like a normal rink, but it was still ten feet away, and Chaz was right behind him.

"You've ruined *everything!*" Chaz yelled, another shot cracking through the air and ricocheting off the slippery ice. "Why couldn't you have just done what you were told?"

As he dove into the fake pine trees and landed on the wood chips, Kamran heard more people yelling. He rolled and tried to scramble to his feet. The trees weren't very dense, but he'd rather have them between him and Chaz than nothing. Except Chaz was crazed, flinging himself onto the ice, waving his gun around, and he flailed like Bambi trying to stand upright.

"Why didn't you just do the job?" Chaz screamed.

"Why didn't you just leave me alone?" Kamran yelled back

as he ran through the trees. "You fucking dumbass! In fact, you know what? *You're* the one who decided bank robbery was an exciting career choice. That's *all* on you, not me!"

"Shut up!"

Kamran couldn't tell where Chaz was behind him, but Kamran had reached the other side of the fake woods and prepared himself to launch himself back onto the ice. Except that a shot cracked through the air, sending chips of ice flying right where Kamran had been about to put his feet.

He jumped backward, his arms pinwheeling. *Fuck.* He snapped his head around, eyes darting back and forth, but he couldn't see where the goon was. He couldn't see anyone. Where were Lee and the cops? Was he all alone?

Had Lee left him after all?

He ran to the other side of the fake forest island, but he couldn't see who was lurking in the gloom, ready to take a crack at him as soon as he stepped onto the ice that illuminated him under the emergency lighting. He'd stranded himself on this damn patch of woodland, and it was only a matter of time before Chaz and the others honed in on him.

Speaking of Chaz…

Kamran spun around, just in time to see him lunge forward, swinging the butt of his gun at Kamran's head.

Thank fuck for small mercies. He had to be out of bullets.

That didn't mean he wasn't still dangerous.

He missed Kamran's head by inches as Kamran dodged and threw himself out of the way, grabbing onto the nearest fake tree. Thankfully, it was bolted into the floor and didn't just fall over as he used it to propel himself away from Chaz. But Chaz was obviously way more accustomed to scrapping than Kamran was and recovered quickly, lurching after him.

"Get *back* here!" he shouted.

"No, thank you!" Kamran replied.

He hopped over a log and decided to try and make a

break for it back the way he came. But he couldn't see shit among the trees in this creepy red lighting. Without warning, his foot caught on something – a fake root, an electricity cable, who knew – and went crashing into the ground. He tasted blood as he groaned, attempting to make his limbs move the way he wanted and get back up, but it was as if he'd turned to Jell-O all over.

Until Chaz grabbed him by the scruff of his neck and hauled him up to his knees. Then he remembered just how much he was made of flesh and bone.

"You! Asshole!" Chaz shrieked, punctuating each word with a fist to Kamran's face. Pain exploded everywhere as he tried to slap and scratch against Chaz's arms, scrambling to get free. But Chaz's grip was like a vise. "Ruined! Everything!"

"Fuck you!" Kamran screamed right back. *"Lee! Help me!"*

Chaz laughed. "Nobody's coming to save you, Kamran. You're nothing. I was the only one who wanted you, and you threw it all back in my face." He shoved Kamran back onto the ground, managing to straddle him before Kamran could scramble away.

Then he wrapped his hands around Kamran's throat.

"No one will even miss you," Chaz whispered with an evil glint in his eye. Kamran coughed and pulled as hard as he could against his wrists, but his cold fingers weren't budging.

His vision started spotting.

"No one will even *remember* you," Chaz purred, looking utterly wild. "You should have stuck with me, baby. I would have taken you places. Now you're going *nowhere.* I was the best thing to ever happen to your pathetic little life, and now I'm going to snuff it out like a candle—"

Kamran didn't know what happened. He just knew that suddenly he could breathe and was gasping for air, rubbing his neck to get the blood flowing back through it. He wheezed and rolled onto his front, not caring that bark chips and fake dirt pressed against his cheek.

Chaz was nowhere to be seen.

But Kamran could hear something.

He coughed and sputtered but managed to get back on his knees, looking around to see where Chaz had gone and what the hell was going on.

He didn't have to look far.

It was Lee. He hadn't abandoned Kamran. Of course he hadn't. He'd dragged Chaz onto the ice, a trail of blood smeared on the luminescent surface from Chaz's mouth. He appeared dozy as Lee's massive bulk pinned him down and cuffed him.

"You have the right to remain fucking *silent*," he was saying, a look of fury on his face that Kamran had never seen before. "But anything you do or say can and *will* be used against you in a court of law, you piece of *shit.*"

"Okay, all right!" a cheerful voice rang out. Kamran crawled forward and slumped at the edge of the fake woodland, looking at the slim woman in her mid-forties waving at Lee with her detective's badge. "I think I can take it from here, Agent Marshall. Want to make sure those Miranda rights are read properly with – you know – a little less color, perhaps."

Holy fuck. It was that detective who had arrived in the nick of time to help with that Scout and Emery business a couple of years ago. Kamran wouldn't have thought it could be possible to be more relieved to see her than he had been then, but that was before he thought the man of *his* dreams might die.

There would be no dying today, motherfuckers.

The detective looked down at the ice, then at her heeled boots, then back at the couple of officers behind her. "Uh, okay, boys. Go do the thing." She waved at the ice that she was clearly not going to step on.

They nodded at her and carefully began making their way across the rink. Lee seemed to have been in a trance, not taking his eyes off Chaz until the officers physically reached him. Then he blinked and looked around.

"Detective Padilla?" he asked, looking at the chick with the ponytail.

She saluted him. "Hi, Agent Marshall. Thank you so much for bringing this shit show to my town. It's not like I have a life or anything." She sighed. "That's a dirty lie. This job is my life."

"How did you know to come here?" he asked, sounding bewildered.

What, so – Lee *hadn't* called her?

Padilla scoffed as another officer appeared out of thin air and pressed a huge steaming takeout coffee into her hand. She winked at him, then flicked her gaze back to Lee. "Because I got a call saying you'd told your friends to wait half an hour, but they worked out that was a really *dumb* idea and called me right away. My personal cell," she added with a raised eyebrow. "You were lucky I wasn't on a date."

"A date? You, boss?" one of the officers joked. Kamran laughed, but then he *almost* felt bad at the look the Padilla shot the cop.

Anyway, what friends? Was Padilla talking about Lee's family?

"Ah, speaking of which," said Padilla. She sighed as she looked over her shoulder, then took a large sip of coffee. "Why is everywhere I go, it's *always* you guys? Oh!"

The proper lighting suddenly came on, and Kamran blinked as he looked around from his vantage point perched at the edge of the fake woodland. His heart leaped as he realized that more officers were marching all three of Chaz's goons forward in handcuffs toward the door, but then he did a double take when he realized his friends – literally *all* his friends – were pushing past them, coming the other way so they could get inside The Lodge.

"Kamran!" Emery yelled, waving like a maniac as he led the throng. "They finally let us in! Are you *okay?*"

Kamran's mouth dropped as he watched Emery and Scout run right onto the ice. Behind them were Jay and Angel, looking frantic. But also Robin and Dair, Ben and Elias, Taylan and Hudson, and Ava and Peyton. No Swift and Micha, but they'd probably had to stay home with Imogen. Aside from that, though, Kamran was looking at pretty much all the people he cared about in Pine Cove.

"W-what…what are you all doing here?" Kamran managed to stammer.

He jumped as an arm slipped around his waist. Somehow, Lee had been able to get from the ice to Kamran's side without him noticing. He pressed a kiss to Kamran's temple, and Kamran melted against him like ice cream on a warm summer's day. "I think they came for you, sweetheart," he said in a low rumble, running his hands up and down Kamran's arm and sighing deeply with contentment. "It's a long story, but they tried to help me find you."

"Yeah, sure," Padilla cried in exasperation, throwing up her hands. "Just walk all over my crime scene."

Ava paused and raised an eyebrow at the detective. "You gonna get fingerprints off an ice rink?" she asked as the last of the gaggle began sliding their way over to the fake forest center.

Padilla smirked. "No, I just like bitching." She waved her hand toward Kamran and Lee. "I still need to question you both, though! Don't melt away."

As Kamran's friends made it over the ice and piled on him and Lee one by one, he really couldn't promise anything.

19

LEE

"IT'S ABOUT DAMN TIME!"

Lee blinked as he paused where he was helping Kamran to walk through his parents' entrance hall. Kamran didn't really have any trouble walking, but it just made Lee feel better to hug him to his side after all he'd been through.

There were a few lamps still on in the hall, but they generally stayed on all the time. It was just after midnight, so Lee had assumed most people would have gone to bed.

He'd assumed wrong.

His gamma came out from the reception room brandishing her fist, her eyes a blazing. "It's been hours, Leopold! You didn't think to text or call your old grandmother? I almost had a heart attack!"

"Stop threatening to have a heart attack, Gee-Gee," said Mia, rolling her eyes as she followed Gamma out into the entrance hall. Sugar trotted by her side, the tags on her collar jangling cheerfully. "You're going to live forever. Whoa!" Her mouth dropped open as she saw Kamran propped up against Lee's side. "What *happened?* Are you guys okay?"

Kamran laughed weakly. "You should see the other guy."

Lee shuffled uncomfortably on his feet. He might have used *slightly* excessive force on Bolt, but he couldn't say he regretted it. He just hoped he didn't get in trouble. But after what Bolt had put Kamran through and all those disgusting things he'd said about him, Lee figured he'd had it coming.

Kamran managed to smile at Mia as a number of Lee's other family members came flooding out of the reception room as well. Florence was surrounded by the rest of her pajama-clad children with her husband by her side. Aunt Ginny peered owlishly through her round glasses, a gin and tonic clutched between both hands, and behind her...

Lee raised his eyebrows at his dad. In return, his dad nodded slightly before turning away and disappearing behind all the other aunts and uncles and cousins. But Lee's heart swelled.

That was probably about as close as he'd ever get to a 'well done' from his old man.

He'd take it.

"Oh, Kamran!" Lee's mom cried, rushing up to him where Mia and Gamma were already fussing. His mom fluttered her hands around his face. "Let me get some frozen veggies to put on that."

Lee winced, *hating* that he hadn't been able to stop Bolt from getting his hands on Kamran. He'd only landed a few punches, but enough to give Kamran a fair number of cuts and bruises that were starting to blossom. Lee hugged him tighter to his side, feeling a caveman-like urge to protect him now, even though the danger was long gone.

"It's okay, Cheryl," said Kamran. "I've already had an ice pack on it for too long. Any more and my face will go completely numb."

She bit her lip and nodded. "Okay, well, I'm going to put the veggies in the top drawer of the freezer and leave out a clean dishtowel to wrap them in just in case you need them in the night, all right?"

Lee's heart swelled. "Thanks, Mom," he said.

"Thanks, Cheryl," Kamran said as well.

Lee couldn't quite believe it. He'd explained to Kamran on the drive back from The Lodge that he'd had to confess to his family that they'd started off faking their relationship, but apparently, everyone had believed him when he'd said that what they had was real now.

Or almost everyone. It was conspicuous that Mikey was missing from the welcoming committee, but Lee couldn't say that he cared. He was done trying to win over people who had never had his best interests at heart.

"What happened?" Mia demanded.

"Mia, leave them be," said Florence sternly.

"But it was obviously serious!" Mia protested, her eyes wide as she studied Kamran. "Did the bad guys do that? Did you catch them, Uncle Lee?"

"Yes, and yes," said Lee, then he looked out over the crowd. "Which is why Kamran needs to rest. I'm going to take him upstairs."

"Yeah, sure, 'rest,'" said Gamma, using air quotes and everything, threatening to make Lee blush.

"Gamma!" he said, scandalized.

But she just grinned and shooed them off. "I was young once too, you know," she said. "Off you go now. It's very good to have you back in one piece, Kamran. I'll make you breakfast in the morning, okay? Old Joy will fill your stomach up so much you'll forget all about your face."

Lee laughed and glanced over at Kamran. He was surprised to see his eyes were glassy and he bit his lip. Carefully, he untangled himself from Lee, then moved over to Gamma and wrapped his arms around her in a hug.

"Thank you, Joy," he said thickly.

She patted his back as Sugar rubbed her head against his jeans. "You call me 'Gamma' now if you want, ya hear? You're a part of this family. My little Lee is just crazy about you."

Kamran sniffed, then smiled at her. "I'm pretty crazy about him, too, Gamma," he said before looking over at Lee.

Lee felt a lump rise in his throat. He reached out a hand, and Kamran took it, hugging him against his side again. "Good," Lee murmured, kissing his temple gently. "Now let's go get you taken care of."

Kamran shivered against him, nodding and sighing, sounding content. "Good night, everyone," he said as Lee moved them through the crowd toward the stairs.

A few people called out 'good night' back and Lee was vaguely aware of them moving back toward the reception room. But his sole focus was on Kamran, making sure that he managed the steps okay.

Kamran obviously noticed.

"I'm not made of glass, you know," he said with a faint laugh.

"I don't care," Lee said, kissing his hair and rubbing his arm. "You were incredibly brave tonight and did the right thing, even when I let you down—"

"Hey," said Kamran, stopping on the first landing and pointing a finger at Lee. "Let's get one thing clear, okay? You did *not* let me down. You saved me. *And* you finally arrested Chaz. So none of that crap, all right?"

Lee chuckled and pulled Kamran into a hug. He still felt guilty, but he figured he could make it up to Kamran in a hundred different ways later. Right now, he really did want to bask in the fact that they were okay.

Better than okay. They were together.

"All right," he repeated. "Just so long as you also accept you were brave and didn't do anything wrong."

Kamran sighed as they continued walking up the stairs.

While waiting for him to respond, Lee slipped his hand against Kamran's, entwining their fingers and rubbing Kamran's knuckles with his thumb.

"I think I was wrong for not speaking up against Chaz before," Kamran said eventually. "I was complicit. He hurt people, and I let him pay me off to keep my mouth shut. That feels wrong."

"But you're making it right now," said Lee gently. He knew Kamran wasn't an angel, but if he was honest, that was one of the things that he liked most about him.

That he loved.

Kamran wasn't perfect, and he didn't try to pretend to be. Unlike Lee's awful brother who had apparently convinced everyone that his damn wife was at the reunion when she was somewhere else entirely, divorcing his ass. Lee figured that was probably what happened when you tried to present some perfect imitation of life to the world. It all came down like a house of cards eventually.

Kamran was rough around the edges and didn't expect a damn thing from the world, which kind of made him perfect in Lee's eyes anway. Lee wanted to give him everything he'd never had. A loving home and a caring if slightly nutty family. Practical things like financial stability, but also a warm bed every night with more cuddling than he could probably stand. But Lee was going to cuddle the crap out of him anyway, every chance he got.

Kamran was never going to want for anything again.

He led Kamran to his room, pulling him inside and firmly locking the door behind them. Wordlessly, Lee guided Kamran to the bed. He turned on a single lamp, then dropped to his knees to unlace Kamran's sneakers, a thrill shooting through him when Kamran allowed him to do so without comment. He toed his own loafers off, then lay down on the bed, hugging Kamran tightly against his side.

For a while, they just stared at each other, their fingers gently caressing over clothes and through hair. It hurt Lee's heart to see the blemishes on Kamran's face, but he was still utterly stunning as far as he was concerned. Breathtakingly beautiful, in fact.

"I'm in this for real," he said, done dancing around the issue.

Kamran stared at him. "'This'?"

Lee smiled, then pressed a soft kiss to Kamran's forehead before replying. "Us. You and I. I know there's a distance issue, but quite frankly, Kamran, I don't care. I'll make it work. I want to be with you. I *need* to be."

He held his breath, watching Kamran's face as he waited for a response.

"Oh, Lee," he said finally, choking back a sob as he buried his face against Lee's neck, clinging to his shoulder and throwing his leg over Lee's. In other words, getting even *closer* to Lee than he had been before. "I want that, too. Are you sure? I'm…we're not…"

Lee pulled his head back and touched his thumb and finger to Kamran's chin. Kamran blinked, his dark lashes spiky and wet as he met Lee's gaze. "You're *perfect*," Lee said firmly. "We're *serious*. Okay? My only hesitation about being with you was an ethical one, and now that Bolt is in custody, that's not an issue anymore."

Kamran frowned at him. "But what about the trial?"

Lee growled and tickled Kamran's side where he knew he was extra sensitive. Sure enough, Kamran squealed until Lee stopped, then placed a gentle kiss on his sore face.

"Who's the FBI agent here?" he asked.

Kamran sighed happily. "You," he said. "Did I mention how fucking sexy it was when you grabbed Chaz's gun off him? I mean, in the moment, I wanted to piss my pants, but now I can safely say it was hot as fuck."

Lee chuckled and rolled his eyes. "Only you would think almost dying was sexy."

Kamran arched an eyebrow. "I think you'll find that most of Hollywood agree with me—"

"Shut up," said Lee, grinning as he kissed him again, this time with a little more heat. "I don't care if it was sexy. I never want you in that kind of danger again, okay?"

Kamran looked at him. "You're not going to make me be a little house husband, are you?" he asked dubiously. "I still want to work."

Lee really did throw his head back and laugh at that, rubbing Kamran's side. "No. Someone made me realize what ridiculous expectations I had of my imaginary future husband. I want you to work as well, but not because you have to for minimum wage. What would you do if you could?"

"I'd get more training for stunt work," said Kamran immediately, his eyes lighting up. "I'd get some *real* driving qualifications and attend some of those fighting workshops. The kind of stuff Angel does."

That was the friend from the party who'd asked about the protestors on a film set, Lee had learned. He smiled, thinking about all those friends who Kamran had assumed didn't really think much of him literally *running into an active crime scene* for him.

They seemed like great people. Lee hoped they'd be seeing a lot more of them in the future.

"So, no more Uber?" he prompted.

"Hell no," Kamran grumbled with a little pout that Lee found utterly adorable. "Don't get me wrong. I'll always drive my friends places. But *having* to do it for the money was getting kind of old."

Lee stroked Kamran's hair back, feeling warm and tingly. Of course Kamran would still want to help his friends out.

For someone who continuously called himself selfish, he really wasn't.

"Good," he said. "That makes me happy."

Kamran narrowed his eyes at him. "I mean it, though. I won't be some 'kept' man or whatever. I've got my own life. I don't need a sugar daddy."

Lee raised his eyebrows. "So…you don't want me to spoil you with all the money that my family has too much of and doesn't know what to do with?"

Kamran chewed his lip. "I mean…a *little* spoiling might go a long way," he admitted.

Lee grinned before kissing him tenderly. "That would make me very happy," he mumbled into his mouth.

"Well, if it'll make *you* happy," Kamran mumbled back.

For a while, there was no talking, only kissing. There was heat to it, but Lee didn't feel like it was building to anything despite their earlier plans.

He groaned.

"What?" Kamran asked, sounding concerned, but Lee laughed.

"I just remembered that *incredible* picture you sent to me before, and now I'm mad all over again that we got interrupted."

Kamran also groaned and ran his hand over Lee's chest. "I don't think I can tonight…" he began, but Lee was already shaking his head.

"No, no, definitely not," he insisted. He wanted their first time to be really special, not hopped up on adrenaline and with the memory of Charles Bolt fresh in their minds.

But that didn't mean he didn't want *anything* to happen tonight.

"How about a shower?" he asked, caressing the side of Kamran's neck. "Let me take care of you?"

Kamran sighed and dropped his head onto Lee's shoulder.

"That sounds great," he said sleepily. "I need to wash all that awfulness off me right the hell now."

"Come on, then."

Lee escorted Kamran to the en suite, then sat on the edge of the tub as Kamran stood in front of him, letting Lee undress him. It wasn't exactly sexy, but it was incredibly intimate. Lee loved every second of it.

Once Kamran was naked, Lee ran his hands over his body, inspecting it for any other damage at the hands of that psychopath. But Kamran was just as beautiful as always, and Lee was grateful that his injuries hadn't been any more serious.

He got the water running hot, quickly yanking off his own clothes with Kamran watching him attentively. "Like what you see?" Lee asked him, eager to get their playfulness back after the seriousness of the evening.

Kamran didn't need much encouragement, that sparkle finally back in his eyes. "You don't even know, Agent Marshall."

"You're going to show me, then," said Lee, pulling him under the cascade of water with him.

It was a lazy mess of kissing lips and hands skimming all over each other's bodies. Lee took charge of the products, making sure their hair and bodies got lathered enough to thoroughly rinse off all the sweat, blood, and tears from earlier. But then he had one arm wrapped around Kamran's back and the other hand brushed over Kamran's stiff cock, jutting up toward Lee's own length, rubbing them together.

"Is this okay?" he asked between kisses.

"Hell, *yes*," Kamran hissed, thrusting against Lee's palm. "I need you, baby."

Lee paused, looking down at Kamran, unable to stop himself from blinking.

Kamran seemed to realize what he'd said, too. He

squeezed his eyes shut with a little whimper and dug his fingernails into Lee's chest. "I-I want..." he stammered through a grimace. "I think I want...to be...I mean..."

"Baby?" Lee tested, trying out the word that had felt so natural to call Kamran for days now, but he'd held off because Kamran had been so adamant that he hated it.

Except now, a desperate sob escaped his chest, and he threw himself against Lee, nodding emphatically. "It's *different* when you say it," he choked out. Lee moved his hands to embrace his lover, wrapping him tightly in his arms, nuzzling his cheek against Kamran's wet hair.

"Different in a good way?" he asked softly over the running water.

Kamran shook. *"You came for me,"* he whispered. "I needed you, and you *came.* When you call me that, I feel safe. It's not a broken promise anymore. It's...it's *everything."*

Lee's chest threatened to break open. His heart was so overflowing with love and affection. "Because *you're* everything," he said. He kissed Kamran's cheek and rubbed his back. "You hear that, baby?"

Kamran's whine was almost like a small scream. He grabbed Lee's face and began kissing him passionately, pushing Lee back against the tiles as he rutted his cock against Lee's thigh.

Well then. If Kamran needed release right now, then that was what Lee was going to give him.

He firmly took hold of Kamran's hip to steady him, then put his other arm between them to encircle both their cocks again.

"Lee, please," Kamran begged against his lips. "I need you."

"You've got me," Lee promised him. They weren't going to last long, he could tell. So he didn't bother worrying about finesse as he jerked them off. All that mattered was that they were close and safe and suddenly had a future unfolding out before them. There was no longer a ticking clock creeping up on them.

Even though the time pressure didn't matter as much anymore, there was still an urgency as Kamran clung to him, kissing him frantically as they both chased their releases, thrusting into Lee's hand. Maybe it was all the pent-up fear and anger needing to find an outlet, but within no time at all, Lee could feel his heavy balls contracting.

"Kamran," he grunted.

Kamran bit Lee's lower lip, dragging it through his teeth. *"Lee,"* he cried, sounding close as well.

Sure enough, within seconds, Kamran started spilling out between them, his cum hitting their chests and the tiled walls before getting washed almost immediately away with the water. Lee was close, and he kept pumping Kamran's cock against his own as Kamran shuddered through his climax. But then suddenly he dropped to his knees without warning, shoving Lee's hand away and replacing it with his own at the base as he swallowed the rest of Lee's dick down with gusto.

Lee yelled, slamming his palm against the bathroom wall to steady himself. He'd been so close anyway, but Kamran's hot, eager mouth tipped him over the edge. He came with a bellow after only a few seconds, spilling down Kamran's throat. As usual, Kamran didn't appear to mind in the slightest. He gulped everything Lee gave him down with enthusiasm, stroking the base of Lee's length, milking every last drop from him.

Lee blinked, gasping as he came back to his senses. Kamran was wobbly, trying to get back to his feet. When Lee realized, he gripped the top of his arm to help haul him up, then hugged him tightly, kissing that perfect mouth of his, trying to pour all of his love into that one act.

"Be my boyfriend," he mumbled between kisses along Kamran's jaw.

Kamran snorted tiredly. "What are you? Twelve?" he said with a sleepy chuckle. "Are you going to ask me to go steady?"

Lee bit Kamran's ear, earning himself a satisfying yelp. "Kamran…I'm serious. I would like it if we just…I want to be exclusive."

Kamran's mirth faded, and he looked at Lee tenderly, trailing his fingers down Lee's cheek as their gazes locked. "I want that, too," he said sincerely. "Yes, I like a lot of sex. But I'm perfectly fine getting all that sex from one place. Especially if that place is as big as a mountain with a cock that—*mph!*"

Lee cut him off before the almost-romance talk could completely evaporate. His heart sang as he claimed Kamran's mouth thoroughly.

"Be a good boy and just say 'yes' already," he growled.

Kamran giggled, batting his wet eyelashes at him. "*Yes,* I will be your boyfriend, you big nerd."

That was all Lee needed to hear.

KAMRAN

"WHAT'S THIS?" KAMRAN ASKED AS HE LOOKED UP FROM WHERE he'd been tying his shoelace.

He was perched on the side of Lee's bed, *finally* dressed after Lee had kept him naked for most of the day. But now he was showered and smelling fresh after a long hot shower (alone, so as not to be tempted.) The laces on his fancy new shoes felt particularly slippery to him, but perhaps that was because Kamran's hands were shaking ever so slightly.

It wasn't that he was *nervous*, exactly. But…it was just this was the end of the big family reunion, and the Marshalls had invited all kinds of fancy-schmancy people to their big formal ball-type party. Kamran had just about gotten used to some of Lee's family, but there were still certain people he'd shied away from, feeling completely out of his depth. Now he was going to be surrounded by even more mega-rich people, and they were all going to be judging him and—

Breathe.

Lee was standing in front of him, looking incredibly handsome in his tux but also strangely coy, almost like he was nervous. Why would he be nervous? Oh, right, the box he was holding out in front of Kamran's face.

"It's a present," said Lee.

Kamran was tempted to tease him. After all, the box was wrapped in pretty silver paper with a purple bow. But despite the obviousness of it all, Kamran didn't feel like joking around.

"You didn't need to get me anything," he said, reaching out and placing his hand over one of Lee's that was clutching the box. "You already bought me so much."

Kamran looked down at the fancy suit that he'd put on. Trying on this thing had been the moment when he'd finally allowed himself to admit that he really wanted Lee and for more than just one night. It felt significant. In fact, it was almost like armor, helping Kamran to temper his nerves for the party. Wearing it felt like he was wearing a neon sign saying, 'property of Lee, so I belong here!'

Lee licked his lips, then moved to sit beside Kamran on the bed. He held out the box for Kamran to take.

"I know," he said. "But remember how we agreed that you'd let me spoil you every now and again?"

Kamran bit his lip and tried not to let the warm pride that swelled within him manifest as a blush. Oh, he'd talked some talk about not wanting to be a kept man and all that, but the truth was he was *very* quickly becoming okay with Lee surprising him and lavishing him with tokens of his affections. Because they also came with sweet kisses and deep sighs and all that other lovey-dovey crap that Kamran had told himself he hated when, in fact, he liked it all quite a *lot* when it came from Lee.

Because Lee meant it. Everything about the man was real and sincere. How funny that this had all started out as something fake between them. There was nothing pretend about the way Kamran felt now.

Kamran accepted the present, surprised at how heavy it was. It kind of looked like a shoebox from the size of it, but you could put anything in a shoebox and wrap it up. He bit his lip, wondering what it could be.

"Can I open it now?"

Lee smiled fondly at him, then reached up to brush a lock of hair back from Kamran's forehead. Kamran quivered with pleasure that wasn't quite lust, but it definitely fell under the category of 'I am crazily attracted to this man.'

"That's kind of the point of giving it to you now," Lee said with a smile.

Kamran frowned at him, not done with trying to guess what he was up to yet. "Is it for the party tonight?"

"Not exactly," Lee said, indulging his questions. "If you open it, you might be able to find out."

Kamran rolled his eyes at the sarcasm, but at the same time, his heart fluttered.

How the hell had he managed to accidentally end up with a man who came up with thoughtful, surprise presents for him like this?

"I, um, didn't get you anything," he said, still not ripping open the wrapping paper.

He was nervous about what might be inside. He wasn't sure why he would be. Perhaps he was still just getting used to this whole 'being in a relationship' thing. As if he was still waiting for the other shoe to drop like he'd learned to expect from Chaz.

Urgh. He mentally spat out the word. No more thinking about his ex, not when he had Lee right here with him.

"Kamran," Lee said firmly, making him look up. Lee rubbed his knee and looked him in the eyes. "You don't need to get me anything. But it would make me really happy if you opened this now. I'm nervous you won't like it."

"Oh," said Kamran, feeling his eyebrows rise. "What? No! I'm sure I'll love it. Okay…if it'll make you happy"

Kamran wasn't an idiot. He'd picked up that Lee tended to say something would make him happy if Kamran was stressing himself out whether he deserved it or not. The funny thing was, it worked, even though Kamran knew what he was doing. Because he always wanted to make Lee happy, and if that meant accepting being a little spoiled, well… Kamran would just have to get used to it. He was sure Lee knew that full well.

It was dastardly, really.

So Kamran stopped protesting and slid the bow off the box before ripping the end of the paper. It was indeed a shoebox – a large one, bigger than a normal sneakers box – but a quick glance at the branding on the brown cardboard told Kamran what *kind* of shoes these were.

His heart skipped a beat.

He looked up at Lee, who smiled at him. "Go on," Lee said, nudging the corner of the box.

With trembling hands, Kamran pushed the lid up on its folded hinge, revealing a layer of tissue paper. He bit his lip as he pushed it aside to uncover…

"Oh, Lee," he said, doing his best not to get emotional but not really succeeding.

They were ice skates. Light powder blue with white laces and fur trim, and a warm brown wooden heel. The blades shone like polished mirrors. Kamran reverently touched one of them, then looked back at Lee, blinking his tears away.

"I love them," he said.

He'd never had his own skates, always borrowing them from the rink as a teenager. He'd dreamed of having sleek black ones, but now these pretty ones were his, he loved them even more than something that might have been considered more masculine. With Lee, he finally felt safe in expressing himself in ways that he would have been screamed at for when growing up.

That was almost a bigger gift than the skates.

Except he really, *really* loved the skates.

"If they're the wrong size or whatever, we can change them," Lee assured him, hugging him to his side and resting his chin on Kamran's shoulder. "I got the same size as your dress shoes we bought, but if that's not right—"

"I'm sure they're perfect," said Kamran, resisting the urge to shove them on his feet right that moment. "Will The Lodge be open by tomorrow? Can we go?"

He felt like a small, excitable child, but he didn't care. No one had *ever* cared about his skating until Lee. Kamran had gotten a similar thrill from driving as he did skating over the years, but he felt as if he'd finally unlocked a part of himself that he thought he'd never find his way back to. Now that he had, he'd discovered that it was still filled with impossible joy.

Except now it was even better because he got to share it with Lee.

"The Lodge will still be closed tomorrow," said Lee apologetically. "Not just for the refurb. We did some damage catching Bolt and his men. But I promise I'll take you as soon as it's open again, and in the meantime, maybe we can find another rink."

But Kamran shook his head. "I'll wait for The Lodge," he said. That was their special place. He wanted to erase all of the memories of Chaz's presence by going skating with Lee there for the first time with his present. He smiled at Lee, leaning in to kiss him. "Thank you."

Lee cupped the side of his face and rubbed his thumb over Kamran's cheek. "You're very welcome. Now, let's get down to the party, or we'll never leave this room."

Kamran had to admit that he was tempted to just stay

hidden away for a second, but they *had* to at least make an appearance. So he put the lid back on the shoebox and stood up, smoothing his tux down.

"Are you sure I look okay?" he asked.

Lee scoffed. "No, you look stunning, baby."

Urgh, that *word*. How Kamran could feel so different now was nothing short of a miracle. All he knew was that when Lee called him 'baby,' it made him feel all warm and syrupy, immediately wanting to melt against Lee's side.

So he did.

"Let's go, baby," he whispered, then kissed Lee's lips gently. Just enough to give him a little tease but not quite enough to completely rev his engines.

That would come later, Kamran hoped.

He moved to give himself one last look over in the mirror. Thanks to a rigorous icing regime over the past few days, his face was looking pretty damn good, considering Chaz had used it as his own personal punching bag. There was hardly any swelling, and although there was some bruising, Mia had come up a little while ago and used some of her makeup to cover the worst of it. Kamran felt like his old self.

Or rather, he felt like a brand-new version of himself. The clothes made him look fancy, sure, but that wasn't really it. He felt loved, and that was something that shone from within.

"Ready?" he asked.

Lee held up his arm so Kamran could take it.

"Ready," Lee agreed.

There were still butterflies in Kamran's stomach as they made their way down the stairs, the sounds of music and people's voices getting louder as they descended, but they were just little baby butterflies now. He may be very different from a lot of these people, but that didn't mean he didn't belong there tonight.

He belonged wherever Lee was.

He bit his lip. For so long, he'd tried to convince himself he wasn't jealous of what all his friends had. But now he could totally admit that he'd been a big green-eyed monster as they'd all fallen in love, one by one. Now it was finally his turn, and he was ready to shout it from the rooftops.

Not that he'd needed to. What with all his crazy buddies following Lee to The Lodge and throwing themselves onto the ice the second that Chaz and his goons had been arrested, they knew *all* about Kamran's not-so-fake FBI boyfriend. They'd all tripped over themselves to tell Kamran how much they approved and how happy they were for him.

And Kamran was happy, too. Even though the week was coming to an end and Lee would have to go back to Seattle first thing on Monday morning. Kamran told himself for the thousandth time not to worry about all that. Lee had promised him time and again that he was *in* this. That they were going to make it work.

Kamran just wasn't sure how.

He pushed all those thoughts away, though, as they entered the reception room. There were so many people attending tonight that the Marshalls had organized for a tent to be set up in the grounds out back. However, there were still plenty of guests present in the reception room, mostly seated on the plush couches and armchairs.

One of which was Gamma Joy, gossiping conspiratorially with Mia as Sugar munched on what appeared to be a French macaron at their feet. Kamran bit his lip. Mia had no idea what danger she'd been in, and he hoped she never would.

"There are my boys!" Gamma called out, waving them over to her and Mia. She had a glittering shawl on over her dress and a peacock brooch in her hair.

"Don't you look glamorous?" Kamran commented as he leaned down to give her a kiss and a squeeze of her shoulders. "And Mia…I wanna say handsome? Is that cool?"

She was wearing pants with a button-down and suspenders, topped off with a pinstriped trilby hat on her shining long brown hair.

"Hell, yeah," she enthused, offering up her hand for a high five. "Not too shabby yourselves, guys."

She winked at him and Lee, and Kamran loved how people talked to them as a couple now. They had before, but he and Lee had been pretending then. Now it was *real*, and the fact that Lee's family accepted Kamran was with Lee meant everything to him.

"Well, this is quite the shindig," said Kamran with a nod as he looked around. Lee picked up two glasses of Champagne from the tray of a passing waiter, offering one to Kamran.

Gamma scoffed. "All a lot of pomp and nonsense," she said, shaking her head. "I'd prefer a nice game of cards and some brandy."

"I'm sure we can sneak off and do that later," Kamran told her with a wink.

"Oh, damn," said Lee, suddenly reaching into his breast pocket for his phone. Although he was still technically on vacation, he was coordinating with the local PD to process the transfer of Chaz into FBI custody and all that other red tape stuff they had to do. Sure enough, Lee nodded. "It's Padilla. Do you mind?"

Kamran kissed his jaw. "Go fight crime," he said, really not minding. He was still apprehensive when it came to a lot of Lee's family, and he had no idea what he'd say to most of their fancy guests, but here with Gamma and Mia, he felt safe.

Even when a certain somebody approached him.

"Good evening, Mr. Amir."

Gamma rolled her eyes. "It's *Kamran*, Donald, as you well know."

Lee's dad gave her a tight smile, then nodded at Kamran. "Yes, Kamran. I apologize."

Kamran shrugged, taking a sip of cold Champagne, the bubbles fizzing pleasantly down his throat. "No sweat. What can I do for you, Mr. Marshall?" He noticed Gamma didn't try and correct him to call him 'Donald.'

Lee's dad glanced at Mia and Gamma (and Sugar, who'd hopped up into Gamma's lap) and sighed. He probably realized that he wasn't going to get away with asking to talk to Kamran in private.

"I owe you an apology," he said with a slight bow. His eyes met Kamran's briefly before flicking to the floor. Kamran wondered if his wife had bullied him into coming over here. In any case, Kamran was already enjoying the moment immensely.

"You just apologized for the name thing," he said, knowing full well that wasn't what Donald meant.

Sure enough, Donald grimaced but tried to turn it into a smile. Either way, his eyes remained narrowed. "I spoke out of turn the other night," he said, his voice clipped. "I said a number of things to you I regret."

"Such as?" Kamran prompted, sipping his Champagne.

Donald cleared his throat. "Oh, there's no need to—"

"You called him a gold-digger," said Aunt Ginny as she tottered past, wearing a bright yellow sixties shift dress, waving her glass of G&T like a baton. "And Kamran told you to keep your nose out of Leopold's business. Hi, Kamran, dear."

She grinned at him as she carried on wobbling on her heels toward the party outside, grabbing a second G&T from a passing tray, despite the glass in her hand still being almost full.

"Yes, *thank you*, Ginny," said Donald through gritted teeth. "What I mean to say is I think some snap judgments might have been made—"

"By you," Mia interjected cheerfully. Gamma snorted into her Champagne.

"—but perhaps those judgments were unfair," Donald continued as if she hadn't spoken. The vein throbbing in his temple suggested that he'd very much heard her, though. "It seems my son cares deeply for you and you are sincere in your affections for him. I wish you every happiness."

"Gee, thanks, man," said Kamran cheerfully, clapping Donald on the shoulder. Donald blinked slowly, like he couldn't believe that Kamran had just touched him. "So you're not going to be cutting Lee off from his trust fund or anything?"

Donald's nostrils flared. "I would never do anything so crass."

Kamran winked at him, not entirely sure he believed him. "Good to know," he said, at least hoping that *now* he wouldn't do anything like that.

Donald hummed before sweeping away, heading to the nearest member of the waiting staff, no doubt to demand a ridiculously large and expensive whiskey. Kamran chuckled, not caring if the old man liked him or not. Just so long as he wouldn't punish Lee for being with him, that was fine.

In fact, if he could get off Lee's back altogether about his various life choices – like, say, his career – that would be really great. But one step at a time.

Speaking of which, Lee suddenly appeared at Kamran's shoulder, frowning. "What did my dad say?" he asked warily.

"He wished you and Kamran every happiness," Mia said, gleefully bouncing on the sofa. "He looked like he'd swallowed a lemon."

Gamma snorted again, then schooled her features when

Lee raised an eyebrow at her. "Mia, behave," she said, sounding vaguely serious.

Mia rolled her eyes and grinned. "So, Uncle Lee – what did the cops say? Have they handed over that douchebag yet? Are you *finally* going to get that promotion you've been working all these years for?"

"Umm…" said Lee. He frowned at his phone before pocketing it, then turned to Kamran with a strange look on his face. "Actually, can I talk to you for a second?"

Kamran's stomach dropped. He'd been trained to expect the worst, and he'd been waiting for the other shoe to drop. But he tried not to let his mind run away with anxiety before he'd heard what Lee had to say.

"You can totally say anything in front of us," said Mia eagerly, raising her eyebrows and giving Lee a pleading look. "We won't tell anyone. Will we, Gee-Gee?"

Gamma raised her hand in a salute. "Girl Scout's honor."

Lee laughed at them, his eyes full of skepticism, then put his hand on Kamran's arm to gently steer him to a quieter corner of the room.

"Is there something wrong with Chaz's case?" Kamran asked before Lee could speak. He'd be lying if he didn't admit that the thought of the case falling through and Chaz coming after him again had crossed his mind once or ten times.

Lee frowned at him for a second, apparently not quite understanding what he'd said before raising his eyebrows and shaking his head. "Oh, no, nothing like that," he said with a laugh. "It's actually about that promotion I've been after."

Kamran had been prepared for this. He kept his smile firmly in place, even though fear was threatening to make him panic. Just because Lee was getting more responsibility didn't mean their relationship was doomed. Just because he'd always been a workaholic didn't mean he was going to fall back into those ways so soon. This was fine. It was *great,* actually. Lee deserved it.

"You got it," he said warmly, squeezing Lee's arm. "Congratulations."

Again, Lee looked mildly confused. "No," he said slowly. "Well, I mean, yes, maybe." He shook his head. "That's not what I'm asking."

It was Kamran's turn to raise his eyebrows at him. "Okay?"

Lee chewed his lip and studied Kamran for a second. "Would you be disappointed if I didn't take it?"

That hadn't been what Kamran had been expecting. His mouth fell open. "But…you've worked so hard for it? Chaz's whole case. You deserve it!"

Lee sighed and shook his head, more subdued this time. "I've made my whole life about work, and I don't want that anymore."

Kamran jabbed a finger at Lee. "Don't you dare turn down an opportunity like this because of me," he said crossly. "I *never* want to hold you back. I want you to fly! You should—"

"Padilla just told me that a detective's position is going to be opening up right here, in Pine Cove."

Kamran blinked. He couldn't have just heard that correctly, could he?

"W-what?"

Lee nodded, a smile creeping onto his face. "One of her colleagues is retiring. I mentioned how I wasn't sure how I'd be able to juggle splitting my time for work in Seattle and seeing you here, and she just casually mentioned it in an 'FYI' sort of way."

Kamran's heart was starting to race. "But…that would be such a step down for you."

Lee scoffed and held his hand out, indicating the house. "I

don't *need* to work at all," he said. "Mikey basically doesn't. What I love is helping people, and the FBI seemed the perfect career path for me to be the best of the best. But I want other things now." He stepped closer and took Kamran's hand in his. "I want *you*."

Kamran was aware that his mouth was opening and shutting like a goldfish. As much as he wanted this to be true…

"Lee…" he said weakly. "I – I love you. I want this to work out, believe me. But we've only known each other for a week. Are you really going to change your whole life for me?"

Lee arched an eyebrow. "I told you I wanted to spoil you, didn't I?"

"But, *Lee—*" Kamran protested.

Lee cut him off with a kiss. "I know this is different from a pair of skates," he murmured sweetly against Kamran's mouth, stroking his chin. "But I've lived my whole life trying to impress people who I'll never win over. I want to win *you* over, and that means being *here*. If that's what you want?"

Doubt flickered through his eyes, and Kamran made a split-second decision. "Of course it's what I want!" he cried incredulously. "But I'm a selfish asshole. Just because it's what I want – what I'd *love* – doesn't mean you should just drop everything and do it!"

Lee grinned, the doubt completely gone. "That sounds like an *excellent* reason why I should drop everything and do it. If we both want to be together, then I can't help but feel like the universe has just dropped the perfect solution into our laps. Kamran, we could move in together – share a place. Doesn't that sound amazing?"

Good things didn't happen to Kamran. He chewed his lip, waiting for the other shoe to drop. But he suddenly realized that with Lee, there was a very real chance that it never would.

"You mean…we'd share a bed? A *big* one?"

Heat flashed through Lee's eyes now, and he subtly rubbed his hip against Kamran's, putting other body parts into excitingly close proximity. "One with the kind of headboard we could attach handcuffs to," he growled into Kamran's ear.

Kamran gasped, his pants suddenly feeling *very* tight. "Uh, yeah," he said, clearing his throat. "That sounds like something I'd really want to share."

Lee's grin was huge and unashamedly happy. He leaned down and kissed Kamran's lips with possessive urgency. "And I'm making a new rule," he mumbled against Kamran's skin as he kissed along his jaw. "You are *not* allowed to call yourself a selfish asshole ever again, understood?"

Kamran opened his mouth to protest, but Lee talked over him.

"*No.* You gave yourself up to Bolt to save your friends and my family. You are full of love and compassion. I knew it before then, but now I have irrefutable proof. I don't want you talking trash about yourself like that. Okay?"

Kamran stared at him a second. How – *how* – had he been so lucky to find such a generous, kind man?

"Okay," he whispered, rubbing Lee's chest.

"Good." Lee sighed happily. "Padilla's captain doesn't need an answer right away, and I'd still have to work out my notice at the Seattle office…but can we call that a tentative 'yes,' *boyfriend?*"

"I'd say that's a strong possibility of a 'yes,'" said Kamran, feeling giddy. How was this his life? How had Lee walked into a bar and walked into the rest of his life at the same time? It was crazy.

But it was real. And Kamran wasn't letting it go for anything.

2 1

KAMRAN

"SHH!" LEE HISSED AS THEY STUMBLED THROUGH HIS BEDROOM door some hours later.

Kamran grinned as he kissed his mouth. "You shush," he said, feeling tipsy from the Champagne but also just from life in general. He was so happy he could die.

But there would be no dying before they finished the night with a bang.

With the door firmly closed and locked on the rest of the world, Kamran felt a freedom he wasn't sure he'd ever experienced. He'd made it through the party. Lee's dad had *sort of* given them his blessing. Lee wanted to take the job in Pine Cove. He wanted to *move in together*.

Kamran felt like he'd hit the jackpot.

And now he was going to get his prize.

"Come here," he growled, dragging Lee by his shirt over to the bed.

They grinned as they kissed sloppily, hands fumbling with each other's shirt buttons. They managed to kick their shoes off before they tumbled on top of the mattress, Lee rolling them until he was on top of Kamran, kissing him fiercely and grinding their hard lengths together through their dress pants.

"You're fucking gorgeous, and you're all mine," Lee said, his voice low and rumbly with desire as he nipped at Kamran's earlobe.

Kamran panted and nodded. "Yep. Definitely. One hundred percent," he squeaked.

Lee chuckled, a low rumble that went straight to Kamran's balls. He groaned and tried to get his hands back on Lee's damn shirt.

"Be more naked," he grumbled into Lee's mouth.

Lee laughed good and proper at that. "You know what? You're right. We've had *way* too much foreplay – a whole week's worth. Clothes off, now."

Kamran scrambled to help Lee attack his shirt and bow tie. When those were completely undone, Kamran lifted his torso so he could pull his shirt off while Lee made short work of his own shirt. Now their bare chests rubbed together as Lee dropped back down to kiss him, sending shivers all over Kamran's body, but it still wasn't enough. His cock was threatening to burst out of his pants, and he was already making a mess of his boxer briefs, he could tell.

He made a whining noise and tried to wiggle so he could get his hands between them to get to his pants, but Lee laughed softly at him. "Shh," he soothed, taking Kamran by the wrists and moving his arms to place them above Kamran's head on the pillow. "Let me take care of it."

"Okay, Lee," he said breathlessly, more than happy to comply.

Lee gave him a heated look, not breaking eye contact as he slid Kamran's zipper down over his straining cock. "Good boy," he murmured.

Kamran whimpered and squirmed, biting his lip as Lee held his gaze while he tugged Kamran's pants down over his hips. He pulled them all the way off along with Kamran's socks, then crawled back up the bed. He nuzzled Kamran's hard length through his tented underwear, licking at the already wet patch.

"Lee," Kamran begged in a thready whine.

"Baby," Lee rasped back, squeezing Kamran's hips. "I need you."

He pulled at Kamran's side, encouraging him to turn over onto his belly. Kamran hugged the pillow and moaned with pleasure as Lee peeled his briefs over his ass and down his thighs. Kamran couldn't stop himself from rubbing his throbbing dick against the bed, needing some release. That was until Lee swatted his bare cheek, making Kamran gasp and tremble all over.

"I told you I'm going to take care of it," said Lee in a bossy voice that got Kamran even harder, if that was possible. He panted and nodded, looking over his shoulder to see Lee kneeling above him, still in his dress pants. His expansive chest glistened with perspiration in the lamplight, and Kamran wanted so desperately to lick and scratch it.

Later, hopefully.

Right now, he was going to do what his boyfriend said and let him take charge. "Please, Lee," he said, his voice catching with pure want. Lee smiled down at him, then lowered himself to begin kissing his way down Kamran's spine.

Kamran made fists against the bedsheets like a cat flexing their claws. His skin felt like it was on fire as Lee kissed the soft flesh of his ass, kneading both sides before pulling the cheeks apart and breathing against his most intimate area.

Kamran gasped and felt his hole clench against Lee's gaze, hardly daring to breathe. Sure enough, Lee hummed, sounding like he greatly approved, then began kissing and licking closer and closer…

"Lee," Kamran moaned, screwing up his eyes and shuddering as Lee licked a stripe over the tight ring of Kamran's entrance. He'd prepared himself in the shower earlier in anticipation that this was where the night might end, wanting to give Lee a head start with the stretching. But now, Kamran had to say he hoped Lee would take his time rimming him to loosen him up. His tongue and lips were like magic as they worked Kamran's hole.

"Taste so good, baby," he murmured from between Kamran's cheeks. "All mine."

"Y-yes, Lee, yes," Kamran stuttered.

He was trying really hard not to rut himself against the bed, but his dick was so desperate for friction that he didn't even realize how much he was grinding until Lee suddenly let go of his ass to grab his hips and yank him up to his knees, shoving his face more into the pillow.

"Bad boy," he growled, swatting Kamran's ass again.

Kamran blinked and gasped, "S-sorry, Lee," he said. "I'll be good, I promise."

Lee chuckled and kissed the cheek he'd just smacked, rubbing it gently with circular motions. "I know you will, sweetheart. You know I'll look after you, right? It's my job to take care of you now."

Kamran felt like he was melting like butter, moaning and nodding and waggling his ass for Lee to command. *"Yesss,"* he hissed.

He closed his eyes, so he heard rather than saw Lee moving. But the next thing he felt after the bed decompressed behind him was Lee's fingers pressing against his hole, slippery with the lube they'd been using all week. He gnashed his teeth as Lee pushed his finger inside with one hand, then reached around with the other to give Kamran's cock a stroke.

"You're not getting bored with me, are you?" Lee asked, a hint of teasing to his voice.

"Never," Kamran promised, looking over his shoulder to make sure that Lee knew he meant it. He loved being naked and vulnerable for Lee like this, submitting to him and trusting him. Because Lee had proved that he would take care of Kamran no matter what. That his love was true and not just for show.

Kamran wanted to give him everything. Maybe even the rest of his life.

He knew he was flying on the high of the night, but he was pretty sure he meant that. He'd never met anyone who felt like they fitted so perfectly into Kamran's world. Better than that. It was as if being with Lee was already molding Kamran into the best version he could be.

Soon his thoughts simplified as Lee stretched him with two and then three fingers. Kamran kind of wanted to just impale himself on Lee's impressive girth, but the last shed of his logic told him that preparation was a much better plan so that Kamran didn't get hurt, and therefore they could go for round two much sooner.

And then round three…and four…

"Ohh," he wailed as his thoughts were snapped right back to round one. He'd somehow missed Lee suiting up with a condom, but there was no missing the blunt head of his cock as it pressed against Kamran's hole, lube dripping down his sensitive balls. Lee held his cheeks apart and slowly pushed the head of his length through Kamran's tight ring, both of them gasping as he breached the entrance.

"Holy fuck, Kamran," Lee rasped, rubbing up and down his spine. "You feel amazing. Are you okay?"

Kamran nodded, looking back and smiling at his lover

with tears in his eyes. "So perfect," he mumbled. "I'm okay. Keep going. I trust you."

Lee's chest heaved, and he dropped down to capture Kamran's mouth for a deep kiss. Then he straightened up again and wrapped his hands around Kamran's hips, slowly pushing himself in farther.

The burn was almost too much, but Kamran allowed himself to breathe and relax against the intrusion, welcoming Lee inside him. *This* was his home, in his lover's embrace. A calmness settled over him as Lee continued to ease his way in.

There was no rush.

They had all the time in the world.

Lee wanted to entwine their lives. He seriously wanted to move back to Pine Cove to be with Kamran. There was no second shoe that was going to drop.

This was it.

Kamran allowed that knowledge to envelop him, relaxing him fully as Lee bottomed out, gasping and squeezing Kamran's hips as they both adjusted. "Fuck," Lee gasped, his dick fully nestled all the way up Kamran's ass, throbbing with a visceral need. He moved, rubbing over Kamran's prostate, and Kamran let out a filthy moan that he really hoped no one else would be able to hear over the party still going on downstairs.

Scratch that. He absolutely definitely did not care if anyone heard his man claiming him. He wanted the whole damn world to know.

"Kamran, baby," Lee gasped, rocking his hips and hitting that magic spot deep within Kamran's body that immediately set him on fire. "C'mere."

He pulled Kamran up so his back was pressed against Lee's expansive chest. Their skin was slick, sliding together as Lee rolled his hips. Kamran turned his head over his shoulder so that Lee could kiss him messily as he thrust inside him. Lee splayed one big hand over Kamran's stomach, and the other he used to encircle Kamran's cock, jerking him off slowly as they found their rhythm.

Kamran was in heaven.

This wasn't fucking. It was making love. He could feel it pulsing between them. A promise they were making to each other that this was the realest thing in the world. Pure and uncomplicated, a connection that wasn't ever going to break.

That didn't mean Kamran was opposed to being ravaged, however.

"Fuck me, Lee," he begged into his mouth. "Show me I'm yours. Claim me."

Lee bit Kamran's lower lip, dragging it through his teeth as he grunted, piercing Kamran with a scorching look through his dark lashes. "On your hands," he commanded.

Kamran dropped like a stone, bracing himself on all fours as Lee began to piston into him right away. Kamran was too full and yet not enough. He rocked his body frantically, matching Lee's pace as his balls got tighter and heavier.

Lee had both his hands on Kamran's hips, holding him so he could fuck him as hard as possible. Their desperate cries mingled in the air that was thick with the scent of their sweat, punctuated by the slapping of skin on skin.

"Kamran, baby," Lee said. "So good, good boy. All mine."

Kamran couldn't make that many words happen. *"Yesss,"* was all he was able to hiss, perspiration dripping down his face. He was getting close.

Suddenly, Lee pulled out. Kamran had barely registered what had happened, let alone found the strength to protest, when Lee flipped him over, causing him to drop onto his back. In the next second, Lee was back between his legs, crowding his space as he loomed over Kamran. He bent Kamran's legs so his knees were by his shoulders at the same time as he lined his raging erection back up with Kamran's needy hole.

"Have to see you," Lee gasped, forcing his way back inside.

Kamran couldn't agree more. He leaned up to kiss Lee, grabbing his shoulders and digging his nails into his skin. A primal part of him wanted to mark his lover, to show the rest of the world that this man was *his* and no one else's.

Lee broke the kiss, but his lips stayed hovered over Kamran's as he began to pound him again. His panting breaths tingled over Kamran's lips, their gazes locked in an elevated moment of intensity as Kamran's orgasm rose inside him.

"Lee," he pleaded. "I'm close."

Lee took charge of his cock again, jerking him frantically as his thrusts got even faster. "Come for me, baby. Give me everything. I've got you."

Kamran knew that oh-so-well.

He let go, his climax surging through him as he began spurting all over his belly. Lee's hand faltered as he wailed and gnashed his teeth, his cock throbbing inside Kamran's ass as his orgasm chased Kamran's. The moment seemed to stretch on forever...

Until Kamran's legs dropped back down to the bed and Lee collapsed on top of him. He held some of his weight so Kamran wasn't crushed by his bulk, but Kamran had to admit that he really liked being pinned down by his enormous boyfriend as he floated back from his epic orgasm.

He stroked Lee's back and pressed his lips to his smooth cheek. "I love you," he said serenely.

"I love you, too, baby," Lee said back with a sigh, turning his head and giving Kamran a sleepy smile before kissing his mouth sweetly. "So much."

Kamran hadn't had much luck with love, but from now

on, that was going to change. He wasn't going to keep the world at arm's length anymore. He was going to let love in. Lee's love. His friends' love. And maybe even the love of Lee's family as well. He wasn't sure exactly what the future held, but all he knew was that he was ready for it.

And that was more than good enough for him.

EPILOGUE – A YEAR LATER

LEE

LEE HAD DEDICATED HIS LIFE TO LAW ENFORCEMENT. HE'D faced off with numerous scumbags, worked undercover, been in gunfights and high-speed pursuits. It was all in a day's work.

So why the hell was he so nervous now?

He glanced over at Kamran, who was happily singing along to the music playing through the Bluetooth speaker. Lee still found it oddly endearing that Kamran loved driving – it was his job, after all – but whenever they went anywhere, he always liked Lee to drive.

Some of his worries eased a little. Despite his initial protests, Lee knew that Kamran loved being spoiled and taken care of by Lee. One of the earliest ways Lee had spoiled Kamran was by getting his Mustang key replaced after Kamran had so cleverly used it to slow down Chaz's abduction of him. When Kamran realized Lee's gifts didn't have to be outrageously expensive but could just be thoughtful and only marginally pricy, he'd become more open to them.

But a big extravagance every now and again was also

appreciated, he was sure. Lee had nothing to be nervous about.

Probably.

"Huh," said Kamran, frowning as Lee pulled the Jeep into the parking lot at The Lodge. "It seems kind of quiet for a Saturday. Are you sure they're not doing their seasonal swap-over yet?"

"Not according to their website," said Lee, trying to play it cool as he picked a parking spot. "Maybe people have decided to go to the boardwalk instead. It's a lovely day."

That was true. It was a beautiful spring day. But Lee knew it wasn't the reason that there were hardly any cars in the parking lot. He bit his lip, wondering if Kamran had recognized any of the vehicles. *Damn it.* That was the kind of thing he'd notice.

Indeed, he was squinting as he looked around the place, so Lee quickly killed the engine of his car and pulled Kamran over to him for a searing hot kiss.

"Hello," Kamran rasped a couple of minutes later, his hair mussed up and his lips slightly swollen. He grinned at Lee, his pupils blown with arousal.

Nicely distracted.

"Shall we head in?" Lee suggested, handing Kamran the bag with his ice skates inside.

Since Lee had moved back to Pine Cove and taken up his full-time position with the local PD, he and Kamran had come skating almost every week if they could manage it. For Christmas, Lee had even gotten Kamran a course of private lessons with a former championship skater to hone his talents. It had started out as something just for fun – because Lee loved the joy it brought his boyfriend to be on the ice – but he'd already had his first stunt double offer to skate for a TV show.

So despite the lack of cars in the lot, Kamran shouldn't be

too suspicious of them coming here today. At least, Lee hoped not.

He checked his watch. They were right on time. But his nerves were back with a vengeance, making him want to fidget. So instead, he took Kamran's hand as they crossed the lot to the front entrance, rubbing his thumb over Kamran's knuckles.

Kamran laughed at him. "If I didn't want to skate so much, I'd suggest taking you right back home, Mr. Handsy."

Home. They'd been sharing a house for the last several months now, and Lee had to admit it was better than he ever could have imagined. He'd been wary that Kamran wouldn't be suited to a domestic, monogamous life, but he'd taken to their cohabiting like a duck to water. It helped that neither of them exactly had routine careers.

Plus, Kamran certainly knew how to keep things spicy in the bedroom. Lee had never been so satisfied in his whole damn life.

"We can get handsy tonight," Lee promised, kissing Kamran's hair as they made their way up the steps to the front door.

This was it.

Kamran paused as he reached for the handle. Probably because he'd spied the sign on the glass that said, 'Closed for a private function.' But Lee just reached up himself and opened the door, giving Kamran a smile.

"Come on," he murmured, indicating for Kamran to step inside.

The ticket barriers were up, and there wasn't anyone in sight. Kamran frowned at Lee as they walked into the main building.

They'd had the scariest moment of their lives here. Thank fuck that Chaz and all his lackeys were behind bars now –

including that creepy bouncer who had been spying on Kamran. They were safe now.

And that nastiness had paled against all the many memories they'd made here since. Yes, that night had been scary, but it had also signified the end of Kamran's troubles with his ex and the end of Lee's career with the FBI. It was the place where Lee had fallen in love with Kamran as he skated for the first time since his childhood. Where Kamran had finally been able to flourish in his long-forgotten passion. There had been countless date nights here, so many little presents bought, and miles skated around and around the rink.

And now, today, it was going to signify something else for them.

"What are you up to, Detective Marshall?" Kamran asked.

A slow grin crept onto his face, but Lee said nothing, choosing to simply take Kamran's hand again and lead him to the nearest entrance onto the ice.

"Lee?" Kamran tried again, looking around. "Shouldn't we put our skates on first?"

Lee had thought about doing this at the diner where they had their big New Year's Eve party or on the boardwalk by the town's lake. He'd even thought about the Ridgeway, where he'd driven to meet Kamran on that fateful night they'd met. But this was where their hearts belonged, in this beautiful Bavarian dream. It was a fairy tale brought to life – just like Kamran was to Lee.

He'd found his Prince Charming. There was only one thing left to do.

The lighting was down low with a hint of blue, the way they set up the rink for Friday and Saturday nights. Over the sound system, a love song was playing. Lee wasn't sure which one. He was just glad his thumping heart wasn't competing with an intimidating silence. None of the usually bustling stalls were manned. It was just him and Kamran as they stepped onto the ice, carefully making their way a few feet in.

Before Lee turned around to face Kamran…

…and got on one knee.

Kamran's face dropped in shock. Lee's nerves were like an entire kaleidoscope of butterflies in his belly as he held Kamran's hand in both of his. "Kamran Amir," he said, trying to keep his voice from shaking. He'd practiced these words for so long. Now it was time to finally speak them. "When I first saw you, I thought you were the most beautiful man on the planet. It didn't take me long to realize you had the most beautiful soul, too. It was easy to pretend to love you. It was impossible not to fall for you for real. You complete me, in every way. I can't imagine my life without you in it. Will you do me the incredible honor of becoming my husband?"

Kamran's throat bobbed as he swallowed. Wide, wet eyes looked down at Lee. "You want…to marry…*me?*" he said in disbelief. It broke Lee's heart that even after all this time, Kamran doubted his love for him.

Lee would just have to spend the rest of their lives convincing him.

"Desperately," he said, his voice catching.

He reached into his jacket pocket, and Kamran gasped as he opened the box that had been hiding there. Inside was a platinum ring with a band of crushed gems set all along the middle. They glinted black and blue with a touch of green. Lee had felt like he was looking up to the night's sky when he'd picked it, much like the fake sky above them in The Lodge.

Sometimes 'fake' was better than the real thing.

"Kamran Amir," he said firmly, his voice not quivering one bit. "Will you marry me?"

"Oh, baby," Kamran cried with a sob, dropping down onto the ice and flinging his arms around Lee. *"Yes!"*

"He said YES!"

Lee chuckled as Kamran's head whipped around to see the few dozen people jump up from behind the partition wall that surrounded the rink. Naturally, it had been Emery who had shouted, and he was now clapping and crying all the glitter off his face.

"Of course he said yes," Gamma scoffed as she wiped her own eyes. "My Kamran has *sense.*"

Kamran was crying openly now, clinging to Lee as he took in all the people currently applauding, cheering, waving 'Congratulations' banners, and also crying. All of Kamran's friends were there, including the entire Coal and Perkins families. Florence was there with her husband and all her kids (another baby bump visible under her dress), Aunt Ginny, several of Lee's other cousins, aunts and uncles, and of course, Sugar the chihuahua, who was standing on the partition wall by Gamma, wagging her tail.

Mikey wasn't there, but Lee didn't care. Because also by Gamma was his mom and dad. His mom had tears streaming down her face as she clapped her hands red. But Lee's heart swelled as his dad nodded at him. They were never going to be the closest, but his dad loved him, and that was all Lee needed to know.

The romantic music changed to a cheesy pop song as disco lights suddenly illuminated the whole room. Vendors popped up at their stalls (literally), and then there were trays of food and drink being carried into the crowd. It took three people to bring out the cake that Ben had made in a stunning replica of Kamran's beloved Mustang. Mia unfurled a twelve-foot-long banner with the help of Imogen and Kestrel Coal that read 'Lee and Kamran FOREVER!' in rainbow glitter that covered all three girls as they hung it on the wall for everyone to see.

Kamran turned to Lee, astonishment written all over his face. "You rented the entire place out for us?"

"Of course," he said, feeling a little breathless. It had happened – after all this time, he was sliding the ring onto Kamran's finger. "It took forever to get a date where everyone was going to be here, but today is pretty close to our anniversary, so it seemed like fate."

Kamran laughed, wiping his eyes. "You really got *everyone* here, didn't you?"

Lee grinned, noticing who had just run onto the ice. "I tried my best, including…"

"Cameo!" Sabina Max – the international Hollywood star – shrieked as she slid the last few feet into Kamran, knocking him over with the force of her hug. "Congratu-fucking-lations!"

"You're here?" Kamran cried in disbelief as they righted themselves. Lee caught Ava hugging her partner, Peyton, closer to her out of the corner of his eye, and had to laugh at the possessiveness. But Sabina only had eyes for Kamran in that moment.

"Duh," she said, clapping Kamran's arm. "I told Angel this was going to be the best proposal ever. I couldn't miss it! Unfortunately, Bella's filming right now, but she demanded we FaceTime her later."

Kamran wiped his eyes, looking around at everyone again, then fixed his gaze on Lee. "I can't believe this is my life," he whispered.

Lee took his hands between his as Sabina rubbed his back. "This is your *family*," he said thickly. "And they love you."

"Especially you?" Kamran asked.

Lee beamed. *"Especially* me, shnookums."

Kamran dropped his head back and laughed. "I love you, baby."

"Not as much as I love you, baby."

Lee leaned in to kiss his fiancé, half hearing Sabina laugh and say something about getting off the damn ice before she froze her ass off.

Lee didn't even feel the cold. As he held Kamran to him, a warmth filled him that he knew was going to last for all time. He didn't even recognize his life compared to how it had been a year ago. All it had taken was one crazy fake boyfriend to make Lee realize what was real and true.

It wasn't his career or his reputation. It wasn't the approval of people he didn't even like.

It was love. And now he was overflowing with it, just like Kamran. This was where they belonged, with their family – whether blood or chosen family, it didn't matter – this was home.

And it was forever.

THANK you for reading Kamran and Lee's story. If you enjoyed it, it would be super awesome if you'd leave a review on your favorite website!

Go BACK to the beginning of Pine Cove:

#1 – Safe Harbor – Robin and Dair

#1.5 – Sweet Spot – Robin and Dair's Halloween fun!

#2 – Troubled Waters – Emery and Scout

#3 – Homeward Bound – Micha and Swift

#4 – Bright Horizon – Ben and Elias

#4.5 – Crossed Paths – Raj and Antoni (a Bright Horizon companion)

#5.05 – Midnight Sky – Taylan and Hudson

#5 – Memory Lane – Jay and Angel

FOR GIVEAWAYS, sneak peeks, ARC opportunities and general fun times, please join my Facebook group! Helen's Jewels. We're very friendly! For more of my books, take a look below...

MORE FROM HJ WELCH

SHARED UNIVERSES

HJ WELCH HAS WRITTEN in two shared universes with multiple authors to create incredible worlds! You can find the links to her contributions below:

ROSAVIA ROYALS

Welcome to the tiny European country of Rosavia, where roses ramble over alpine slopes and princes fall for the men of their dreams. Every Rosavia Royals book happens simultaneously, so books can be read on their own, or in any order... but keep an eye out for familiar faces around the palace!

- Reign or Shine

HIDDEN CREEK

Welcome to Hidden Creek, Texas, where the heart knows what it wants, and where true love lives happily ever after. Every Men of Hidden Creek novel can be read on its own, but keep an eye out for familiar faces around town!

- Season 1: Storm
- Season 2: Ashes
- Season 3: Masterpiece
- Season 4: Reveal

ACKNOWLEDGMENTS

Cheerleaders: Ed, Amelia, Conrad, Mum, Hubby, kitty cats
Cover Artist: AngstyG
Beta Reading: Amy Pittel
Editing: Meg Cooper
Proof Reading: Tanja Ongkiehong
Special thanks to Christine for inventing Kamran's NASCAR sponsor: Excalibur!

ABOUT THE AUTHOR

HJ Welch is a contemporary MM romance author living in London with her husband and two balls of fluff that occasionally pretend to be cats. She began writing at an early age, later honing her craft online in the world of fanfiction on sites like Wattpad. Fifteen years and over a million words later, she sought out original MM novels to read. By the end of 2016 she had written her first book of her own, and in 2017 she fulfilled her lifelong dream of becoming a fulltime author.

She also writes contemporary British MM romance as Helen Juliet.

You can contact HJ Welch via social media:

Website – http://www.hjwelch.com/

Newsletter – https://www.subscribepage.com/helenjuliet

Facebook Group – Helen's Jewels

Facebook Page – @HJWelchAuthor

Instagram – @helenjwrites

Twitter – @helenjwrites

Email – helenjulietauthor@gmail.com

www.ingramcontent.com/pod-product-compliance
Lightning Source LLC
Chambersburg PA
CBHW030806210726
48290CB00002B/459